Temporary Shift

E.V. Baugh

DEDICATION

For Mum and Dad

ACKNOWLEDGMENTS

Special thanks to my friends: some faraway,
some near, some new, some old, but all to me
so dear. For making me laugh and smile,
and picking me up when I'm down. Sarah, Anna,
Sharon, Maud, Tanya, Jaime, Angela (my 'Old *Deer*
Friend'), and Niki (my friend/sister)… to name a few.
To Paul, for twenty years of love and friendship,
and our three boys: Toby, Oliver & James, so
different but alike in awesomeness. And my brilliant
niece, Robin.
You are all shining stars.
Thank you Rachel (my cover girl, and soon to be
sister in law), for gamely running around in your
office clothes whilst Ben photographed you!
And to my parents; John & Wendy, for a
childhood of happy sunny memories. For your
patience and love, support and understanding. To you
I owe everything.

xXx

i

CONTENTS

1 ~ PRESENT-TEMP ~ MONDAY

Sally Sullivan gazed through her reflection as the bus tumbled along in the damp British countryside, and she wondered – not for the first time – where her life was going.

Sometimes she felt as though she'd been born missing the instruction manual. She had pictured herself having life sorted by thirty. But here she was; almost thirty-three, single, living in a dilapidated rented flat above a curry house and scraping by, working for a temping agency on minimum wage, taking whatever work they could throw her way. Every decision she had ever made in her life had led her to this point in time. But where was she?

Where was she? With a jolt Sally realised she had nearly missed her stop. Pressing the bell and grabbing her bag in a panic, she hurried to the front of the bus. She mustn't be late today. Present-Temps were giving her one last chance. It wasn't that Sally didn't try hard. She was honest and conscientious, and possibly one of the nicest people you could meet. But as a teacher had once said, years ago in one of her school reports; *"Unfortunately nice people don't always succeed in life."*!

Sally's whole life sometimes seemed a series of ill fortune and wrong decisions. She had certainly had more than her fair share of bad luck. But she didn't dwell on things or let life get her down. Her real problem was her acute clumsiness – which came from her lack of confidence and self-esteem – which in turn came from her acute clumsiness. It was a vicious cycle, and the harder she tried the worse it got.

Thanking the sullen bus driver and bracing herself for the wind and rain, Sally bundled off the bus, and stepped straight into a muddy puddle. Cold water seeped over and into her comfy work shoes. Sally jumped back in surprise and just as she did so the bus doors concertinaed together catching a corner of her raincoat. Her raincoat firmly trapped between the doors the bus started to pull away, yanking Sally with it. Frantically trying and failing to get the bus driver's attention, she stumbled, half dragged alongside the front of the bus. The few passengers on-board seemed as equally oblivious as the driver. The bus was starting to speed up. Sally wrestled with her zip and in her mind's eye pictured the headlines in tomorrow's news. She was suddenly determined; *I am not going to die like this!* A surge of adrenaline powered through her. She tugged and wrenched, and with a twist and a turn she finally broke free.

Sally stood – her heart hammering – and stared after the bus as it sped away along the road, dragging her rainbow-striped raincoat along with it. The wind whipped her hair across her face, the misty rain plastered it in place, and as a final insult a passing car drove by through an enormous puddle and drenched her from head to toe. Sally staggered to the edge of the road gasping and wiping bedraggled wet hair and muddy puddle from her flushed face.

The car that had just sprayed her came to a stop, reversed back along the road and pulled up beside her. Electric windows wound down, a clean worried face leant across regarding Sally. 'I am, so, so sorry!' the man stammered, his earnest eyes round with concern.

Sally straightened her clothes and smiled self-consciously. She had the strangest sense of déjà vu – did she know him from somewhere? 'It's okay, really. I'm fine, please don't worry. I, ehrm, left my coat on the bus… I'm starting a new job today, well temping. It's at a lab of some-sort somewhere around here…' she said in a rush, and trailed off searching her soggy pockets for the job details.

'SALL?' he asked.

Confusion flickered across Sally's face, 'Sal, yes some of my friends call me Sal, how…?' She caught the amused look in his eyes.

'The Lab. Scott Addison Lockhart Laboratory?' He picked up a notepad from the passenger seat and flipped through its pages, 'Are you, by any chance Sally Sullivan from Present-Temps?'

'Yes, oh, yes I am,' embarrassment crept upon her and she tried again to straighten her sodden clothes, her blouse and knee length skirt clinging to her awkwardly.

'My friends call me Lockey,' he smiled warmly. 'I, work at SALL. Can I give you a lift? It's a good twenty-minute walk from here still. Please, it's the least I can do.' Lockey leant across the passenger seat and opened the car door.

'I'm saturated,' Sally warned.

'It's not a problem, company car, leather seats. Really, hop in.'

Sally gratefully slid into the car beside him, instantly relieved to be out of the cold wind and rain. As they pulled away she surreptitiously glanced in the visor mirror and wiped at her smudged mascara. 'I look a state,' she laughed self-consciously. 'Will there be somewhere I can have a bit of a clean-up before I meet the boss?'

Lockey smiled again, 'I really am so sorry, what a start to your day! I have some clean clothes at the lab you can put on when we get there, until we get your things dry and... don't worry about the boss, he's pretty easy going.' He looked a little embarrassed for a moment, and then they fell into a brief comfortable silence as the car sped along.

They passed through a small village and then back out into green countryside. The sun broke through the clouds, illuminating the freshly rain washed trees and fields with an almost fluorescent viridity. Lockey broke the silence, 'So, do you know much about SALL, Sally? and what we do there?'

Sally mentally kicked herself for not reading the notes properly that Present-Temps had emailed her, she had been in such a rush to get out of the flat on time that morning, what with the toaster catching fire and everything. She smiled apologetically, 'Not much at all really. What sort of work *is* it that you do?'

Lockey checked the rear-view mirror, indicated, and turned off onto a smaller road. 'We specialise in Particle Physics. We've been working on a pretty revolutionary project. Have you heard of the Large Hadron Collider? We've nothing on that scale, but it uses similar principles… Particle accelerators have had some pretty bad press over the years. The papers seem to love nothing more than selling scare stories about how the LHC is going to create a massive black hole, ending the universe or some such science fiction nonsense. But what we're doing here is science, not fiction, and it's ground breaking stuff. The conclusions could have huge, far reaching implications, positively changing the world as we know it; not ending it!' Lockey realised he was starting to rant and saw from Sally's slightly bewildered expression he was losing her. 'Sorry, as you can possibly tell it's my passion. We're right on the brink, and our research here at SALL is at the very forefront…' He smiled. 'So, have you done any Lab work before?'

Sally felt a spike of anxiety rise, she thought she'd just be answering phones or something. 'To be honest, I've never even been in a lab, unless you count my old high school science room…' She cringed inwardly, *what a stupid thing to say.*

Lockey didn't seem to mind and chuckled, 'It's fine Sally. It's just going to be filing mostly and a bit of tea making, if you're happy with that. We have a huge report we're preparing and need a little help organising the office. Carol – our Administrator – has gone off on unexpected maternity leave. Well, unexpected for us; she didn't tell us she was even expecting a baby until last week when she went into labour, a week early, at work and was rushed away by ambulance. She said she meant to tell us… I had wondered about the increasingly baggy clothes, but she also seemed to be constantly eating, so I'd just put it down to that.'

They chatted companionably for the rest of the short journey, conversation easy, as though they had always known one another. At a similar age to herself – Sally thought – Lockey was an attractive man. He had a well-proportioned face, short dark brown hair and kind hazel eyes. But there was more than that – Sally could tell he was a good man. She felt something warm and familiar about him, something happy and safe and strangely, for the first time in years, Sally had a feeling like she was at home.

2 ~ SAL AT SALL

Before Sally knew it, they had arrived. She hadn't even really noticed the rural countryside giving way to the industrial looking area. A variety of warehouses and modern buildings clustered together, clean and stark looking, sharp lines softened by trees and flowerbeds. The car crunched up a short stony driveway and pulled up outside a single storey structure, its metal cladding shining in the early spring morning light.

'Here we are.' As Lockey pulled on the handbrake he turned to Sally, 'This is it, let's go on in and get you sorted out.'

Lockey led the way and Sally rushed to keep up with his stride, noticing for the first time how tall he was. At probably over six-foot, he had broad shoulders and a naturally athletic looking build. Swiping a card and entering a key code with practiced fingers, he pushed the door and held it open for Sally. 'Welcome to SALL,' he beamed proudly. 'Come on in.'

Inside, Sally found herself in a bright and airy

reception area, flooded with natural light that poured in through a row of large windows, high up on one side of the room. 'Before I give you the tour, let's get you cleaned up. Just wait here a moment.' Lockey was already rushing off and called over his shoulder, 'I'll be right back. Put some coffee on if you like.'

A large desk dominated the room, its surface cluttered with letters and invoices, a telephone and laptop almost lost on the surface beneath the haphazard piles of paper. Sally located the coffee machine in a small kitchen area to one corner of the room, checked the water level and flipped it on to warm up. She found the coffee in the under counter cupboard, along with a collection of mismatched mugs. Something pink caught her eye, and reaching out she found herself holding a small tatty pink bear with two overlapping hearts appliqued on its belly. Sally didn't hear Lockey return, she was miles away – transported back to her childhood.

'What have you got there?' Lockey laughed.

Sally jumped. 'Love-A-Lot,' she answered distractedly.

'I beg your pardon?' Lockey raised an eyebrow.

'Sorry – the bear. It's a Care-Bear, called Love-A-Lot.' Sally smiled at the bear fondly, 'I used to have one *just* like this.'

'It must belong to Scott's little girl,' Lockey smiled. 'Sorry I was so long. Here, I found these… not the most attractive of outfits, but I'm sure they'll do while we get your clothes clean and dried.' He passed her a small pile of clothes, 'There's a little washroom just around the corner there, first on the right. You go get yourself cleaned up, no rush. I'll meet you back here when you're ready. Just leave your wet clothes in there, I'll get someone to get them dried for you.'

Inside the washroom, Sally tutted at her reflection in the mirror and picked a stray leaf from her hair. Her long auburn tresses hung like curtains of seaweed around her mud and mascara streaked face. Rummaging in the depths of her bag, she found some emergency supplies and wiped her face, and fixed her makeup. By crouching awkwardly under the hand-dryer she managed to dry her hair – but unfortunately this puffed it into a wild frizz-ball. She tried taming it with her fingers for a moment to no avail – thinking wistfully of her hair-straighteners and expensive conditioning spray at home – she didn't even seem to have a hairband anywhere. It would just have to do, she told herself firmly and pulled on the clothes that Lockey had lent her. The long sleeved shirt and the trousers swamped her, but with a few turn-ups on the trouser legs it wasn't that bad and she was grateful to be warm and dry again.

When she returned to the reception area, Sally found Lockey talking to a short balding man, his portly belly buttoned into a white lab coat. Lockey trailed off losing his thread of conversation, a little taken aback by her appearance.

Sally approached the older man her hand extended, 'You must be Professor Lockhart,' she said, clutching the man's hand before he had a chance to speak. 'So nice to meet you, I'm Sally Sullivan...'

He was an odd, nervous little man. He seemed a little befuddled.

'Present-Temps sent me?' Sally offered helpfully.

The two men exchanged a glance and Lockey broke in, 'Sally this is, Roy, he's... uhm, my assistant,' Lockey looked sheepish. 'I'm so sorry for not introducing myself properly earlier. I'm Professor Lockhart, but really, everyone just calls me Lockey. It's a name that just stuck years ago. My first name is… well, I don't like to go by it.'

'You're, *the Boss*?' Sally exclaimed in surprise.

Lockey laughed, 'Well, I suppose, I'm one of them at least. But It's all a bit more informal than that here.'

Sally raised her eyebrows and then smiled at Roy, 'Well, lovely to meet you Roy.'

Roy stepped back nervously and nodded his head in reply. He seemed eager to get away, but reluctantly shook Sally's hand, 'Well… I'd better get back to work…' he glanced at Lockey, 'I'll double check those figures Lockey and get back to you ASAP.'

Alone again in the room, Sally turned to Lockey. 'Well that was embarrassing! Why didn't you tell me in the car that you're Professor Lockhart?'

Lockey regarded her beseechingly, 'I'm sorry Sally, my friends *do* call me Lockey.'

'Hmmm,' Sally didn't sound convinced. 'So, you were going to give me a tour?' she asked somewhat coolly.

'Yes, ah, yes-yes a tour.' Lockey showed Sally out of the reception area and into the corridor. There were numerous doors: the washroom, a few store cupboards, and a couple of small rooms with computer monitors and odd gadgets in that Sally didn't recognise. They came to a larger door, this one Lockey had to swipe his card to enter. Inside was a small cloakroom, a bench on one side and a row of hooks with white coats hanging on the other. Lockey handed Sally a coat to put on and pulled one on himself. He tapped in another code and pushed open one of the double doors at the end of the room. He beckoned for Sally to follow.

After the reasonably small corridor, this room was vast – easily the size of a sports hall. Sally was taken aback by the sheer size of the laboratory, and in its centre a huge shiny machine of some sort took up almost the entire length of the room and half of its height.

'What on earth is this? It looks like a time-machine!' Sally exclaimed, before she could stop herself.

'Ha, well you know what, you're not far off there, Sally. This, is ALICE. It's our very own little particle accelerator here at SALL.'

'Little! It's enormous!' Sally gazed in amazement.

Lockey laughed, pleased she was so impressed, 'Well you know, compared to other particle accelerators, ours is remarkably small. The LHC is a twenty-seven kilometre ring and the proposed ILC would be possibly thirty to fifty kilometres long.'

'Can I have a closer look?' Sally asked.

'Yes, but not too close. Come on.'

The two of them strolled down the side of the room, Lockey explaining things to her enthusiastically, most of it going over her head, and she was so in awe of it all she realised she had entirely forgotten to be annoyed with him. Sally adopted her most sensible voice, 'Well, It's all very fascinating, Professor Lockhart.'

Lockey looked crestfallen, 'Sally, please – it's Lockey.'

'I tell you what Professor Lockhart,' she challenged. 'Tell me your first name and I'll call you Lockey. But I'm sure it can't be *that* bad.'

'It *is* Sally, it really is,' Lockey grimaced.

'Oh come on! Tell me! I promise not to laugh!'

Lockey sighed in resignation, 'Horace.'

'Horace! But that's so cute,' Sally laughed, and caught herself, and with mock seriousness added, 'It's a fine name, Horace!'

Lockey rolled his eyes. 'Well it's an old family name, goes back generations. Now please, call me Lockey… friends?' he held out his hand.

'Friends.' Sally took his extended hand and as their fingers touched, a little static spark crackled between them. They both jumped back slightly and laughed.

'Well that was weird!'

Their laughter fizzled out and Sally found Lockey regarding her enquiringly, a tiny furrow forming between his brows, 'You know, it's funny Sally, I really feel like I've known you for a lifetime.'

Sally did know what he meant, and it wasn't funny – she felt the exact same way. Before she had a chance to reply, they were interrupted by Roy, who had silently shuffled up and cleared his throat to get their attention. 'Ah Lockey.' Roy glanced at Sally. 'Could I have a word for a moment please?'

Lockey looked apologetically at Sally, 'I'll be right back.'

The two men turned their backs and fell into conversation, 'I've been over and over the numbers and just can't get them to add up…'

Sally stepped away, allowing the men to talk in private, their words almost immediately drowned out by the hum of machinery. As she looked around, her attention was caught by a soft ticking sound. Ears straining to locate the source of the noise, she found herself approaching the machine. ALICE; Lockey had called it. The ticking grew louder as she got nearer. It now felt as if it were filling her head rather than her ears, but it drew her in, its pull almost magnetic. Mesmerised, she found herself right up by the machine in front of a panel with buttons and flashing lights. Sally suddenly became aware of a vibrating against her thigh and with a jolt, she remembered she had put her mobile phone in the pocket of the trousers when she got changed. Panicking and remembering guiltily the *Strictly No Mobile Phones* signs on the way in, she fumbled in her pocket.

'Not now,' she muttered, discreetly taking her phone from the trouser pocket, hands trembling slightly. The vibrating stopped almost immediately as the phone touched her fingers. *At least it was on silent,* she thought. Glancing at the screen she saw it was a missed call from Aunty Mary; she'd call her back at lunch time. Deciding she'd better turn the phone off completely for a while, she pressed the little off button. But before she could turn it off properly the phone slipped from her hands and clattered to the floor. *Stupid slippery mobile phones.* Glancing over her shoulder quickly, to check no one had noticed, she bent down and reached forward.

Several things happened in quick succession at this point; as Sally leant forward her elbow brushed the control panel. Unaware, she crouched and edged forward further trying to reach her phone, which had skidded just under the machine. Finished talking with Roy, Lockey turned to see Sally, several metres away from him, on her hands and knees reaching under ALICE. His mouth fell open as he heard the warning signal sounding. She must have activated the machine somehow. No one should be in the room even, let alone in the area, with the machine fired up. Sally, oblivious to any danger, reached a little further and triumphantly retrieved her mobile. Still on her hands and knees, she suddenly found Lockey jumping on top of her shouting her name, and at the very same moment she felt her phone vibrate in her hand. A bright white light burnt in from the corners of her vision, until everything was blank and all that was left was the ticking – now amplified and magnified as though a thousand clocks ticked and tocked in chorus through every molecule in her body.

3 ~ THE HIGH FLYER

Sally came-to face down, her cheek pressed against the cold hard floor. Head pounding, she ached all over. With some effort she rolled herself onto her back, groaning involuntarily. She struggled to open her eyes, but muzzy headed she felt as though she were engulfed in a cold fog. She couldn't see straight and everything was blurred and spinning. A door opened somewhere, footsteps approached and she was vaguely aware of her name being called.

'Sally... Sally? Are you okay?' his voice, gentle but insistent.

Sally could just make out the blurred figure hovering above her. Groaning again, she rubbed at her temples. The aching was ebbing away now and the world coming back into focus – fuzzy lines sharpening and the spinning decelerating to a slow rotation. Befuddled, she found herself being helped up by the strong arms of, of *who*? Not Lockey. The man in front of her now, was a stranger. Late fifties maybe; slick silver hair, smart suit, clean shaven.

'Sally are you all right?' the stranger asked again.

He's probably another of Lockey's assistants, or a colleague maybe? she thought. 'Yes… I think I am, thank you,' Sally smiled weakly, but faltered as she looked around the room. She struggled to make sense of her surroundings. It wasn't just the man that was a stranger. Nothing was familiar.

The room Sally was in appeared to be an office; hardwood laminate flooring, expensive looking highly polished furniture. But most alarming was the view from the huge windows, which ran along the back of the room. A cityscape. An almost birds eye view cityscape. She must be twenty floors up at least.

'Where *am* I? How did I get here? And where's Professor Lockhart?' Sally demanded.

The man regarded her, his concern turning to real worry. 'Sally I think you should sit down; you've had a bump to the head or something. And who the hell is this Professor Lockhart?'

Alarm bells started ringing in Sally's head. 'Lockey?' she offered, hoping it may help jog his memory.

But the man just looked at her blankly, 'I'm sorry, never heard of him. Look Sal, it's been a stressful month. And about last night—'

'What happened last night?!' Sally asked in confusion, 'And why are you calling me Sal? … I'm afraid I have no idea who you are!'

He looked taken aback and cleared his throat nervously. 'I'm sorry Sally, I know we said we should pretend it never happened. But there's no need to be childish.'

Baffled, Sally rubbed her temples again.

His face softened, 'Look, just sit here,' he pulled

the chair from behind the desk. 'I'm just going to pop out and get you a nice cup of tea, and see if Karen the first-aider is about.' He led her to the chair and sat her down gently. 'I'll be back shortly, okay?' He stroked the side of Sally's face, smiled and before she could say another word, he strode from the office and quietly closed the door behind himself.

Sally leant forward and absentmindedly set off the Newton's Cradle desk-toy in front of her, sending its silver balls clacking from side to side. *This must be some sort of elaborate prank,* she thought, as she glanced around trying to work out what was going on. Her eyes caught a framed photograph on the desk, and she froze, the fine hairs on the back of her neck standing on end. The photo showed a happy family, two smiling children; a girl and a boy of about three and five, and a tall man; beard and glasses, with his arm wrapped around a lady, who looked, *remarkably like herself.* Shorter darker hair perhaps. Sally leant in closer to get a better look, her hand going up to her own hair. She stopped dead. Her usually longish shoulder length wavy hair, was now cropped to a short sharp bob, just like her double in the photograph. She felt a prickly heat rising and loosened the buttons at the neck of her blouse. Her blouse? This *wasn't* her blouse. Sally looked down and took in her outfit in bewilderment. It wasn't just the blouse; the outfit Lockey had lent her was gone, and she was now wearing a knee length pinstriped pencil skirt, stockings, and a pair of shiny grey high-heels with red soles.

Sally jumped to her feet and stumbled from the desk. An icy wave of fear and nausea rolling through her, what *was* going on?! But nothing could have prepared her for what happened next. The office door flew open and in marched, her father. Her *dead* father. Older; his once dark hair now peppered with grey. His face weathered, but the same bright blue eyes. He was, unmistakably, her father.

'Daddy?' Sally's voice was small and thin.

Her father stopped in his tracks, as he saw the look on her face.

Sally blanched, the blood draining from her head, her vision pixelating.

'Sally, what's up old girl?' But it sounded as though he spoke from far away and she could barely hear him. 'Sally, shall I fetch you a doctor? You don't seem yourself at all...'

Sally felt her knees go weak as the dizziness overwhelmed her, and she dropped to floor once more.

4 ~ MEDICATION TIME

When Sally awoke the next time, she found herself in hospital. A stiff white cotton sheet and cellular blanket tucked around her. A friendly looking nurse busying about, noticed she had woken.

'Good morning Sally,' the nurse said cheerily. 'Gosh you slept like a log last night, well that's good, you needed it. How are you feeling today love? Do you want some toast?' She fussed about her kindly, adjusting the metal framed bed's backrest and plumping the pillows. 'Doctor will be along shortly on his rounds. I'll get you a cuppa tea love.' She smiled warmly at Sally, turned, and bumbled from the room.

Sally took a deep breath and sank back against the pillows. What *was* happening? She screwed her eyes shut and tried to think. There had been an accident at the laboratory? She had a faint memory of Lockey shouting her name and throwing himself at her, before everything had gone blank. An explosion? Yes, she decided. There must have been an explosion. Lockey. Was he okay?

The nurse appeared, clattering in with a tray; teacup and saucer, and a plate of slightly burnt white toast. 'Here you are dear,' the nurse said, pulling the over-bed table across the bed, and setting the tray upon its surface. 'A nice cuppa, and your meds.' She handed Sally a tiny cup with three pills in and poured her a glass of water.

Sally swallowed the pills and glanced at the nurse's name badge. 'Thank you Brenda,' she said a little croakily, and tried a smile. 'Please, can you tell me... Is Professor Lockhart okay?'

The nurse stopped in her tracks, taken aback, 'Gosh, that's the first I've heard you talk in all these months you've been here. You must mean Doctor Lockhart, lovely? He's off today I'm afraid.'

'Months? I've been here for... *months*? But how could that be?' Sally asked perplexed.

'Oh dear, don't you remember? The accident?' The Nurse looked at her with sympathy and growing concern.

'Yes, the accident, at the laboratory... I sort of remember. That's why I need to see Professor Lockhart. Horace Lockhart?'

'I don't know about any laboratory accident Sally. You do remember why you're here don't you? The car crash... It was touch and go for a long time you know.'

'Car crash? How can that be? This doesn't make any sense! I need to see Professor, Horace Lockhart. I need to know what's going on. Please!' Sally demanded, her voice rising.

The nurse looked uneasy, 'I'll fetch the Doctor for you Sally. Try not to upset yourself dearie.' She hurried from the room.

Pushing aside the over-bed table, Sally pulled back the covers to get out of bed. But her legs wouldn't cooperate. In fact, she realised now, she couldn't even *feel* her legs. She tried to wiggle her toes. Nothing. She physically picked up one leg at a time and manoeuvred them off the bed, letting them dangle to the floor. Shunting herself with her arms, she pushed herself from the bed to stand. But her legs, useless beneath her, buckled and she crumpled to the floor. Nurse Brenda returned with a doctor, they rushed to her side and called for help.

Back in bed and sedated somewhat, Sally stared at a stain on the suspended ceiling. A silent solitary tear tracked across her cheek and down towards her ear. Nothing she had been told made sense. According to the doctor, she had been involved in an incident with a car, nearly twelve weeks ago. Her bike had been hit side on, as a car ran a red light. No one else had been injured, but Sally, was apparently paralysed from the waist down. The Doctor tried to reassure her that some impaired memory was to be expected, with the physical and mental trauma she had suffered. But nothing seemed to add up. Yes, she knew her name. But that was about it. They even said her brother would be in to visit this afternoon – but Sally was an only child. A wave of all too familiar anxiety gripped her. *So this is it*, she thought, *I am finally completely losing my mind.*

Nurse Brenda returned to take her blood pressure. 'I shouldn't have really, but I got a message out to Doctor Lockhart that you were quite insistent on seeing him. He's a good doctor. I've seen how much he's helped you through it all recently. He's certainly been the only one that's managed to get any smiles from you, so I've seen.' Brenda smiled and un-velcroed the blood pressure cuff.

Sally was barely listening. What did any of it matter? Either this was all a dream, or, she had completely lost the plot. Either way, she couldn't see how meeting some doctor, who happened to share the same surname as Lockey, was going to help.

'There, all done. Shall I open the privacy curtain? Or do you want it left closed love?'

'Closed will be fine. Thanks Brenda.'

'Okay love, we'll leave it shut for now. Lunch shouldn't be long.' The nurse swished out through a gap in the curtains.

Sally heard her talking to someone on the other side of the cubicle curtain, voices hushed. And then he appeared, Professor Lockhart. Lockey.

5 ~ DOCTOR LOCKHART

'Sally, it *is* you! Thank God! Do you remember me?'
He looked pretty much the same, apart from the
beard – that was new, as was the weariness he wore
under his eyes.

'Yes, I do. What's going on Lockey? They said I
was in a car crash and I'm paralysed, and I've been in
here for *three months*? But how could that be?'

Lockey pulled a chair over and sat by her side.
'Well, they're right and they're wrong – I'm pretty
sure *you* haven't been here for three months. By my
estimation, it's nearer three hours. Look, I'm not
really sure what's going on myself yet, but I'll work it
out Sally. It was ALICE I think; the machine. I don't
know how it happened, and you may be the only sane
person in the universe that will be able to believe me,
but I'm seriously thinking we've slipped *sideways*
across time, into an alternate reality.'

Sally reeled, this wasn't the explanation she'd been
hoping for. She wasn't sure which one of them were
crazier. But then, what explanation *could* she hope for?

Sally recalled the office, the photograph, and seeing her father. A dream she had thought, but it had felt so real. Surely not. She looked hopelessly at her useless legs.

'Sally, I'm going to sort this out. I promise. I'll find a way.'

Sally sighed. 'Please tell me this a joke Lockey.'

'Believe me, you don't want to *know* where *I* woke up before here,' Lockey grimaced. 'And then I collapsed. The next time I woke, I was in a strange house – strange, but mine it seems. I had a bit of time to look around and work things out. You know, I found photo albums and all sorts of mementos of a lifetime I haven't lived. It was surreal. And I look the same.' He stroked his beard thoughtfully, 'Well, almost the same,' he laughed, and Sally laughed too, a little. 'I'm a Doctor here it seems – swapped one white coat for another.' He gave a thin smile. 'Someone from the hospital called and left a message, said you wanted to see me. I was so surprised. I was starting to think it was all a dream, you know? It took me a while to piece it all together. I'm so glad I've found you Sally.'

Sally was glad too, this was insane – but at least she didn't feel so scared and alone now. 'Me too. I thought I was going out of my mind. The doctor who came around earlier thinks I'm suffering some sort of delayed memory loss – *Post-Traumatic Brain Injury Syndrome,* he said. He was asking me all these questions, and pretty much the only ones I got right were my name and date of birth. You know, they told me my brother's coming in to visit this afternoon. I'm an only child Lockey. My parents… they died when I was eight.'

Lockey nodded with understanding and squeezed her hand, 'I'm so sorry Sally.'

Sally looked away and took a steadying breath. 'It's okay, it was a long, long time ago.'

They heard someone approaching. Lockey released her hand and said in a lowered voice, 'We just have to go along with this all for now, until we work out what's going on.'

The Doctor that Sally had seen earlier returned. 'Doctor Lockhart. Can I have a word?'

Lockey glanced at Sally nervously, 'Err, yes, yes of course.' And to Sally, 'I'll be back later, okay?'

Sally nodded mutely.

Alone again, with the modicum of privacy the thin partition curtain allowed, Sally reached across to the small cabinet beside the bed and picked up a wash-bag. She stared at the stranger in the mirror. Her face pale and washed out, an angry scar ran across her cheekbone and down towards her chin. Hair; scraggly, bleached blonde with a couple of inches of dark roots. 'Nice to meet you Sally,' she muttered.

Lunch was brought around and cleared away, and still Lockey had not returned. The ward was abuzz with visitors now. A little girl – half shyly at first – approached the lady in the bed adjacent, a bunch of flowers in her hands and a broad grin on her face. Sally looked at the clock; quarter-past two. *Where is Lockey?* she wondered anxiously.

Sally didn't see him approach until he was almost by her side; a young man in his early twenties, a dark mop of hair and bright blue eyes. Sally had gazed for hours at the old albums; her parents, young and happy, her parents on their wedding day – he looked remarkably like her father. A strange rush of emotion came across her and somehow, *she knew*, She knew him, and so much more.

'Cal,' Sally found herself saying.

He smiled and ruffed the top of her hair, 'Alright Sis.'

6 ~ THE BROTHER THAT NEVER WAS

It was strange, Sally had never had a brother – and yet, she had. As she looked at him, she saw flashes of the boy he had been. A lifetime of hazy, barely tangible memories flitted across the peripheries of her mind. Sally realised now, that she had lost *three* people in the car crash, on that fateful day in June all those years ago; her father, her mother, and her unborn baby brother.

Her father had died on impact. It had been a head on collision. Her mother had been rushed to hospital, her life hanging in the balance. But there had been nothing they could do, they'd said. No one had ever told Sally that her Mum had been pregnant. Sally was sent to live with her aunt and uncle. Conversations had been in hushed whispers when Sally was out of the room. But somehow, in this reality, her mother had survived – And her brother.

The year he had been born had been a hard one. He had arrived on Christmas day into their little fractured family. He had been Sally's only gift that year, but she had loved her little brother with all of her heart, from the first moment she had seen his little pink face. Nearly nine years between them, but always thick as thieves – Sal and Cal. Her crazy-silly, annoying at times, but big-hearted, little kid brother.

Sally was overwhelmed and felt simultaneously devastated to have lost him, and overjoyed to have found him.

'Why *are* you looking at me like that Sal? Is there something on my face?'

Sally laughed and wiped at her welling tears with the back of her hand, and swallowed against the lump in her throat. 'No you're good, it's just so good to see you Cal.'

Cal smiled at Sally fondly and sat on the edge of her bed. 'You only saw me a few days ago, you big soppy thing.' He wrapped her in a brief warm hug. 'Mum phoned last night.'

'Mum?' Sally's heart raced.

'Yeah, they're in Paris. She reckons they'll be back by the weekend.'

'Mum… and, Dad?'

Cal looked at her oddly. 'Mum and *Troy*. Ha-ha Sal, hilarious – I don't think we'll be seriously calling "The Toy Boy Troy" *Dad* any time soon!'

Her mother had become detached after her father had died, of course, it had been a lot to deal with. She just needed a little time, they had told her. Time to grieve. But by the time she was done with grieving, she just seemed to move on. Sally and Cal trailed along with her as she remarried, and divorced, twice. And now there was Troy; the twenty-seven-year-old bartender she'd picked up on a package holiday in Tenerife.

Sally tried to compose herself. It was so confusing, to have these conflicting memories. 'Of course, yes,

I… forgot.'

'You all right Salamander? You seem *odd* today, what's up?' Cal asked with concern.

'It's just, been a strange day.' And not even knowing where she'd start, Sally changed the subject, 'So, what's new with you?'

They chatted for over an hour. Cal had a new job he was revved up about, DJing at a local club. He had met a new girl. His friend Mike did something hilarious the other night. Not all of it Sally took in, she just enjoyed being with him, his words washing over her and somehow soothing away her fears. He had so much energy and enthusiasm, it was contagious, and they laughed so much. Sally couldn't remember the last time she had laughed until her ribs ached, maybe years. Too soon, visiting hours were over.

'I'll be back in to see you the day after tomorrow,' Cal assured her.

Sally found herself hoping that she'd still be here. She watched him leave, tall now, over six foot. He looked over his shoulder as he left the room and grinned, mock marching behind the stern Nurse who had broken up their little party of two.

The ward filled with the smells of potatoes and gravy as the dinner trolley clattered around. The sun was just setting. Its soft golden light leaching in through the windows. Sally's head was still in a whirr. It was just all too much to assimilate. More and more memories had filled her head since Cal had left and Sally was struggling to process all of the new information. Pretty much everything she had known about the last twenty-five years was different now;

two completely conflicting stories danced around in her head. Maybe the doctor had been right and she *had* suffered some kind of brain damage. Or, was she relapsing into the mental breakdown she'd suffered a few years ago? Surely that would make more sense than what Lockey was suggesting. She just didn't know what was real anymore.

The ward door opened and there he was, finally. Sally glanced at the clock; quarter to six, 'Lockey! Where have you *been* all afternoon?'

'Sorry Sally, I got back as soon as I could,' Lockey apologised. 'I've just been trying to work some things out.' He sat on the chair beside her bed.

'I met my brother,' Sally said simply.

Lockey looked at her sadly.

'I never had a brother, he never even *existed*. Or, I never *knew* he existed. I didn't even know my mum was expecting. I'm so confused Lockey. Somehow I'm remembering things that I've never experienced. All these memories. Tell me, am I losing my mind?'

'No Sally. I'm experiencing similar myself. I think they're the memories stored in the old grey matter.' He tapped his head. 'Borrowed memories, you could say. Sally, I was thinking, where did you wake up first?'

'I, I woke up in a strange office. There was a man there I didn't recognise, but he knew my name. And then, my Dad was there... I was so shocked. I think I must have fainted.'

Lockey nodded thoughtfully. 'Yes. I think, somehow, your fainting triggered us to shift sideways again; into *this* reality.'

Sally felt the tightness of a headache coming on, she rubbed her temples and humouring him asked,

'But how many realities could there be?'

'An almost infinite amount. Although, I think we can only move into realities which we inhabit in similar form, an identical genetic match I suppose. If I'm right, I think that when we go to sleep tonight, we'll leave here, we'll lose hold of the consciousness of these bodies and well, I don't know what. Maybe we'll get back to our own reality? Or, maybe we'll shift again.'

Sally thought of Cal. 'But I've only just found my brother.'

'But he's not *your* brother. He's the brother of your alternate-self. Even if we wanted to Sally, we couldn't stay here. Look, you're a Temp right?'

Sally nodded.

'So, you're obviously adaptable. Think of this like you're temping; only, now you're temping in another life. In a way we're all temping. Everything is temporary; our lives in the grand scheme of things are pretty short and insignificant really, just a spark in the passage of time. I'll be honest with you – I don't know where all this is going. But, this is monumental Sally. Not only did we succeed in creating a black hole with ALICE, we somehow opened a portal across the multiverse. We're in unchartered waters here, in a realm merely theorised and there's not much we can do at this point other than learn as much as we can from it all, and try to enjoy it maybe.'

Sally looked down at her useless legs and felt a new wave of tears sting her eyes, 'It's not that easy Lockey.'

Lockey gave her a sympathetic smile. 'We'll find a way to get back, Sally. We have to.'

Sally took a deep breath. 'I wonder where we'll be

tomorrow,' she mused.

'We may still be here; I could be wrong… Or, maybe we'll be home,' he added hopefully.

'But what if we're somewhere else entirely? – *if* this is really happening, I mean… We could be anywhere. How will we find each other Lockey?'

Lockey looked at her solemnly, 'I'll find you Sally; I'll find a way. I'll keep looking and looking until I find you. Look, I don't know what things will be different now, but I'm originally from Hampshire. I grew up on an Estate m—'

'Oh, I grew up on a council estate in Hampshire too! Millside?' Sally interrupted.

'Ehrm, no. Wentworth Hall. My parents have a manor house in the New Forest. It's not all as grand as it sounds. But anyway, it's pretty easy to find. Just remember the name. So how about you? Millside Estate was it?'

'Well, I didn't start-out there. I was born in Surrey; a large Tudor-style house in a pretty village within easy commuting distance of the city… for my father. I don't remember that much about it really – I was packed off to Easthampton boarding school when I was seven.'

'Easthampton?!' Lockey cut in excitedly, 'I went to Easthampton too Sally! *That* must be where I know you from!'

Sally shook her head, 'But I was only there for two terms. Then there was the accident the following summer, and everything changed. It turned out my parents had been up to their eyeballs in debt, just hanging on to the house and everything by the skin of their teeth. It all went, one way or another; the house, the money. I was packed off to live with my aunt and uncle in their two-up two-down on the Millside estate and moved to a local school.'

They looked at each other and the sense of what could have been, hung in the air. Sally hadn't been at Easthampton long enough to work out many names even.

Sally changed the subject, 'So, Lockey, where was it *you* first woke up on this crazy adventure of ours? I'm intrigued.' She watched him expectantly.

Lockey drew a long breath. 'Okay, no laughing... I came-round and I was gaffer-taped to a tree in a town park somewhere. Don't laugh Sally! Apart from the tape, I was completely naked! A stag-do I'm guessing, and it had my brother Teddy's name written all over it I'm sure. Anyway, this old lady walking her little dog comes right up to me. She didn't bat an eyelid, I'm telling you – and just like it was the most ordinary thing to come across on a Monday morning stroll in the park – she nonchalantly asks me if I need some help. It turned out she was really handy. She had a pen knife in her handbag (for sandwich making she assured me) and cut me free. She even fashioned me a modesty outfit out of a jute shopping bag... Stop laughing Sally! It really wasn't funny!'

'Oh Lockey! I'm sorry, but that really is!' Sally spluttered.

Lockey gave in to it and they both laughed, for a little while. Sally grew serious again.

'And what about *this* Sally? If we do shift again?'

'Well, hopefully, she'll just get back to *her* normal. I spoke to that doctor earlier Sally. He said some recent tests have come back with really promising results, they're really hopeful they'll have you... *her*, back on her feet. In-fact, they're going to start some physiotherapy tomorrow.'

Tomorrow, who knows what tomorrow will bring? Sally thought.

They heard the ward nurse approaching – the stern one, not the kindly Brenda.

Lockey leant in closer. 'Everything is going to work out, one way or another, I'm sure of it. Look, just get some sleep okay. I'll find you.'

After Lockey had left, Sally found a mobile phone in the bedside table drawer. She scrolled through the contacts list, found Cal's number and tapped in a text message;

'So lovely to see you today Cal. They're going to start me on physio tomorrow! X' She sent the message and a moment later the phone pinged with his reply.

'Wow! Amazing! That's huge news Sal! I'll come and see you Weds – you can tell me all about it! :-) Good luck tomorrow! Love you Salamander. x x x'

'Take care little brother. Love you too Cal,' And then she added, *'Calamari. <3 Xxx'* and tapped send.

The ward grew quiet. Lights were dimmed. Sally lay and thought of her bizarre day. More memories had come to her, the picture filling in like a paint by numbers. Maybe she would wake up tomorrow and it would have all been a dream after all. She tried to stay awake for a while, but she couldn't fight the tiredness. It had been an emotionally exhausting day. Her eyelids grew heavy and she fell into a deep dreamless sleep.

7 ~ FLOATING ON A STARRY SEA

Sally awoke, her senses alert. Had someone called her name? It was pitch black and the world was swaying and pitching from side to side. What *was* happening? She lay in the dark – her head rhythmically rolling against something soft – and listened to the peculiar sounds all around her. She could hear odd creaking noises and the sound of water moving, close by; swishing and gurgling. It sounded as if she were in a washing machine. *Is that the sound of the sea?* – the sound of waves splashing and lapping, not only in the distance but all around, as if played in stereo surround-sound. *Am I dreaming?* Sally tried to get her bearings. She wasn't in hospital, that much was clear.

'Sal?' There it was again; a loud whisper. And then, she felt a hand on her shoulder. 'Hey, Sal? ... wake up. It's your watch?' the stranger said softly, his voice laidback and distinctly Australian. Sally's eyes had adjusted a little to the dark and she could just make out the outline of the shadowy figure before her now. She tried to swing her legs from the bed, but she couldn't. She seemed to be restrained. *Am I still paralysed?* she thought. Feeling a cold panic rise, she wriggled and writhed and tried to free herself. 'My legs…' her voice came out in a rasp.

The hand had moved from her shoulder. He fumbled for a moment and then there was a loud unzipping sound, and her legs were freed. 'Got yourself all tangled up in your sleeping bag again?' he laughed. He sounded kind and a little rough around the edges. In the semi-darkness, the stranger offered Sally a strong weathered hand and helped her out of the ridiculously narrow bed; there was a stiff canvas panel along her outer side, which she had to clamber over to get out.

So this is really happening? she thought. *But, where am I?* He passed her something, a lightweight jacket – Sally pulled it on. She seemed to have been in bed fully clothed. Her bare feet found a pair of leather shoes on the floor and she slipped them on. The shadowy figure was moving away. Sally stepped into the dark to follow him and lurched to one side, she grabbed out to steady herself. *Am I drunk? Or drugged?* And it was only then that she realised, that she was on a boat.

Sally felt her way across the dark cabin, walking toward a faint light in the same direction that the stranger had gone in. Her legs seemed to have become accustomed to the pitching and rolling motion already and she found that instinctively, on the whole, she could steady herself. Her fingers found the bottom rung of a wide, smooth wood ladder. Sally paused and looked up to a rectangle of starry sky – with the rocking motion of the boat the stars almost appeared to be moving – she took a deep breath and clambered upward towards the open hatch above her.

Sally poked her head out of the hatchway. The salty wind whipped at her hair. Fingers gripping tightly to the wooden surround, she stood on the top step. The sea was louder out here and swished and rushed in whispers all around. Sally was alarmed to realise how close the water was – she could just make out the dark shapes of the waves rolling by, on a black bubbling sea; It was a small boat. She looked about wildly, her grip tightening as the boat pitched suddenly.

There was a dim orange glow coming from a display panel beside the hatch, which was lit up with all sorts of numbers and symbols that meant nothing to Sally. In the faint light she could just about see him now, sat behind a large steering wheel. He was older than her; ten, maybe twenty-years even, it was hard to tell. But even in the low light, she could make out the friendly lines around his eyes. He had lightish hair; either dark blonde or light brown, and a strong jaw. In this light he looked not dissimilar to a younger Robert Redford.

'Aren't you coming out?' he smiled.

Gingerly, Sally made her way a little further out of the hatchway, moving her hands along a metal railing. The boat lurched alarmingly and smacked down against a wave. Sally sat down hastily in the cockpit, opposite the man. A fine salty spray spritzed her face, but strangely it wasn't cold out here, there was a soft wind which carried a warmth on it; promises of sunny distant shores perhaps.

'It's a beautiful night.' He fell silent for a moment.

Sally looked up, she could make out the dark triangle of the boat's sail against the night sky – a sky studded with a billion stars, which twinkled and blinked overhead and all around, right down to the horizon of the dark sea. Replaced by awe, her fear ebbed away.

'Shall I make you a coffee? – before I turn in?'

Sally was surprised to realise he had almost disappeared entirely down into the cabin already, only his head remained in view. *Is he planning on leaving me out here? All alone?* Her fear sprang back; *I can't sail a boat!*

'Um, coffee… yes please – if you don't mind…' She hoped this would stall him while she worked out what to do.

He smiled. 'The self-steering's doing a good job – I doubt you'll even have to steer. Just keep us heading west.' And he disappeared down into the boat's cabin.

Sally shuffled along the cockpit seat, until she was behind the wheel. She put a hand on the wheel lightly and felt it making small adjustment movements, as if helmed by an invisible captain. She looked back up at the stars. A shooting star flickered across the sky and once again she forgot her fears. The sea didn't look quite so black and terrifying when she looked back down. In fact, she realised, it wasn't entirely dark, there seemed to be glowing stars shimmering across the waves, glittering and sparkling. Was it a reflection of the sky? She strained her eyes to see better. These sea stars were moving and seemed to be brightest where the boat was rushing through the waves. They glimmered in a trail in the boats wake.

'The phosphorescence are amazing tonight aren't they? Here…' he passed her an insulated mug of hot coffee, rotating the cup so the handle faced toward to her.

Sally took the mug gratefully. 'Thank you.'

'We'll probably be able to stay on this tack all night, the wind's ideal.' He looked out across the sea, 'I saw some dolphins earlier.' And then he yawned. 'I'm bushed,' he rubbed his eyes, 'I'm gonna get some shut-eye. Have a good night.' And before Sally could even reply, he was gone – leaving her alone on deck, the boat steadfastly bashing on into the night, across the seemingly infinite dark and starry sea. Rather than feeling scared or alone though, Sally was full of wonder. She gazed at the dark and sparkly world around her. She had read about bioluminescence, but she could never have imagined anything quite so beautiful.

Sally wondered; *How had this Sally come to be here now? And where is this little boat sailing to?* She wondered where Lockey was and where she would end up next. She had plenty of time to wonder all sorts of things, as the boat bashed on into the night.

Sally hadn't a clue what the time was, or how long she had been sat out in the cockpit for. Time seemed irrelevant out here. The sky had gradually lightened. The shadowy sea had turned to an inky blue. The sky, now a soft golden pink as the sun glinted up above the horizon. As it had got lighter, the details of the boat had filled in. It was a modern looking yacht; sleek lines, smooth white moulded topsides with pale wooden decking strips, neatly coiled ropes and taught creamy sails. A Dutch flag flapped out at the boats stern. The entire boat was probably only the length of a bus, but this solitary island upon the vast undulating ocean, had become Sally's entire world. She had become rather attached to the boat and felt almost as if they were a team, racing unfalteringly through the waves together across the sea. Her trusty steed.

The sun had inched up further – now a glowing ball upon the sea – and painted the wave tops with a dancing orangey light. Out of nowhere, there suddenly came a loud *chuff* sound. Sally started. *What on earth did that noise come from?* There it was again, closer this time, almost right beside her. Sally looked over the side of the boat into the waves, and then she spotted it, a fin – a shark? Sally felt alarmed, although she knew she was probably safe out of the sea. And then there was another, and then another and she realised, that they weren't sharks at all, but dolphins.

Sally watched the pod of dolphins, enthralled, as they gracefully slipped through the water, racing beside the boat, ducking and diving playfully in the boats wake. She was mesmerised. Every now and then she would catch a glimpse of a smiley eye, as if they were just as fascinated by her, as she was with them. And then just as suddenly they departed. Sally watched the sea hopefully for their return – heart brimming with love and wonder – but they were gone.

'Hey, you still up?' Australian Robert Redford had appeared in the hatchway rubbing his eyes and looking less like Robert Redford in the light of day. 'Did you not wake Quinn? You must be shattered. You'd better go get some sleep?' He yawned, and then Sally yawned too and she realised that she was actually, completely exhausted.

Sally had wondered briefly if she could stay awake for a while longer, to see if she could tune-in to the memories of this Sailor Sally. But there was no way. She was ready to drop. She zipped up the sleeping bag and felt sleep washing in before she had even closed her eyes. She felt as if she were weightless, floating on a soft warm sea. And like a baby in a cradle, the boat rocked her. She could fight it no longer. She closed her heavy eyes and surrendered to oblivion.

8 ~ DEAR OLD FRIENDS ~ TUESDAY

When Sally woke next it was morning and it took her a moment to come-to. She lay in bed and waited for her surroundings to become familiar. But they didn't. She sat and rubbed her eyes. Dust motes danced in a bright shaft of sunlight, which streamed in through a crack in the long heavy curtains at a large bay window opposite the double bed she was in. Where was she now?

Sally hadn't seen the fat tabby cat curled up asleep at her feet, and when she threw back the patchwork quilt the cat jumped from the bed and meowled loudly at her. Sally shrieked and jumped up on the bed in a fright, knocking the paper ceiling light shade and sending it swinging wildly. The cat turned and glared at her as it sat before the bedroom door and then proceeded to preen itself, still eyeing her disdainfully.

Sally laughed with relief, 'Hello Cat.' She climbed down from the bed and reached out to stroke it, but the cat hissed at her and arched its back as she approached. Sally stumbled back across the room in surprise and almost losing her balance, reached out frantically and grasped hold of a fold of curtain to steady herself. The curtain rail gave way and peeled from the wall. The curtains slid to one side, her arms went up instinctively and she caught the rail mid fall.

Sally found herself looking out from a ground floor window and to her dismay realised that she was standing in full view, wearing only a pair of knickers, her hands still above her head clutching the curtain rail. A postman walking by outside gave her a cheery smile and a nod. Sally yelped and half wrapped herself in a corner of curtain. The bedroom door flew open.

'Not again Sally!' Nita laughed, her eyes sparkling.

Nita; Sally's oldest and dearest friend. She looked much the same as the last time that Sally had seen her at Christmas – apart from the fact that her short hair was now dyed a deep shade of claret with fine pink and purple streaks. But this wasn't out of the ordinary; Nita changed her hair colour more often than her boyfriends – and she got through plenty of them. 'Nita! You're here!'

'Yeah, I'm running late… did you just flash the postman!?' Nita asked with a laugh. The two of them were laughing so hard now Sally could barely get out a reply.

'Here.' Nita threw Sally a dressing gown.

Sally held her sides, tears of laughter streamed down her face. Nita's laugh was infectious; a raucous, dirty cackle. After a couple of attempts, they regained themselves.

'Oh God I love you Sal, you're bloody hilarious!' Nita gave her a hug and glanced at her watch, 'Shit, I've got to go. I'll see you later.' As she hurried from the room she called over her shoulder, 'I'll see you later on. Looking forward to tonight!' she sang the last few words.

No clue what Nita was referring to, Sally found herself shouting, 'Yeah sure, see you later.' It was so good to see Nita. It had been far too long.

Nita had taken Sally under her wing on her first day of Primary school, when she'd moved to Millside. It had been friendship at first sight. Nita had a confidence which Sally admired. She had marched straight up to her, on that first day and fell into conversation as though she already knew her, introducing herself only as an after-thought. And it had been a relief for Sally. Nita didn't give her the pitying looks that others did. Most people seemed wary of Sally's grief – as though she may have something contagious – kids and adults alike.

Sally's whole world had rocked on its axis when her parents had died. They hadn't been that close. Her father, although he doted on her when he was around, was away on business a lot. Her mother blew hot and cold; one moment loving and kind, the next closed off and snappy – some days it seemed as though she could barely bring herself to look at Sally. But they had had their good moments, and they were her family. They were all she had known.

Sally's mother's sister Mary and husband Joe, were appointed as her guardians. They turned up at Easthampton, packed Sally and her small collection of possessions into their rusty Lada Estate and drove her away from the life she had known, to their little terraced house in Millside.

Mary was a no nonsense sort. Sally had met her only once before. She showed Sally up the steep narrow stairway, to her new little room. 'You can call me Aunty Mary,' she had told Sally stiffly and gave her an awkward hug.

Joe was lovely, a great bear of a man, with more hair on his chest than his head. A week or so after her parents' funeral, Joe drove Sally out to the countryside with a small tree and a couple of spades, and they had planted it together in memory of her Mum and Dad. They returned home that day, firm friends and covered in mud. She didn't feel so alone in the world anymore and felt a new lightness from saying a proper goodbye to her parents. Aunty Mary had glared at the two of them and muttered disapprovingly. But Uncle Joe had winked at Sally conspiratorially and nothing could have dampened her spirits.

Sally looked out of the window. The sea; blue and sparkling, stretched out to the horizon. Brighton. Sally recognized the iconic pier not far off – she had visited Brighton on a school trip, some twenty years ago. There was a small white sail on the sea in the distance. Sally thought of her night out on the waves. What a magical night it had turned out to be. She still wondered if it were all a dream. She looked around the room, taking in her surroundings properly for the first time. It was decorated simply and furnished with a haphazard shabby-chic mix of vintage and new.

Sally went to the wardrobe and stood before its full length mirror. This Sally's hair came to just above shoulder length; a good four or five inches shorter than her own, and the fringe was new. It suited her. She tamed her hair with her fingers. The cut was better, soft layers gave her waves more bounce.

When Sally opened the door she gasped. The wardrobe was almost bursting at the seams. Its contents, a vivid rainbow of colour and pattern. She thumbed through the beautiful collection of garments inside: a variety of blouses, shirts, trousers and skirts, playsuits, jumpsuits and dresses – so many dresses. Dresses in almost every length and style. Sally's regular look consisted of not much more than jeans and t-shirts for the weekends and plain skirts and blouses for work. She had never had much time or money to think too much about what she'd like to wear. Her hands paused at a blue fifties style polka-dotted dress. Sally couldn't remember the last time she'd worn a dress. She smiled. *Why not?* she thought, and pulled it from the rail. She found some underwear in a dresser drawer, and with the dressing gown still half on and her back to the window, she wriggled awkwardly into the dress.

The full skirt swished out as Sally twirled in front of the mirror. It fit her perfectly. She pulled on a fluffy yellow cardigan and stepped into a pair of canvas pumps she'd found by the door, and she was just about to leave the room when she noticed a framed photograph on the wall; Nita and Sally, graduation outfits and beaming faces.

Sally had wanted to go to university, Nita had almost convinced her. But she couldn't just go off and leave Mary and Joe. Joe had suffered a massive heart attack that year, he had survived, just about. Sally owed a lot to Mary and Joe, and money had been tight. So, although it had been heart-breaking, Sally had stayed. She'd taken a job as an office junior at a local insurance firm and said her goodbyes to her friends as they headed off for their new futures. Nita and Sally had kept in touch as much as they could, but it wasn't easy and they had inevitably gone their own ways, more or less, for a few years. After that Nita had moved away and they barely saw each other these days.

So what kind of life has this Sally had? she wondered. Sally closed her eyes and tried to search for any new memories, but none came to her. Taking a deep breath, she headed out of the bedroom to explore.

Sally's ground floor bedroom led into a small hallway. There was a bathroom off to one side and through the next door, another bedroom. Smaller than her own, every surface was cluttered. There were more clothes strewn across the floor than in the drawers that hung open. The whole room was in disarray, apart from one wall; completely lined with shelves, on which, an impressive shoe collection had been painstakingly arranged in colour order. This was unmistakeably Nita's room. Not wanting to nose around Nita's space too much, she shut the door again quietly.

A narrow stairway led up to the next floor. Sally found herself in an impressive, bright and airy open plan area – a kitchen come diner at one end, and a generous comfortable looking lounge to the other. Another large bay window framed the breath-taking sea-view. *Sally must be doing well to afford the rent on this place*, she thought.

Sally stopped in her tracks, her attention drawn to a large painted canvas, hanging on the wall behind the sofa. It was beautiful. An abstract seascape. Thick layers of oils; bright cobalt, ultramarine and cerulean blues, led down to meet a beach of ochre and gold.

A telephone started ringing, snapping Sally from

her reverie. She located the old rotary-dial telephone on a small table beside the sofa and hesitated before lifting its receiver. 'Hello?' she answered warily.

'Sally? Sally, is that you?'

'Lockey? Yes, it's Sally. How did you find me?'

'Ah-ha, the good old internet. You were pretty easy to find. Didn't take me long at all to track you down actually. How is everything? Are you okay?'

'Yes, I'm fine. It's weird, but yes, everything's okay.' Sally thought of the last time she'd seen him in the hospital, 'It's good to have my legs back I'll say that much. How about you? Where are you?'

There was a little pause. 'I'm at Wentworth Hall… Look, I'm coming to find you. Brighton, right? I'm going to hop on a train. I'll be with you just after midday. Will you come and meet me at the station?'

Sally's heart lifted. 'Yes, of course. That's great Lockey. Thank you.'

'No, don't thank me, we're in this together. It may not always be possible, but we should stay as close as we can. Sally, do you know much about yourself here yet?'

'No, not a lot, other than I'm as clumsy as ever and I'm sharing an apartment with my old school friend Nita, in Brighton, obviously. Why, do you know something?'

'You're a really successful artist Sally! That's why you were so easy to find. You've got an exhibition opening and there's going to be a private-view party thing this evening.'

'What! Really!? I've barely picked up a brush since school…'

'Not in this reality. I have to go. My train should get in at twelve eighteen. I'll see you soon, okay?'

'Yes, I'll meet you at the station. See you soon.'

Sally put down the phone and took a closer look at the painting on the wall. In the bottom right-hand corner, a signature was scrawled; Sally Sullivan.

9 ~ TWO PEA-FRITTERS IN A POD

The morning passed by surprisingly quickly. Sally had helped herself to breakfast and made coffee, and though she did explore, looking for little clues about her life here, she felt a little uncomfortable nosing around. She was both at home and an intruder here. She didn't discover an awful lot, but there were more photos. Photos of this other life; Sally on holidays that she had never been on, of the University days she which had never had, of friends and of boyfriends. It looked as though this Sally had had a pretty nice life.

Sally thought of the night before again, of a Sally somewhere sailing across a wide sea. And she wondered how Sally in hospital was getting on. Were the other *hers* back? And did they remember anything about their missing time? There were so many questions buzzing around her head, but no one to give her any answers. Maybe Lockey would have some more theories.

Before she knew it, it was almost time to head up

to the station to meet him. In her room she found a handbag; a mobile phone, keys and a purse inside. She flicked through the purse briefly. Three different bank cards in her name – *this Sally is doing all right*. The mobile phone had a keypad lock. Sally entered her date of birth and the phone sprang to life. There was a new voicemail waiting and without meaning to she pressed the voicemail icon.

'You have, one, new messages. New messages. Sally Daarling, It's Abigail,' a plummy voice declared. 'We're all set for this evening. There was a little issue with the caterer, but it's all sorted now so not to worry. I'll see you at the gallery around seven. Ta-ta. Ciao for now. *End of messages. You have, no, new messages.'*

After finding her home address on some letters by the front door, Sally called a taxi (she had found the number saved under TaxiMike on the mobile) and she arranged a lift up to the train station. With a few minutes to spare, she rushed to the small bathroom to get ready.

Sally felt odd using makeup and a toothbrush that didn't belong to her. But she guessed the toothbrush was familiar with this mouth already. She knew it was silly, but she gave the toothbrush a really good clean before she used it, disinfecting it liberally with some extra strong mouthwash she'd found. She applied just a touch of makeup; a little mascara, a light dusting of face-powder and she was just dabbing on a little lip gloss when she heard the taxi toot outside. Grabbing her handbag, she rushed out and slammed the front door behind herself.

'Alright?' the driver greeted her. 'Where you off to today love? Somewhere nice?'

'Just meeting someone off a train.' Sally smiled amiably.

The Taxi was at the station in hardly any time at all, she could have easily walked it.

'Thanks, that's great,' she paused for a second, '…Mike.'

The Taxi driver beamed, 'No probs. You need a lift back down?'

'No, I think we'll probably walk. Thank you.' She handed over some money and climbed from the cab.

Sally wandered into the bustling station. Its high ceiling, a lattice of panelled glass, criss-crossed with ironwork supports. She looked up at the antique four faced clock; quarter-past-twelve. With a few minutes to spare, she bought herself a coffee. She didn't see him approach. He was suddenly behind her. 'Sally!'

She spun around sloshing most of her coffee on the ground. 'Lockey! You're here.' So glad to see him, Sally wrapped Lockey in a half hug with her free arm and breathed him in. He smelt warm and familiar like gingerbread.

'Liking the look Sal,' Lockey pulled away and gestured to her dress and hair.

'Thank you,' Sally flushed happily, 'I hadn't worn a dress for years… You don't scrub up too badly yourself.' She took in his cleanly shaven face, smooth and soft looking. His chestnut brown hair, neat and well cut. He wore an expensive looking wool coat, a blue and white checked shirt and a pair of navy cotton trousers.

They found themselves walking. Sally drained her cup and threw it in a nearby bin. 'So where did *you* wake up this morning?'

Lockey didn't answer immediately, he looked

troubled. His eyes clouded over, stormy suddenly. 'Well… it seems, I'm married.'

Sally wasn't sure how she felt about this, *not that it has anything to do with me,* she thought – *but Lockey certainly doesn't look happy about it.*

'Who's the lucky lady?' she asked lightly.

Lockey looked at her, his face softened slightly and he sighed. 'Patricia,' he spat the name out crossly.

Sally waited for him to elaborate with growing concern.

'We nearly married. We were engaged. Luckily for me I discovered her for the shallow, manipulative, money-grabbing, two-timing, sociopath she was, just in time.' He let out an angry snort, 'It seems I wasn't so lucky in this life.'

Sally didn't know what to say. She rushed to keep pace with his increasingly fast stride and touched his arm. 'None of this is easy. But hey, let's just go with the "It's all just a dream" option for now.'

Lockey slowed his step and turned to face her. 'I'm sorry Sally. I shouldn't take it out on you. I just, can't believe I'd be *so stupid.* I didn't see her; seems she's off at a spa for the week.' He smiled grimly and changed the subject, 'So how about you? An Artist Sally! I saw some pictures of your work online. You're amazing Sal, why were you temping?'

'There's nothing wrong with temping,' Sally replied defensively.

'That's not what I meant. It's just, you're obviously talented. I just wondered why you never found your calling in our own reality, that's all.'

'I don't know,' Sally said simply. She didn't know much of anything at the moment. Everything she had thought she had known, had come unstuck around the edges.

They fell into step and made comfortable small-talk as they ambled along, and before long they found themselves on the seafront. The salty sea air mixed with the smell of cooking chips and vinegar, and both realising they were ravenous they were drawn to a little Fish and Chip shop. 'I could murder a portion of chips and a pea-fritter,' Sally laughed wistfully.

'Ha, me too! Pea-fritters are my absolute favourite!'

There was a slight chill still in the air, but the sun was shining and it was pleasantly warm for early March. They took their warm paper wrapped bundle to the beach. Lockey lay his coat on the stones for Sally and they sat side by side and ate their chip-picnic looking out to sea. It was quiet on the beach, just the soft sound of the waves sighing against the shore. They both reached for their pea-fritter's at the same time and accidentally brushing fingers they laughed.

'I'm glad it's you that's here with me Sally. I know we just met yesterday, but it really doesn't feel like it. I'm still trying to work out if we maybe did meet somewhere before, or some *time* before?' Lockey laughed, 'It seems anything's possible.'

Sally gazed out over the sparkling sea to the horizon. It was so easy talking to Lockey. The only other people Sally remembered feeling this comfortable with were: Nita, Uncle Joe and in her borrowed memories of Cal, the brother from her other life.

'It's my birthday on Friday. I wonder where I'll be then,' Sally mused.

'Seriously? This Friday? It's *my* birthday on Friday too!'

Sally turned to Lockey, 'No, you're joking!' she studied his face to see if he was serious.

'I kid you not. So how old will you be? If you don't mind me asking?' He bit into a chip.

'I'll be thirty-three'

Lockey nearly choking, laughed. 'Ha, crazy! Me too. What are the odds!' Then more seriously, 'Did you have anything planned?'

'No, not really, probably tea with my aunt. How about you?'

'I probably would have just worked late. Although, my mother always likes to throw me an elaborate party.' Lockey seemed absorbed in thought, 'You know, in a way, we've been living parallel lives to each other in our own reality. Both born on the same day thirty-three years ago. Our lives have taken such different paths.'

They watched an old couple making their way along the beach slowly, arms linked. They seemed in their own little world, totally absorbed with each other. 'That's sweet. I'd like to find that one day.' Sally looked at Lockey and ventured, 'Will you tell me about Patricia? You don't have to, if you don't want to?'

Lockey didn't answer immediately, he was still gazing at the old couple walking into the distance. He closed his eyes for a moment and then sighed. 'We met at a party through friends. I was twenty-five, she was a year younger. She was different back then vivacious, sweet and funny. I thought she was the girl of my dreams.' He looked thoughtful for a moment and then continued, 'I fell for her, totally, from the first moment we met. I didn't know love like that existed outside of fiction. We were inseparable, we did everything together. The cracks started to appear a few years in. We were engaged, wedding plans were being made, rings had been bought. My parents were updating their wills. Being the eldest Son, it was always presumed I'd take on Wentworth Hall one day. And I didn't realise that this was what Patricia had presumed too. My parents were hoping I'd start helping with the running of the estate, but it wasn't what I wanted. I have absolutely no interest in a life like that, Sally. My work is my life. I live for it.' Lockey picked up a stone and turned it in his hands deep in thought.

Sally couldn't see his eyes, but she could feel his sadness.

'I didn't go through all those years of education to just sit back and run Wentworth Hall. My little brother Ted, on the other hand, was born for it. Fortuitously I was approached by an investor, around this time, interested in my work and wanting to back the lab. That was how SALL began. And I went to my parents and convinced them to leave the entire estate to Ted.' He discarded his stone, tossing it towards the sea onto the beach. 'Patricia lost the plot when I told her what I'd done. She raged! Threw plates. Screamed at me. I was pretty surprised. She'd had more than her fair share of tantrums. But this was new. She tried every tactic she could, over the following weeks. Even telling me she was pregnant and that our baby deserved a secure future. I mean, it's not like we'd be living on the streets without Wentworth. But no, she had it all planned out. I was really in two minds, she nearly had me convinced. That's when I found her with Ted. They were alone in the library and didn't see me. She had him cornered, she was literally all over him, poor lad. I heard her saying that she had never loved me, it was him who she'd always liked. He said; "What about the baby?" and she laughed, she *laughed* and said there *was* no baby. To his credit, Ted pushed her away, disgusted, and told her in no uncertain terms that he wasn't interested.'

Lockey took a deep breath and looked out across to the ruins of the old burnt pier. 'I just threw myself into my work. I've been pretty wary of women since then, to be honest…'

Sally was incensed, 'I'm not surprised, what a cow! We're not all like that you know.'

'I know, you're not.'

They didn't talk for a while, they just sat companionably.

Then Lockey turned to Sally, 'Okay your turn, how about you Sally? What happened so differently in our own reality? You seem to be doing so well *here*, shining.'

'I don't know really.' Sally searched for the words. 'I had wanted to go to Uni, but, there just wasn't the money. And I felt like I owed it to my aunt and uncle to stay and look after them, too. They'd been there for me all those years. Then Uncle Joe died about four years ago. I was devastated. He was such a great man…' Sally paused, wondering whether to tell him about her *breakdown*. But that was a whole other story. She wasn't sure she wanted to open that can of worms right now. She had, after all, only met Lockey the day before. And how many people have a complete mental breakdown and disappear for months and months, and then return with no memories at all?

57

They said it had been the stress of her job, combined with the emotional trauma of losing her uncle. Sally just upped and left – she didn't pack a bag or leave a note. She simply vanished from the face of the earth, for eleven whole months. A Fugue State they called it. And then just as suddenly as she had left, she returned – physically at least, but mentally, it took her far longer. At first she didn't even remember her own name. For weeks on end, apparently, she had just stared blankly into space, unresponsive. But day by day she had returned, until eventually she was almost entirely back to her old self. However, the missing months remained lost to her, like a torn out page. Though she had long since been signed off by the mental health team, she had been left with panic attacks, a gaping hole in her life and an underlying anxiety that she was missing some undefinable part of herself. She lost not only her confidence and self-esteem, but also her appetite for everything in life that used to bring her joy; painting, music, food. Friends, she now unintentionally pushed away and kept at a distance. She was unable to hold down a fulltime job – even the temping agency were losing patience with her. And this, was the true reason that she was where she was in her life. But how could she tell Lockey any of that?

Lockey was looking at her expectantly, he could tell she was holding back. 'Go on,' he urged gently.

Sally sighed. 'What was left of our little family fell apart. My aunt, she comes across as tough. But she was broken, and I…' she sought the words. 'I wasn't there for her, when she really needed me. I… I don't know. Then, I guess I stayed around to look after her really… And then the days, weeks, months, years went by. I never seemed to have much luck. Mary won the lottery not long after Joe died – not a huge win, but enough to buy herself a more comfortable house and she went on a cruise for a few months.'

'Didn't she give you any money, then? – to go off to university?'

'No, I was twenty-nine by then – and I wouldn't have expected her to anyway,' Sally sounded defensive, 'She deserved all of it and more – after all she'd been through. She hasn't had an easy life. And she's done far more than her fair share of looking after me over the years. I still feel like I owe her so much. I do what I can to help her. She's got terrible arthritis now. I rent a flat nearby where she lives, so I can check in on her, you know, run errands, cleaning and stuff.'

'Surely she could get a Carer? someone else to help?' Lockey asked.

'But she's *family*, and she's the only family I have left. I feel I owe it to Joe too. He always took care of her, kept her sweet, he'd say,' Sally smiled sadly.

'But you need to start living your own life now Sally. If, I mean, *when* we make it out of this, promise me you'll try?'

Sally thought of her little flat, her empty life. 'Yes, it *is* time to make some changes. Maybe it's time my luck changed.'

'We make our own luck Sally; you just have to believe in yourself.'

A large seagull swooped in and stole a chip from the wrapper. It turned neatly, flapped its wings and flew away, the chip still in its beak. 'Oy!' Sally laughed. 'Cheeky thing!'

'Uhrrgrh! It *pooed* on me!'

Sally turned to see Lockey, crossly wiping at his trouser leg with some screwed up paper.

'*That's* supposed to be lucky,' Sally said consolingly.

'Lucky! I'd say It's far more likely to bring me E. coli, or some nasty viral disease than good luck!'

Sally tried not to laugh. Lockey went down to the water's edge and tried to dart into the shallows between waves, to scoop up a handful of water to rinse off his white streaked leg. He managed it the first time, but didn't see the next wave coming in – the wave caught him off-guard, he lost his balance and ended up in a half press-up plank position in the shallows. He stumbled to his feet and emerged from the sea dripping and gasping, 'It's flipping freezing in there!'

Sally couldn't help herself now, she held her sides as she laughed. Once he got over the initial shock, Lockey laughed too, there wasn't much else he could do.

'So much for the good luck,' he laughed. 'Seems to have washed the seagull poo off nicely though.'

'Oh Lockey, what are we going to do with you?!'

A cloud passed in front of the sun and a chilly breeze blew in from the sea. 'I don't know. I'm absolutely frozen now!' Lockey shivered.

'My place is nearby, luckily for you. Ha, lucky, see.'

10 ~ DRESSING AND UNDRESSING

Sally's house really wasn't far and in no time at all they were at the door. She rummaged in her bag for the front door key. 'Oh no,' she winced. 'I think I must have left the keys inside… Maybe there's a spare somewhere?'

Lockey was already hunting about around the front door; he checked under the mat and under a couple of old plant pots.

Sally found Nita's number on the mobile phone and called it. But it went straight to answer, 'Neetz it's Sal. I've managed to lock myself out. Give me a call will you. Bye.'

Meanwhile Lockey had clambered into the front flowerbed and was trying a ground-floor sash window. With a couple of yanks the window opened up. He looked over his shoulder and grinned triumphantly, and then peered inside, 'It's a bedroom.'

'It's alright it's mine, well, oh you know what I mean.'

Lockey hoiked himself up and slid in through the window, head first. He disappeared out of sight and a moment later the front door opened.

'Ah, well-done Lockey! Surprisingly good at breaking and entering. You sure you're not in the wrong career?'

Lockey mock bowed and stood aside for Sally to pass. He followed Sally through to her bedroom.

'I doubt I have anything you'd want to borrow to wear,' Sally laughed. 'Here,' she chucked him a towel and her dressing gown, 'There's a bathroom through there. Go have a shower if you like. I'm sure I saw a tumble dryer upstairs. I'll go give your clothes a quick wash and get them dried for you.'

Sally stood in the hall outside the bedroom while Lockey got out of his drenched clothes. 'I'm getting a bit of déjà vu to when we first met, Sally,' Lockey called through from the bedroom. He appeared a moment later, the towel wrapped around his waist. He was in surprisingly good shape. Sally gestured to the bathroom door and took his wet clothing.

She was halfway up the stairs when she heard a high-pitched shriek. She rushed back down and Lockey burst from the bathroom, stumbling backwards apologising.

'There's someone in there, Sally!' he flustered. 'In the bath!'

Just then Nita appeared at the door, brandishing a hairbrush like a weapon, 'Who. The hell. Are you!?'

'Neetz, it's okay!' Sally pacified. 'This is Lockey! I said he could use the shower.'

'Bloody hell Sal. Gave me a bloody heart attack! And why couldn't he have used your en-suite?' Nita pulled her towel up a little higher.

'My en-suite…'

'Has he been using my toothbrush too?!' Nita demanded. 'It was all wet and smelt funny, like mouthwash…'

Sally felt her cheeks burning; *It was Nita's toothbrush?* 'No Neetz, we just got here. Lockey fell in the sea. I said he could have a shower.'

Nita turned to Lockey and seemed to see him properly for the first time. She eyed him up and down approvingly and treated him to one of her winning smiles. 'Nice to meet you Lockey,' she twinkled, then gave Sally an enquiring glance, eyebrows raised.

Lockey smiled awkwardly. He held his towel with one hand and offered out his other, 'Nice to meet you too. I'm so sorry for barging in… I had no idea,' he flushed and they shook hands.

'No worries Lockey,' Nita winked.

She is such a flirt, Sally thought, *that girl is incorrigible!*

'I've finished in here now,' Nita purred, squeezing past Lockey a little too closely. 'It's all yours.' She linked her arm through Sally's, 'I'm just going to talk to Sally now. Have a nice shower.'

Nita dragged Sally off to her room, to interrogate her whilst she got dressed. 'Okay, you dark horse,' she grinned, hands on hips. 'Where on *earth* did *he* come from?' she demanded animatedly.

'He's…' Sally searched for the right thing to say. 'He's, a friend. I met him through work…'

'At the gallery?' Nita raised an eyebrow, unconvinced.

'Yes, um no. He wanted to buy some of my work…'

'So, you pushed him in the sea and lured him back here to get him out of his clothes?' Nita chuckled.

'You're a *bad* girl Sal, I never knew,' she teased.

Sally blushed, 'No Neetz, like I said he's just a friend. It's not like that.'

'But he's *well* fit, what's *wrong* with you Sally? Seems like a nice guy too… Ah, of course; he's a nice guy. I remember, you only like arseholes.'

'Nita! That's not very nice.'

Nita rolled her eyes, 'True though.' And then she softened, 'Sorry Sal.' She gave Sally a hug. 'Is he coming tonight?'

'I, I guess, yes.'

'Good! Theo's coming too. Let's all go out for a drink and some food before the party. What do you think? Cocktails first at Cool Bananas?'

'Cool Bananas?'

'Sal. You haven't been out for *way* too long! What are you wearing tonight? by the way.' Nita picked up a tiny, bright, carrot coloured number – which Sally guessed was a dress – and held it up to herself, 'I was thinking of wearing this…' She caught Sally's expression, 'Don't you like it?'

'Well… It's very bright and, very small…'

'Perfect then!' Nita laughed and wriggled into the dress. 'There. What do you reckon?' The tiny orange halter-necked dress skimmed her petite figure and was outrageously short. But somehow on Nita it worked.

'You know what Neetz, on you, it's just right.'

Nita beamed and hugged Sally again. 'Now, to just find the perfect shoes to go with it…' She looked thoughtfully at her huge array of shoes. 'I knew I should have bought a new pair earlier,' she sighed.

'How about these?' Sally absentmindedly passed her a pair of brightly patterned heels.

'I guess.' Nita stepped into the shoes and looked

satisfied. 'How about you?! What are *you* going to wear!?' she asked dramatically, looking suddenly concerned.

'I don't know. This?' Sally gestured to what she was already wearing.

'Sally, no! This is your big night. You have to make an effort!' Nita eyed Sally thoughtfully. 'I will dress you,' she announced magnanimously.

Sally sat down on the edge of the bed and Nita proceeded to search her room.

'How can you find anything in here? It's a mess,' Sally laughed gesturing to the floor.

'That's not mess, that's my floor-drobe,' Nita said defensively.

'And *that?* Sally pointed to the chair in the corner, piled high with folded and unfolded clothes.

'Chair-drobe… Here!' Nita said triumphantly. 'Put this on,' she threw something small and black at Sally. 'No arguments.'

Sally held it up, unconvinced, 'Really?!'

'Yes. Just put it on,' Nita barked bossily.

Knowing there was no use arguing, Sally obediently changed.

Sally stood in front of Nita's dusty mirror and took in her reflection. The dress was well fitting, a little too snug perhaps, but she had to admit, she did look good. It was longer than Nita's dress – which wasn't difficult – coming to just above the knee. It had capped sleeves, with a high neck and three little cut-out triangles at the collarbone. It was pretty modest for something in Nita's collection, Audrey Hepburn-esque even.

'You can't go wrong with an LBD,' Nita said matter-of-factly and came to stand next to Sally in

front of the mirror, 'You look AMAZING Sally!
Please, please, please wear it!'

'Okay. Okay,' Sally laughed and slipped an arm
around her friend's shoulder.

Nita grinned victoriously. 'Yay! And *don't* wear
your pumps,' she said, pointedly looking down at
Sally's canvas shoes in disapproval. 'Wear these!' She
handed Sally a pair of black kitten-heel shoes,
'Perfect!'

'Why are you home at lunch time having a bath
anyway Neetz?'

'The joys of being self-employed. I need to get
back actually. I'll have to take this with me so I can
get changed at the studio. I'll meet you there,' said
Nita; already out of the orange mini-dress and pulling
on a pair of painty jeans and t-shirt. 'Cool Bananas at
seven?' Nita was almost out of the door, then turned
back, 'Oh, hang-on.' She delved into her chair-drobe
pile and pulled some clothes out, 'These may fit
Lockey…' She passed Sally a pair of red tartan
trousers and a black shirt.

'Are these yours?' Sally asked suspiciously.

'Theo's. I doubt he'll mind. He got changed here
last weekend and left them. Oh, he left shoes too…'
Nita kicked some clothes aside on the floor and
found a pair of highly polished, pointy-toed, tan
brogues. 'See, I know where *everything* is – it's all
perfectly organised.'

Nita had rushed off, running late again, in true
Nita style. Sally had given Lockey, Theo's clothes –
another of Nita's many boyfriends Sally presumed –
Lockey eyed the clothes warily.

'It's either these, or we'll have to hang-about here

for ages while your stuff dries. I just chucked it all in the tumble drier, but it's going to take a while.'

'All right,' Lockey conceded.

He returned a few minutes later – Sally did a double take; it was such a different look. 'Wow, you look like a you from an alternate reality.'

'Very funny,' Lockey dead-panned.

'No, I like it; it suits you. Very... Brighton.'

'Whatever *that* means,' Lockey laughed. 'I look like my little brother.'

They were upstairs now in the sitting room, 'Is this one of yours?' Lockey was studying the painting on the wall.

'I think so, yes.'

'It's very good. I'm looking forward to seeing more of your work later. If I can come that is?'

'Of course you can. And yes, I'm looking forward to seeing my work too.'

11 ~ HUMAN BLACK HOLE

They spent a very pleasant afternoon exploring Brighton, meandering the quirky narrow alleyways of The Lanes. They even took a ride on the big wheel. To any bystander they would have appeared to be a regular couple sightseeing.

Before they knew it the sun was setting. Lockey glanced at his watch, 'It's quarter to six already. What time are we meeting your friend Nita and her boyfriend?'

'Seven. We'd better pop back and get ready.'

Back at the apartment they changed; Lockey back into his own clothes, and Sally into the dress she'd borrowed from Nita. Lockey whistled and Sally gave him a twirl. 'What do you think? Too much?' she asked self-consciously.

'Not at all. You look amazing.'

It didn't take them too long to find the bar – Lockey had managed to look it up on his phone. Nita saw them through the window, waved, and beckoned them enthusiastically into the crowded bar. They pushed their way through the crowd to join Nita and her boyfriend. Lockey's eyes widened as he took in Nita in her tangerine micro-dress. Nita threw an arm around Sally and kissed Lockey on the cheek. 'Sal, Lockey... This is Theo.'

Her companion turned – he looked oddly familiar. Sally was trying to place his face.

'Teddy!' Lockey stammered, 'Wha— what are *you* doing here!?'

'I could say the same of you!' Theodore laughed, looking perplexed.

'You two know each other?!' Nita shouted a little too loudly over the music.

'He's my brother!' Theodore answered. 'Craziness! What *are* you doing here Ace? Is Pats here too?'

'No. I uhm, came to buy some of Sally's work, for Patricia. It's a surprise.'

'Well! It's certainly a surprise to see you! A good one though!' He slapped Lockey on the back and pulled him in for a hug. Sally could see it now, the familiarity. They didn't look identical by any means, but there was certainly a strong family resemblance. Theodore's hair was a lighter redder shade of chestnut and his pale skin was sprinkled generously with freckles, but they shared the same kind hazel eyes and aquiline nose. There was no doubting they were brothers. Sally liked Theodore instantly. He was a few years younger than them and had a playful energy; like an overgrown child, he seemed to be constantly moving and was all smiles. He wore a pair of yellow and black checked trousers, with a bright red shirt – which fought with the red in his hair – his look was not dissimilar to Rupert the Bear, Sally thought.

The brothers had gone off to the bar to buy drinks. 'How crazy is that!?' shouted Nita. 'Bumping into each other like that! Theo was just talking about him the other day – *Ace*, Theo calls him. Ha, I should marry him; Neet and Ace,' Nita laughed raucously.

Lockey handed her a yellow drink in a tall glass, 'And *what* are you two laughing about?'

Nita took a generous gulp of the drink. '*Nothing*, nothing!' she laughed.

'God Nita. How many of these have you had?!' Sally eyed her own glass warily, not being one to drink much herself usually.

'Not enough! They're AMAZING. These are *the* cool bananas of Cool Bananas. They're not only banana-ry, but they're cool and they make you bananas.' Nita snorted at her own joke. 'Come on Sal. Live a little!'

The four of them sat around a small table in a quieter corner to the back of the bar. Sally sipped her cocktail tentatively. *It tastes pretty good actually*, she thought, *rather like an alcoholic tropical smoothie*. 'I like it here,' Sally mused. 'Everything is so wonderful. And you and me, Neetz, renting this cool house together… Everything here is how I always wished it could have been. I *am* a little worried about Aunty Mary though…'

'Renting? What has gotten into you Sally? *Your* house is brilliant Sal. And I'm very privileged you let me stay here with you – but you deserved *all* of it. That a*unt* of yours… I just don't know how you could be concerned about *her* after all she did to you. I'm amazed you got away so un-scarred; she ruined your childhood. That woman is a *black hole*.'

'A black hole?' Lockey asked with a laugh.

'Yes, she has an amazing ability to suck all of the happiness and positive energy out of a room, and everyone in it.'

'A human black hole, I like it.' Lockey was thoughtful.

'Don't call Mary a *black hole* Nita, it's not very nice. She *is* my aunty.'

'After all she did to you? Sal... I don't know *how* you could forgive her. I certainly never will.'

And then it came to Sally, in a huge sickening wave of sadness.

By chance Sally had returned home early that day. She had heard their raised voices as she'd let herself in. 'You need to tell her Mary.' Sally's ears had pricked and she'd paused at the doorway. Joe sounded livid. 'I can't believe this. It's not right. You lied. All these years you lied, to her, to me. I feel sick Mary, sick to my core. It stops here. You will tell Sally tonight and If you don't tell her, I will.'

Sally could bear it no more, 'Tell me what?' And the whole terrible truth had come out. Mary had been lying for years. Sally's parents hadn't been on the verge of bankruptcy. There had been money, and plenty of it. Sally had been left everything. Over two-million pounds. There was a trust fund; which allowed a very generous forty-thousand pounds a year for living expenses and school fees, until Sally reached the age of eighteen, at which point she would receive around five-hundred-thousand pounds and then the same at twenty-one and twenty-five. Joe only found out because he'd wanted to find a way to raise some money to send Sally to university. He had visited their bank manager to ask for a loan. The bank manager had been surprised, would Joe not want to withdraw from their joint savings account? he had asked. Mary had been squirrelling away money, it turned out; over three-thousand pounds a month of Sally's inheritance, for the last ten years. Mary had 'saved' over three-hundred-and-sixty-thousand pounds into the account, since Sally had come to live with them. Back home Joe had searched the house and found the paperwork – the original will Sally's parents had left.

Joe had said 'You need to go Sally, you're eighteen, go out into the world and grab every moment.'

Sally clutched the edge of the table to ground herself. The blood had drained from her face. She thought she was going to be sick. *Could it be? Could Mary really have done that to me?* Sally thought of Mary's 'lucky lottery win' and tears stung her eyes, her chest felt tight, she could barely breathe.

'Sal? I'm so sorry Sal.' Nita reached across the table and squeezed her hand.

Sally didn't know what to think. She raised her glass and downed the contents in one, she'd try and work it out later.

Lockey caught Sally's eye, concern wrinkling his brow. 'Are you okay?' he mouthed.

Sally nodded and smiled thinly, and then looking at him gravely she gave him a barely perceptible shake of the head. No, no she wasn't okay. She didn't object to the second cocktail and by the third her troubles were numbed nicely. She jostled in amongst the crowd at the bar to order them all a fourth round of cocktails.

Lockey came up behind her and touched her elbow gently, 'Sally? Come outside? I want to talk, it's too loud in here.' He led her through the crowd and they slipped out through a side door and past a huddle of smokers. When they were out of earshot, Lockey stopped and turned to Sally. 'What happened back there? Did you get some new memories?'

'You could say that.' Sally pulled her arm away. 'I

don't think I can even talk about it Lockey. It's all just too messed up.'

'I know it's confusing, but these memories, they're not really yours. You have to try and separate them from your own reality.'

'But that's the problem Lockey. I think these *are* my memories. I mean, they concern my reality too.'

Lockey looked confused.

Sally sighed, unsure how to explain, or where to even start. 'Look, you know what I was saying earlier; my parents left no money, me not being able to go to university? That's what Nita was talking about in there. It was my Aunty Mary; she *lied* to me. There *was* money, plenty of it. I don't know if it's what she set out to do from the beginning, but she basically stole it all.' Sally felt a sob rising.

Lockey looked aghast. 'But maybe she didn't do that, in your reality?' he offered gently.

Sally snorted angrily. 'The coincidental *lottery win*? I don't know Lockey, I just can't comprehend any of it any more. I feel as if my head's going to explode.'

At that moment Nita burst from the bar and called out to them, 'Hey! *There* you two are! I've just seen the time Sal. We've got to get up the road to your do.' Nita turned to hurry Theodore along.

Lockey took Sally by the shoulders and said seriously, 'We don't have to go, if you don't want to? We could just say you're not feeling well, if you want to talk or get some space?'

Nita and Theodore were approaching them now, sharing some joke, the pair chortling, arms linked. Sally blew out a slow breath regaining herself. 'No. I don't think I do want to talk about it at the moment to be honest, or even think about it. Any of it.'

Nita wrapped an arm around Sally's shoulder, 'You alright chick? I'm so sorry if I dredged up bad memories.'

'It's okay.' Sally gave her friend a reassuring smile. 'We'd better get a move on hadn't we?'

12 ~ ABIGAIL'S PARTY

The four of them walked the short journey. The cool fresh night air welcome, and Nita and Theodore's jolly chatter and banter pleasantly distracting. Before long they arrived at the gallery. Sally found herself being hustled into a brightly lit entrance room, impatiently, by a towering woman with a severe shiny black bob and scarlet painted lips. 'Sally. You're late!' she barked. 'Quick-quick. Let me take your coat. *Everyone* is waiting for you.' The large lady wrestled Sally's coat from her and turned to greet the others. 'Anita,' she said curtly, and theatrically air kissed Nita.

'Abigail. A pleasure as always,' Nita said darkly, taking her own coat off and thrusting it into Abigail's arms.

'And you two are?' Abigail turned her disapproving gaze to Lockey and Theodore.

'Abigail; Theodore, Lockey,' Nita gestured and then turning to the others. 'Theo, Lockey, meet A-*big*-gal,' Nita's eyes twinkled, her tongue in her cheek.

Theodore sniggered involuntarily. Lockey; looking

a little uncomfortable, gently shouldered his brother. Sally suddenly feeling far too sober, gave Nita a look and held her breath. But oblivious, Abigail hurried them all through to the next room.

There was a fair sized crowd gathered in the gallery. Sally felt all eyes on her as they entered the room. Abigail strode off into the throng.

'Here,' Nita thrust a glass of white wine into Sally's hand. 'I don't know *how* you can bear that woman. She's a complete snob.'

'She's not that bad, is she?' Sally answered distractedly, and took a large gulp of the wine. It was an acidic dry white. Sally pulled a face, but took another swig. She really needed not to be sobering up right now. In fact, she decided, she was going to get very drunk.

Sally circled the gallery. It was the strangest feeling, taking in the exhibition of her own work; seeing the pieces with both a familiar and unfamiliar eye, and oddly she envied her own confidence and talent. She vowed to herself to pick up a brush and try her hand again soon.

Time raced away. She found herself on the social conveyor-belt, jostled from one small group to another. She smiled and nodded numbly – it appeared to be enough – and an attentive waiter kept her glass topped up nicely. Sally was suddenly conscious that a hush had come over the room – the crowd of blurry faces turned to her expectantly – and she was vaguely aware that someone had asked her a question, but she had no clue what it had been. She blinked hard trying to focus both her vision and her thoughts. She looked up to see Abigail looming over her.

'Sally?' Abigail said loudly, 'We were wondering if you would care to say a few words?'

Sally looked back over the crowd. She spotted Nita and grinned. Nita smiled back encouragingly.

'Do you need this?' Abigail pushed a microphone into her hands.

'Ehrm,' The microphone squealed and Sally snorted into it, her muffled laugh amplified across the room. 'Well, I'd just like to say thank you, to you all, for coming, really...' she trailed off and looked to Abigail for assistance.

Abigail looking slightly exasperated snatched the microphone from her, 'Yes, thank you Sally.'

Abigail carried on talking and Sally, grateful to be off the hook, drifted away. She drank some more wine, sloshing half of it down her chin.

13 ~ RIDE A PAINTED PONY

Nita found Sally swaying precariously on her feet, staring at one of her paintings. 'Let's get you some fresh air Salamander.'

'Whadi'you say?' Sally asked in confusion.

'I said; let's get you some fresh air Sal, shall we?' Nita repeated. She had never seen Sally like this before. She needed to get her home. 'Come on. A nice walk will make you feel better.' She tucked a supportive arm around Sally.

'Neeeta, I love you,' Sally slurred, smiling blearily at her friend, 'Did I tell you tha' tlately?'

'Yes Sal, love you too chick.' Nita gestured for Lockey to help and he came and supported Sally on her other side.

'Lockey!' Sally laughed. 'I know we just met, but I love you too! You're such a lovely man. You're like the brother I never had. Oh, no Cal was the brother that I never had...' she trailed off, and hiccupped loudly. 'Where's your lovely boyfriend gone Neetz? Theo-Teddy?'

Nita raised an eyebrow, 'He's not my boyfriend Sal. You know that! He'll catch us up in a minute, he's just gone to the cashpoint.'

'Ah but I like Theo. He's a sweetie. Why's he not your boyfriend Neetz, he-shlovely.' Sally hiccupped again.

'I'm not his *type* Sal... you know that!' Nita laughed.

'Whaddoyou-mean you're not his type. You're every man's type! Well every straight man...' Sally snorted with laughter.

'Hmmm, yes, there you go then,' Nita laughed and ruffled her friend's hair, but then stopped abruptly. Sally saw Nita and Lockey exchange a look, but she couldn't decipher it. 'Oh come *on*! Surely you knew!?' Nita was saying in amazement.

Sally had no clue what they were talking about. She pulled away from them, drawn to the bright lights of a carousel. Thrusting some money at the ride attendant, she clambered onto a brightly painted pony. Sally clung on to the twisted pole as the carousel began to turn. Round and around, everything was a blur of bright light and colour. She laughed and whooped loudly, circling an arm in the air – rodeo style – but her laughter died down as the spinning all started to get a bit much.

The carousel stopped. But Sally carried on spinning. She dismounted her pony ungracefully. Sliding to the ground and staggering sideways, she toppled straight into Theodore – who had just caught up with them all – nearly knocking him off of his feet. He caught her under the arms. Sally looked up at him unfocusedly, smiled vaguely and then vomited down his front.

It took all three of them to help Sally back home. Theodore and Lockey supporting her either side as she half-walked, half-stumbled along, head lolling, her feet in auto-walk mode. And Nita talking to keep her awake. Lockey was anxious to get somewhere safe, and quickly; aware that they would most likely both *shift* as soon as Sally fell asleep. He was relieved when they reached the house and Nita unlocked the front door. Lockey and Theodore helped Sally through to her room.

'That girl is going to feel *rough* tomorrow,' Theodore mused as he left the room.

Lockey pitied Sally's alternate-self who would most likely wake up with the almightiest hangover in the morning. He pulled off her shoes and rolled her under the duvet. 'Sally? Are you awake?'

Sally murmured something incoherently. Lockey lay on the bed beside her on top of the duvet.

With a struggle Sally half opened her eyes. 'Hello you,' she muttered dreamily. Her eyes fell closed again.

A moment later when Nita stuck her head around the door, she was surprised to see Lockey curled up on the bed next to Sally, fully clothed and fast asleep. As she found a blanket and tucked it over him, she wondered how on earth he had fallen to sleep so quickly and deeply. Nita gazed at Lockey's sleeping face for a moment, before turning out the light and leaving the room with a sigh.

14 ~ LITTLE MISS CALAMITY ~ WEDNESDAY

Sally stirred, groggy with sleep. She didn't open her eyes immediately – when she did she found herself in a darkened room. Where was she now? She struggled to remember where she *should* be.

There was someone asleep on the bed beside her. She could just make out the outline of a broad shoulder; his shadowy shape silhouetted by the diffused glow of light which seeped in through a gap in the door. Sally closed her eyes again and tried to concentrate her thoughts. The last things she could remember were the gallery and her abysmal attempt at public speaking. Did she ride a Carousel? Foggy memories came to her in waves. *Oh god, I was sick all over poor Theo.* Sally started feeling queasy just remembering. And then, *was I in bed with Lockey?* She looked over to the sleeping figure beside her. 'Lockey?' she whispered.

The shape moved slightly and in reply gave a soft snore. Sally climbed from the bed. She was wearing a long baggy T-shirt, her legs bare. Her feet found a pair of slippers on the floor beside the bed. She shuffled into them and padded over to the door. Tentatively she pushed open the door and looked out onto a landing, dimly lit by a single pendant bulb, hanging in a woven shade over a stairwell. A small window high above the stairs, faintly glowed with the first blue light of dawn. It was eerily quiet here, as if the whole world had stopped. No hum of traffic or sounds life at all. Looking back over her shoulder into the room, she could just about see him now; the light from the hallway softly pooling across the floor to the bed. Sally tiptoed back across the room to study the sleeping form.

He wasn't Lockey, she was somehow both relieved and disturbed to realise. She leant in closer for a better look. Who *was* he? His face – framed by a dark unruly mop of wavy hair – was slightly puffy with sleep and although he may not be considered conventionally handsome, he was beautiful – Sally thought; with a broad open face, a strong brow, dark eyelashes and a wide soft looking mouth. As if he could sense her staring at him he half opened an eye. 'What are you doing? Funny lady,' he asked with amusement, his voice gruff and warm, and unmistakably Scottish. He wrapped an arm around the back of her legs, overbalancing her in a single movement and pulled her onto him playfully. Sally let out a little yelp, but laughed despite herself as he started to tickle her. She squirmed and rolled off him onto the bed and he turned, moving himself over her. Arching back on straightened arms, he gazed deeply into her eyes. Sally felt as if he could see into her very soul, it was electrifying. The particles in the space between them crackled and sparkled indiscernibly to the naked eye. A thrill of excitement coursed through her as he bowed his head, and softly he kissed her.

Sally had never been kissed like that before, so tenderly and lovingly. Her heart ached at the realisation that she had been missing this feeling her entire life, without even knowing. It was as if a final puzzle piece – that she'd never realised had been absent – had slotted into place. She wondered briefly if she should resist. But if her mind didn't know him, somehow on a deeper level she did, and it felt simultaneously thrilling and like the most natural and right thing in the world; to be kissed by this strange man.

'What are you two doing?' a loud little voice suddenly demanded. 'Daddy? Are you eating Mummy?'

Sally craned her neck around in surprise and found a small child standing in the doorway. She caught her breath. There was something startling about this small girl, with her head of flame red curls – surely she *knew* her from somewhere? – she felt an odd squeezing feeling in her heart and strangely, she was happy to see her.

'It's alright bairn. Mummy and Daddy are just playing.' He had already pulled himself up to sitting beside Sally.

The little girl crossed the room and clambered up onto the bed between them. She snuggled in under the covers and blew a stray curl from her eyes. 'I did dream about a angry crocodile,' she said with big eyes, 'He did try an' eat me.'

'An angry crocodile!?' he said in mock-outrage. 'I

hope you chased him away!'

The little girl looked pensive.

'You know, there's only one thing that angry crocodiles are scared of. Do you know what that is?'

She shook her head, sending her tangle of auburn locks bouncing.

'Angry crocodiles may *seem* scary, but they're secretly not very brave. And the one thing that they're *really* scared of is brave little girls, and they're *especially* scared of brave little girls called Flora!'

The little girl giggled. 'But I'm not a little girl, I'm a big girl!' she said boldly.

'Oh! You *are*, are you? Well that's even better, because they're really-*really* scared of brave *big* girls called Flora. So the next time you have a dream about a silly old angry crocodile, you just stand up to him and you say *"I'm not scared of you, silly old crocodile!"* and he'll turn around and waddle away as fast as his short little legs will carry him.'

Flora fell about giggling.

'Oh look, here comes a silly crocodile now!' he clapped his hands from his elbows and the little girl jumped to her feet excitedly,

'I not scared of you silly ol' crocodile!' she yelled, laughing wildly and jumping up and down on the bed a few times, before launching herself at her daddy and wrapping her little arms around him in a great big hug. 'I'm hungry. Can I have pancakes for breakfast?' Flora asked after a moment.

'Come on then little monkey,' he said, scooping her onto his back as he rose from the bed. The little girl clung on, and he turned and winked at Sally as they left the room. Sally heard the pair laughing and chattering their way down the stairs. *So*, she wondered, *wherever am I now?*

Sally found the bathroom along the hallway and closed the door behind herself. She couldn't lock it, as there didn't seem to be a bolt or lock at all. The small room wore all the hallmarks of a family bathroom; a clutter of brightly coloured toys adorned the bath side. An array of bottles of shampoos, bubble-baths and lotions, disarranged on the windowsill, a mug holding three toothbrushes and a couple of tubes of well squeezed toothpaste beside the sink. Sally regarded her reflection in the dusty mirror above the basin. Her hair was longer than it had ever been, coming down well below her shoulders, and although tousled and tangled from sleep, it didn't look bad. Her face was a little plumper – in fact, looking down now, she now noticed she was quite a lot larger all over and could only just see the tips of her toes beyond the curve of her tummy. There were a few new fine lines around her eyes – as if this version of herself had laughed a lot more – and, *is that a grey hair?* She looked tired, but somehow more relaxed. *A happier version of myself? Or is this what motherhood looks like?* she wondered.

Sally sat on the toilet, picked up a little book and absentmindedly flicked through its pages. She turned back to the front cover, which showed a cartoony orange character; Little Miss Calamity, she read – she knew how she felt; what a calamity indeed. Sally thought guiltily of her alternate Brighton self and hoped she wouldn't be feeling too bad today – if of course she *had* been reunited with her own reality – and that she hadn't messed things up too badly last night at the gallery. What would she think when she woke up next to Lockey a stranger to her? And Lockey too; would he wake in Brighton, wondering how on earth he got there? Sally was reminded of her *breakdown* – just disappearing like that with no memories. A black hole in your life and no recollection of where you'd been, or what you'd been doing – it was a terrifying feeling, which she wouldn't wish on anyone. She shuddered. Something important niggled in her mind, but she couldn't quite put her finger on it. And then there had been all that business with her aunt. Could Aunty Mary really have done that to her?

Sally was so deep in thought she didn't hear the footsteps on the stairs and suddenly the bathroom door burst open. The little girl, Flora, stood jiggling in the doorway. 'I need to do a wee-wee,' she announced urgently.

Sally hastily got off the toilet – feeling self-conscious with the girl now standing right beside her – and quickly washed her hands. 'I'll give you some privacy,' she said uncertainly, and left the room closing the door behind her.

Back in the bedroom, Sally drew back the curtains. It was lighter now. The sun was just rising. The window looked out over a fair sized back garden. A large stretch of green lawn, fenced at both sides and lined with mature shrubs and plants, and shadowed at the end by large trees, whose tops were painted gold by the rising sun.

On a chair in the corner of the room, Sally found a small pile of crumpled clothes. *My very own chairdrobe,* she mused, *Nita would be impressed.* A waft of cooking pancakes floated up from the kitchen, and realising she was ravenous, she hurriedly pulled on a pair of trousers and a jumper over the t-shirt she was already wearing. She felt apprehensive to go downstairs, but knew she couldn't hide in the bedroom all day. *Just try to act normally*, she told herself, as she quietly descended the stairs.

Sally followed her nose to the kitchen, and pausing in the doorway, she took a deep breath and entered. He looked up as she came into the room and grinned. 'Wearing my clothes now are you?' he laughed fondly.

Sally felt a hot blush rising.

He came over, spatula in hand, and wrapped an arm around her waist, 'I like it. Reminds me of when we first met.'

As he leant in to kiss her, Sally looked down shyly, and he ended up kissing the top of her head. 'I'm making pancakes,' he said unnecessarily. 'D'you want one?'

Sally nodded, 'Yes please. They smell amazing.'

He returned to the stove. Picking up the frying pan, he tossed a pancake in the air, catching it again easily. 'Where's Flora?' he asked.

'She's in the bathroom.'

He looked at her quizzically.

'Maybe, I should go check on her?' Sally wondered out loud.

'Aye, I think maybe you should,' he chuckled, and continued cooking.

Back upstairs Sally knocked on the bathroom door, 'Are you alright in there, Flora?' There was no answer. Sally put her ear to the door, 'Flora?' There was still no reply, but she could hear noises coming from inside; shuffling and soft banging about noises. Sally pushed open the door, 'Flora?' and was greeted with a sight of chaos.

The little girl was standing in front of the toilet – which was overflowing – a large puddle of toilet water spreading out across the linoleum floor. She looked around innocently, 'I did try and fix the toilet,' she offered as explanation. Sodden hand towels, and soggy rolls of toilet tissue, were strewn about on the wet floor. And inside the toilet bowl itself; more tissue, lots and lots of tissue, and what looked like most of a bottle of shampoo, along with its bottle and, was that a rubber duck?

'Oh,' Sally said simply, wondering what to do. 'Um, should I get your Daddy?'

The little girl shook her head. 'Is my pancakes ready?'

'I think we need to try and clear up some of this mess first. Or at least clean you up a bit.'

Sally helped the little girl wash her hands, marvelling at the tininess of her little fingers, as the warm water washed over them.

'I'll be off to work now Sal,' her, *husband?* called up the stairs. 'There's breakfast for you on the table.'

Flora ran to the top of the stairs, hastily wiping her wet hands on the sides of her pyjamas, 'Bye-bye Daddy!'

'See you later little monkey,' he called affectionately.

Sally peered timidly over the little girl.

'Is everything okay up there?' he asked Sally.

'Um, yes,' she lied, 'We're fine.' And smiling hesitantly added, 'See you later?'

'You certainly will,' he grinned up at her, eyes twinkling. 'Okay. Have a good day. Bye!' And then he was gone.

It dawned on Sally that she was now in charge of this small child. She had no experience at all with children, but then, *how hard could it be?* she thought, *children are after all only miniature humans, right?*

The little girl looked up at Sally, 'Can I go eat my pancake now?'

Sally sighed, 'Alright, you go on down, it's on the table I think. I'll see what I can do about this mess.'

'Sorry Mummy. I won't never do it again.'

Was that an intentional double negative? Sally pondered, as Flora disappeared down the stairs.

Sally found a pair of Marigold gloves and a roll of bin bags in the cupboard beneath the bathroom sink. Reluctantly, she put the gloves on and then reaching into the toilet bowl and pulling a disgusted face, she scooped out handfuls and handfuls of the sloppy wet tissue, carefully transferring it into an open bag.

'Sorry ducky,' she muttered to the yellow rubber bath duck as she chucked it into the bag with the tissue. She delved in again, excavating the shampoo bottle, along with a bar of soap, a pack of dental floss, and a tube of lipstick – it all went into the bin bag. Standing back to survey her progress, she blew the hair from her eyes. It looked like she had removed enough tissue from the toilet bowl for it to flush now. She pulled the handle, and then watched in horror as the water level in the bowl rose and rose, and then thankfully, just as it reached the top, with a glug it sucked back down. She picked up the wet hand towels, wondering whether to wash them, but shoved them into the rubbish bag along with a bath towel, which she had used to mop up the worst of the puddle. After a wipe around with some cleaning spray, she was finally satisfied and pulled off the rubber gloves and washed her hands. *Right, now for some breakfast,* she thought, as she carried the black bag down the stairs.

Sally stopped in her tracks as she walked into the kitchen. The little girl was sat up at the table happily eating a pancake, as if in the eye of a storm, seemingly oblivious of the shambles that surrounded her. Syrup oozed from her plate and dripped off the edge of the table. The Fridge door was ajar, an open carton of orange juice discarded on its side in a puddle on the floor, along with a couple of broken eggs. A chair had been pushed up to the counter and a top cupboard was gaping open, half of its contents emptied onto the countertop below. A bag of flour looked like it had exploded as it fell from the counter.

'I did got you a pancake Mummy,' Flora gestured to a plate in the place next to her, a pancake barely visible beneath a thick slick of syrup and jam. And was that coffee granules?

Sally groaned, 'Oh Flora! What have you done?'

The little girl, sensing Sally's disapproval, looked up at her with hurt in her wide eyes. 'Don' you like pancake no more?' she asked Sally sadly, her bottom lip sticking out.

15 ~ SEAWEED MONSTER

Sally had just finished tidying the kitchen, when a telephone started to ring. Hoping it may be Lockey, she rushed to answer it.

'Hello, its Mrs. Copperpot,' a jovial voice sang, 'I was just wondering if Flora would be joining us at preschool today?'

'Oh, um. Is she supposed to be?'

'She was supposed to start a half an hour ago... For the morning session? Is this her Mum?' Mrs. Copperpot asked uncertainly.

'Yes. Um, sorry. It's been, bit of a hectic morning. Can I call you back?'

'Of course,' the voice sounded concerned now.

'Sorry, can you remind me of the number?' Sally found a crayon and an old envelope and scrawled the number down. Hanging up the phone, she called up the stairs to Flora – who she had sent up to get dressed, to keep her out the way while she cleaned the kitchen. 'Flora? Were you supposed to go to preschool today?' Sally looked at the envelope in her hand that she had written on. It was addressed to Sally Scott – her married name, she guessed – *Mrs. Scott*, she mused.

The little girl came down the stairs. She was wearing the top half of a Viking outfit (complete with double horned helmet), paired with a pink tutu, which she wore over her pyjamas. 'I is dressed,' she beamed proudly.

Sally suppressed a laugh, 'Yes, so I see. I think we need to get you ready for preschool.'

'But I is dressed already.' Flora puffed out her little cheeks.

'You probably don't normally wear that to preschool though, do you?'

'Yes, I does.'

'Oh, well if you're sure,' Sally said distractedly, 'You go get your shoes on then.'

Sally phoned back the preschool, saying that they were on their way. And it wasn't until she had hung up that she realised, she had no clue where the preschool actually was, or how they were going to get there. Flora was by the front door pulling on a pair of gold sparkly welly boots onto the wrong feet. Sally smiled, 'Do you want some help there? Here…' She crouched down and tried to remove a boot.

Flora wriggled her legs and stiffened, 'No. I did do it.' She fixed Sally with a stern glare.

'They might be more comfortable if we put them on the right feet?' Sally gently suggested.

'They don't both go on the *right* feet, 'cause I does have a *left* feet too.' Flora explained patiently. 'They is comfbobble just like this.' The little girl pulled herself up to her feet, 'Come on Mummy. You is going to make us late.'

Sally pulled on a tatty old pair of shoes she found by the door, which seemed to fit. Flora pointed to a bunch of keys hanging on a hook, 'Don' forget your keys 'gain.'

For a second Sally thought of the day before in Brighton, when she had forgotten the keys, but of course Flora didn't mean that.

They left the house and Sally closed the door behind them. She looked around. The house they had just left, was a large red brick semidetached house, set back on a pleasant leafy street. There was a little lane opposite marked as a private road, so, it was left or right on the street they were on. Sally had hoped the way may be instinctive, but she had absolutely no clue where they were. She didn't know where in the world she was, literally. She turned to the little girl, who was now on her knees playing with the little stones of the small driveway. 'Let's play a game Flora, and pretend that Mummy doesn't know the way to school.'

'Preschool?' the little girl eyed her doubtfully.

'Yes, preschool I mean. You show me the way. It will be fun.'

Flora smiled and got to her feet, brushing her grubby hands off on her tutu. 'Okay,' she held up a little hand for Sally to hold.

'Is it far to preschool?'

'No. Preschool is really, really close.' Flora looked up and down the street, as if making up her mind, 'Come on then Mummy. We go this way.'

Flora led Sally down the road along the pavement. It was a sunny spring morning and thankfully warm, as Sally had forgotten to bring coats. The powder blue sky was dotted with a few wispy clouds. The trees were in full blossom, and abuzz with busy bumbling bees. It was a lovely place, wherever this was. The air smelt clean, heavenly; a heady mix of the fragrant blossom and spring flowers, with un undertone of fresh sea air. It was then that she spotted the band of blue sea, sparkling at the end of the street. There was a street sign up ahead. Sally squinted to read it as they approached. It seemed they were somewhere called *Bembridge*, and ahead apparently, was a lifeboat station. Sally could now clearly make out the lifeboat pier, its pillars stretching out across the water to a large curve topped boathouse at its end. They came to another sign saying lifeboat personnel only. Sally slowed, Flora tugged her hand impatiently. There was a little café beyond the sign, so it must only apply to vehicles, Sally decided. But where *was* the little girl leading her? Sally could hear the soft hush of the waves now.

'Are you sure your school's down *here*?' Sally asked uncertainly as Flora pulled her onwards.

Sally found that Flora had led her, as she had started to suspect, to the beach. She turned to the little girl, 'Flora, this isn't your school, is it.'

Flora grinned mischievously, 'Yes. This is my beach school.'

Sally looked around. They were the only two on the stony beach. Flora was already drifting off to explore some rock pools.

'Flora,' Sally called out half-heartedly. She knew she should probably be stern with the little girl, she was obviously playing her, but she was just so joyful and full of life. Sally crunched across the stones to join her.

Flora had found a stick, and was hooking up strands of seaweed with it. She pulled her stick up sharply and a soggy tress of seaweed flicked away, and slapped Sally across the face. She looked up at Sally wide eyed, 'Sorry Mummy.'

But Sally started to laugh, 'Eughrr. I'm the seaweed monster,' she roared.

Flora started giggling. Sally waved her arms about and the little girl ran off squealing delightedly. Sally picked up a large frond of seaweed and chased Flora along the beach.

They played for five minutes before they were both exhausted. They stood panting and laughing. Flora took Sally's hand again.

'Are you showing me the way to school now?' Sally asked hopefully.

'Preschool,' Flora corrected.

Sally nodded.

Flora pursed her lips and nodded too, 'Come on Mummy. This way.'

Their next stop was not, as Sally had hoped, the little girl's preschool, but the little café they had passed at the edge of the beach. Flora had dragged Sally right up to the ice-cream kiosk, before she had even realised where they were headed. 'Hello Flora. What can I get for you today sweetie?' a smiling lady greeted them warmly through the kiosk hatch.

'I would like a whippy ice-cream in a cone, with a chocolate flake on top it too please,' Flora announced.

Sally realised she hadn't a bag or purse, or anything with her at all, 'Oh. Um, no Flora. No ice-creams today. We need to get you to preschool anyway.'

Flora turned to her with large shiny eyes. 'Please mummy,' she said quietly.

'I haven't got any money with me Flora,' Sally explained.

The woman who had been waiting patiently piped in, 'That's okay. She can have one on the house.' And before Sally could even argue, she had turned, and whirled out a soft vanilla ice-cream onto a cone, and topped it with a chocolate flake.

'Oh, thank you very much,' Sally smiled gratefully.

'No probs.' The woman was grinning at her now, 'I like what you've done with your hair today by the way Sally,' she laughed.

Sally's hand went up to her hair self-consciously and she smiled back nonplussed.

They strolled slowly along the road, Flora licking her ice-cream as they walked. Flora had been insistent that they go this way, so they had followed the road around the coast. But they seemed to be getting nowhere fast. Sally realised the little girl had stopped walking. 'What's wrong?'

'I is too tired to walk no more,' Flora huffed, and took another lick of her now dripping ice-cream.

'Come on.' Sally looked about. There was nothing much around, but she could see some buildings up ahead. 'We must be nearly there?' she added hopefully.

Flora shook her head stubbornly, 'I is tired. Can't walk.'

Sally sighed, *what am I supposed to do now?* 'Would you like a piggy back?'

She hoiked the little girl onto her back, and winced as a gloop of ice-cream dripped down her neck. 'Shall we throw the ice-cream away now?' Sally suggested, but wasn't surprised by Flora's reply.

'I is still eating it.'

They walked for ten minutes like that. At first the

little girl had felt tiny and light as a bird on her back. But after five minutes, Sally felt like an old donkey, heavily laden with bricks as she trudged along the road. Each time they came to a junction, Flora would direct Sally which way to go. Sally had a suspicion they had walked a couple of loops, but they seemed to be making progress now.

'Are we nearly there now Flora?' Sally asked, and as she spoke she realised they were on the same road they had started out from – she could actually see the house now and just make out the sea at the end of the street. 'Flora,' Sally groaned. 'Did you take us home again?'

'No. We is at preschool now.' Flora's little arm stuck out and Sally followed her pointing finger.

'Preschool is *here*? But that must be five or six doors up from our house?'

'Yes. Preschool is really, really close.'

There were a huddle of mostly women standing at the front of the preschool gate. They all grinned at Sally as she approached. *They seem like a jolly friendly bunch,* Sally thought and smiled back. The preschool was housed in a large detached bungalow, painted in bright primary colours. Little Rainbows, the sign on the front wall stated. Sally struggled with the lock on the little red gate, until one of the dads came to her rescue, and flipped the bolt across easily. Sally thanked him and crouched down to let Flora off her back. The yellow front door of the preschool opened before Sally and Flora had reached it, and a large lady with a broad smile, dark braided hair, and a psychedelic tabard, called out from the doorway.

'Okay Mummies and Daddies. You can come in to

collect your Little Rainbows now.' Her smile wavered as she spotted Sally and Flora. 'Goodness me!' she exclaimed. 'Whatever's happened to you two this morning? You've missed the morning session...' she trailed off, her face now a picture of concern.

'Oh, yes. I know. Sorry about that. Some things, came up. Um...'

The broad smile returned. 'Oh not to worry. You can come and play next week, can't you Flora. I suppose you popped by to pick up Flora's water bottle?'

'Oh yes... that's it.'

The lady disappeared into the building briefly, and returned carrying a pink sparkly bottle. 'Here you go.' She passed the bottle to Sally and then produced a gingerbread-man, 'And this is for you Flora. See you next week. Take care of yourselves now.' She turned back for one last look and chuckled softly to herself, shaking her head as she walked back inside.

16 ~ WHEN SALLY MET HARRY

There was a car parked on the drive in front of the house when they returned. As Sally fumbled with the key in the lock, the front door opened.

'Hello, my two favourite ladies.' Sally's husband eyed her with amusement. 'What on earth's happened to you Sal?' he chortled, and reaching out he pulled a slimy sprig of seaweed from Sally's tangled hair.

'Mummy is a seaweed monster,' Flora explained.

'So I see.' He pulled Sally in for a hug and shut the front door. Sally thought he was going to kiss her, but surprisingly, he poked out the tip of his tongue and licked her cheek. 'Mmm, Ice-cream. Is Mummy an Ice-cream seaweed monster?'

Flora giggled. 'Yes.' She kicked off her gold wellies, 'Silly ol' mummy!' And ran off into the house.

'How was your morning? Did you get much work done?'

'Work?'

'Yes, yes, I know; your books are not your work, but your pleasure.' He was already walking away and called back over his shoulder, 'Oh, that reminds me. Sue phoned. She had a query about one of the illustrations you sent her. Asked if you can call her back. But I think she said she's out of the office 'til Friday.'

Sally pulled off her shoes and picked up a couple of manila envelopes from behind the front door. She shuffled through them quickly. There was one addressed to Mr. Harold Scott, and the other to Sally Scott. *So that's definitely me then? Sally Scott. Sally and Harold.* Apparently they lived at Seagull Cottage, Bembridge, on the Isle of Wight. Sally had never been to the Isle of Wight. But like many places, it was somewhere she had always meant to visit.

Sally found him in the kitchen, the radio on. He was washing lettuce at the sink. She put the letters on the dresser, and picked up a framed photograph of what must have been their wedding day. Sally wore a simple ivory dress, her hair long and loose, and he was wearing a dark blue suit the colour of his eyes. It wasn't a posed shot; they were both laughing and gazed into each other's eyes, as if sharing some private joke. And a very little Flora was there too – a year old at most – held in the crook of his arm in a little rose pink dress. The three of them in their own happy little bubble.

Sally hadn't heard him approach, but she felt his warm breath on her neck as his arms slipped around her waist. 'Shall we put on a wee bit of telly for Flora, before we have our lunch?' he suggested, picking out yet another wisp of seaweed from Sally's hair.

Sally flushed, her heart hammering. She was just desperately trying to summon up some words, when

Flora came careering into the room on a small orange scooter, and collided into the back of their legs.

'Ow! Flora. What have I said. No scooting in the house!' He rubbed his leg.

'Sorry Daddy.' Flora looked up at them earnestly, her Viking helmet skewwhiff. 'It was a axe-didn't.'

'Come on you, in the garden.' Much to the little girl's delight he scooped her up around the waist, along with the scooter. 'Time for some driving lessons.' He turned and mischievously mouthed, 'Later.' to Sally, and carried a giggling Flora out of the back door.

Sally watched them playing for a moment through the glazed back door, her heart still racing. She had never met a man that had made her feel this way before. It was as though she was properly alive for the first time. But he was not hers, and this was not her life; she was an imposter here.

There was an open laptop on the kitchen counter. Its screensaver fish contentedly swimming their virtual aquarium. Sally touched the keyboard and the screen sprang to life. She glanced out onto the garden again, to check they weren't just about to come back in, and then double clicked the internet icon.

She was so engrossed in reading, that she didn't hear him come back into the room. Lockey it seemed, in this reality as well as the previous, was married to Patricia. There was no mention of his work at all. Just a few high society articles. He was playing lord of the manor here, it seemed. Lockey would not be pleased.

Sally heard a loud sigh behind her and turned, his face had fallen, 'Not again Sally.' He had such sadness in his eyes. 'He doesn't *know* you Sal. We've been over and over this. His wife threatened legal action last time… I'm just, not sure I can go through it all again. Please. I just want *you*. And for the three of us to be happy. You've been doing so well. Have you… have you taken your medication today?' he gently pushed the laptop closed and took Sally's hands. He looked deep into her eyes, 'Do you even know my name, Sally?'

Sally felt cornered, like a rabbit in the headlights, she didn't know what was going on. She tried to avoid his eyes.

'Sally?' he persisted.

'Harold. Your name's Harold.' Sally felt pleased with herself.

But he flinched as though he'd been slapped and took a sharp breath. 'Harry. It's Harry.' He hugged her to him and kissed the top of her head, 'It's okay. Everything's going to be okay. We've got through this before, we'll get through it again.'

Sally wasn't sure if he was reassuring her or himself.

Harry sat Sally at the kitchen table and called Flora in from the garden. He distracted her with something in the other room and then he was riffling through a green box, he'd removed from a top shelf in the cupboard. He unscrewed a lid and shook out a tablet, and then pulled out another packet of pills and popped a couple of capsules from their blister pack. He handed them to Sally, along with a glass of tap water. Sally looked at the three pills in her hand. They looked rather pretty. She wanted to ask what they were, but didn't want to give too much away.

Harry put a hand on her shoulder, and as if reading her mind said, 'They'll make you feel better Sal. You told me to make sure you take them.' He gave her an encouraging look. With nothing else to do she obediently gulped the pills.

Harry had then led Sally through to the sitting room, where Flora was watching a cartoon. He sat Sally beside the little girl on the sofa. 'I'll make us a cup of tea.'

Sally stared at the space in front of the TV screen, trying to work out what had just happened. *I tried to contact Lockey before? What does it all mean?*

Harry returned a few moments later, carrying a tray with cups of tea and chopped French-bread sandwiches. Sally ate her baguette distractedly and realised half way through, how hungry she'd been. She sipped her tea and noticed that he was watching her.

'Better?'

She did feel better. A little floaty and foggy perhaps, but it wasn't an unpleasant feeling. She nodded and smiled, and brushed some crumbs off her chest onto her plate. 'Thank you. That was good.'

Harry took the plate, and then squashed in on the sofa beside her. Sally felt warm and fuzzy now, and like there was nowhere else in the world that she would rather be. She had never felt so content.

Flora climbed up onto Sally's knee and gave her a hug, 'I love you Mummy.' The little girl rested her head against Sally's chest.

I love you, was not something that Sally had heard much of, in her own reality, and her heart felt as if it may burst. And then it came to her. Not like a slap of icy water, but in soft rolling waves. She remembered holding Flora for the first time. And she remembered falling in love with Harry. The details were hazy, but it was a truth she knew with her whole heart and entire being. She loved this man. And this little girl too. She tried to focus her thoughts on all that had happened over the last few days, but it was slipping away. *There was no SALL. I never travelled across dimensions – of course*, it all seemed preposterous to her now – *and Horace Lockhart doesn't even know me. None of that was true. Just a trick of the mind. A nervous breakdown, triggered by work stress combined with the emotional trauma of losing Uncle Joe.* Sally remembered the hours she had spent with psychotherapists – help she had sought herself – when she had finally come to terms with the fact that she was ill. But she could get better, she just had to organise her mind. Her life was here. She kissed Flora's soft little cheek. This was her reality, here, with these two people she loved completely.

'I love you too sweetie.' Sally looked up at Harry, who was smiling now. She had loved this man for over four years. He wrapped a warm arm around her shoulder. Sally leant over and kissed him softly, and then relaxed into his arms. She felt so comfortable now and happy. Everything else in the world slipped away. And it was just the three of them, cosy on the sofa. Sally sighed lightly. She was at peace.

They stayed like that for some time, half watching the television. Sally felt her eyelids grow heavy – she fought sleep briefly, but couldn't remember why she should – And eventually she surrendered to it. Her eyes closed and she drifted off to sleep.

17 ~ LOCO IN TOKYO

Sally had barely closed her eyes, when she awoke again with a start. Her vision was blurry, her head pounding. She winced. It was so loud. Someone, who certainly wasn't Ricky Martin, was singing along discordantly to Livin' La Vida Loca. Harry and Flora were gone. Her head had been resting in her hands, arms propped up on her elbows on a sticky table and it seemed she had been dribbling down her wrist. She raised her heavy head and struggled to make sense of her surroundings and found, that if she closed one eye, she could just about focus.

She seemed to be in a bar of some sort and was sat in a haze of alcohol fumes at a table covered with bottles and glasses. Her mouth felt parched. She reached out to the glass nearest to her and took a tentative swig and grimaced; Rum and coke, not her favourite, but she was so thirsty it was surprisingly quenching.

'Hey Loca Sophia. You drinking all *my* drink now?'

Sally received a friendly slap on the back and

looked up to the face of an odd looking man – his smiling eyes blinking at her through thick lensed round glasses. 'It's your turn now.'

There was cheering nearby and Sally found herself being pushed and pulled toward the stage. Bright lights shone onto her face, she could barely make out the crowd. Someone helped her sit on a stool and passed her a microphone. The very idea of singing in public would usually have horrified Sally. But she felt surprisingly relaxed. She supposed she must be dreaming, but it felt so real. She really did feel quite convincingly, completely off her head. 'Ha,' she laughed out loud, and hiccupped. It seemed like as good a time as any for karaoke.

The music started up. Sally recognised the opening bars of Cyndi Lauper's *Time After Time* immediately. It was one of her favourites. It took her a moment to notice the screen displaying the lyrics and she missed the opening lines. Someone in the audience shouted something she didn't understand, but took as encouragement. She cleared her throat and started to sing, hesitantly at first, but she grew in confidence as she sang and found she was really enjoying herself. She rose to her feet unsteadily and by the time she reached the chorus she really threw herself into it.

Sally was still singing, when she noticed a tall figure standing before her, silhouetted against the bright lights. She tried to shield her eyes from the glare to see who he was, but still couldn't quite make him out. Taking a step closer, she lost her footing and toppled off the front of the low stage towards him.

'Lockey!?' Microphone still in hand, her voice echoed around the room.

Lockey had caught her mid-fall. Sally gazed up at him disbelievingly. 'Is that really you?' she said breathlessly as she righted herself.

But before Lockey had a chance to reply, the man with the round glasses was with them. 'Crazy Lockey!' It was Lockey's turn to be slapped on the back. 'You two, you are both so crazy. This has been the best night of my life. But now I must go. Will you join me? I'm going on to another bar across the city to meet with my colleagues.'

Sally looked up at Lockey, but he seemed perplexed and said, 'I'm sorry, I don't speak Spanish.' He turned to the man and said slowly, and a little too loudly, 'NO HA-BLO ES-PAN-YOLO.'

The man gripped his thighs and roared with laughter. He slapped Lockey on the back again. 'You two! Here,' he passed Lockey a business card and turned to Sally, 'My number. Get him to call me when he's in Madrid. I'll show him my city. Introduce him to a few beautiful ladies perhaps.' He winked at Lockey and then turned back to Sally, 'It really has been a pleasure. I haven't laughed so much since, I don't know when.' He kissed her hand, 'Goodbye my new friends.' And he strode off.

'Funny chap. All I got of that was Amigos.'

'You didn't understand?'

'No, like I said, I don't speak Spanish.'

'Neither do I…' Sally realised that somehow this possibly wasn't true anymore.

'Anyway, more importantly. How are you? Last time I saw you was Brighton…'

Sally didn't know where to start, so much had happened since then, and the alcohol coursing through her veins didn't help much.

Lockey looked how Sally felt; a little dishevelled and ruffled around the edges. His clothes were lightly crumpled; an untucked white shirt – the top two buttons undone – and a loosened tie. His dark hair was scruffy and a little longer than she had seen it before, and it looked as if he hadn't shaved for a couple of days.

'It's too loud in here,' Sally shouted. The music had started back up and someone had started screeching along to Like a Virgin. 'I don't know where we are, but let's get some fresh air.'

They were making their way to the exit, when a young man from behind the bar caught up with them waving a handbag, 'Excuse me. You forgot your bag? Also, you need to pay before you leave.'

Sally made her way back to the bar. 'I'm so sorry...'

'That's okay.' He passed Sally a bill, 'Did you have a good evening?'

Sally nodded distractedly and smiled as she rooted through the handbag. 'Yes, thank you.' She pulled out a wad of notes from her purse, 'How much?'

The bartender took the wad from Sally, counted through them, handed back several notes and smiled, 'You're a good singer. I think I saw you in here a few weeks ago?'

Sally returned the change to the purse. There were several cards slotted into the middle section. She slid out the top one. It looked like a work ID card. On one side there was a small photograph of herself. Sally started when she read; Interpreter. S. Lockhart. Sally *Lockhart?*

'Is everything okay?'

Sally looked back at the barman. 'Um, yes.

Everything's fine.' She hastily tucked the card back into its slot. 'I'm not quite sure how to get home from here…'

'There should be a Taxi up the road. Or I could call one for you, if you like? Whereabouts are you headed?'

'No, that's fine. We'll just catch one from up the road. Thanks.' Sally didn't like to say that she had no clue where she *was*, let alone where she was going.

'Okay.' He smiled, 'I'm hoping I'll see you again sometime soon.' Was he flirting?

Lockey was looking at Sally enquiringly when she returned, 'You speak Japanese?'

'No…I…' She shrugged and pulled a face.

When Sally and Lockey stepped out of the bar, it felt as if they had landed on an alien planet. They were hit by a cacophony of sound and a dazzle of colour. Neon signs illuminated against the dark sky. Bright lights flickering and flashing. And so many people. There was a wild energy in the air, as the crowds drifted by. The karaoke bar, in retrospect, seemed an oasis of calm compared to the hustle and bustle of the chaotic street they'd found themselves on. The cool night air smelt as though it had recently rained. Sally wondered briefly if she had had a coat, but didn't fancy going back into the bar to look for a coat she wouldn't recognise.

'Where are we going?' Lockey had to raise his voice to be heard.

'I don't know.' Sally looked around. 'I don't know where we are.' She pulled out the purse again and started looking through the cards. Along with the work ID there was a bank card, a travel card, a couple of store cards and a Residence Card – they all said

Lockhart. But this one had an address on it too.

'Tokyo?' Lockey suggested.

'Yes, Tokyo. We go here I guess,' Sally showed Lockey the card.

He looked nonplussed, 'That's an address? You can read that?'

Sally took back the card and looked at it again, 'Yes. I can. Come on, we can catch a taxi from around here somewhere.' They rounded the corner, nearly bumping into a group of laughing Japanese students and spotted a taxi.

Sally showed the driver the card and asked him to take them to the address on it. It was a relief to be in the warmth and relative quiet of the taxi, as they sped along the streets. 'Did you see the name on the card?' Sally passed the card to Lockey again, and pulled out the work ID and gave him that as well. Lockey frowned and scratched his head. He didn't say anything, but looked deep in thought.

'What does it mean?'

He looked at Sally for a moment. 'We're married? I guess.'

Sally was feeling increasingly sober. Her head was starting to thump again. She felt, bizarrely, as though she had been unfaithful to someone. To Lockey? To Harry? Her heart wrenched when she thought of Harry. Would she ever see him again? And Flora too... Her throat felt tight. 'Does it even make sense, that we would be together though?' Sally asked him.

Lockey looked slightly wounded. 'Would it be so bad?'

'I just mean, what are the chances?'

'I don't know Sally. This gets stranger and

stranger. Maybe we met at school?'

There was that. Was it really so inconceivable, that they could have met and got together? Sally shrugged.

'I'll say this Sally. You're the nicest, sweetest girl I've ever met. I'd be a lucky man to be your husband.'

Sally felt confused. She wanted to tell Lockey about Harry. But something stopped her. She had never met anyone like Lockey before, and there was undoubtedly something between them; a bond. She had felt it the first moment they'd met. But to Sally, their relationship felt platonic. She certainly didn't feel the way about Lockey as she did about Harry. But maybe she just hadn't remembered Lockey that way yet? Sally rested her head against the taxi window and watched the world slip by. How odd all of this was.

The taxi pulled up outside a block of flats and Sally paid the driver. There was a security code lock at the front door. Sally was just wondering what to do, when the door opened. A small old lady who was just leaving the building emerged. She held open the door for Sally and bowed her head politely. Sally bowed back instinctively as they passed.

It took them a while to locate the right room number, but eventually they found it on the fourth floor. It was the very last door they came to.

The apartment was the smallest Sally had ever seen. It made her flat above the Indian restaurant seem positively palatial. It was a bed-sitting room, kitchen/diner all in one. The bed nestled into an alcove to one side of the room, beside a small sofa. There was a television opposite the bed and beside that a microwave oven on the floor, with a kettle balanced precariously on top. *An accident waiting to happen*, Sally thought. In one corner there was a tiny kitchen area, which consisted of a small stainless steel sink and a two ring hob-top cooker, above a slim-line fridge.

Sally pushed open a door and discovered a miniature bathroom. This little space had everything you could need – Sally mused – except for space itself.

'So, this is home. I guess.' Sally kicked off her shoes and padded across to the kitchenette. She opened the cupboard under the sink, which was crammed mostly it seemed with packets of instant noodles. Sally filled the kettle and carefully switched it on.

There was a large travel bag taking up a fair amount of room beside the bed. Lockey had unzipped it, 'This is odd. Looks like I was going somewhere?'

Sally looked over his shoulder. The bag was stuffed full of folded men's clothing. And he had found his passport on the top. 'That guy in the bar said something about Madrid? Maybe you're going on holiday, or working away?' she suggested.

Lockey slumped down on the small sofa. 'Hey… look at this.' He had picked up a framed photograph, 'Looks like we've known each other for years.' He passed the photo to Sally. It looked like a holiday snap. There were five of them in the photo. All sun kissed and smiling, in shorts and t-shirts. They stood in a huddle before a turquoise sea, on a white sandy beach. To one side of Sally, standing shoulder to shoulder, was a younger Lockey. And on her other side, a woman she didn't recognise with red hair, their arms wrapped companionably around each other's waists. On the outer side, Sally recognised Lockey's brother, Theodore, and behind them all towered a man – who looked not dissimilar to a present-day Lockey – one arm around Lockey's shoulder, the other around Theodore's.

'That's my parents and Teddy there.'

Sally must indeed have known Lockey for years, as she looked to be around sixteen or seventeen. She felt an irrational stab of envy looking at the happy family group. It looked like Lockey's mum had taken Sally under her wing. 'What are they like? ... Your parents?'

Lockey took back the photograph and frowned lightly, 'Well I never saw them looking this relaxed. Don't get me wrong, they're great. But they're pretty uptight, especially my mother. They've got a lot on their plate though I guess, with the estate to run and everything. You'd think that having that much property and money would make life easier. But it's a juggling act from what I've seen.'

'It must have been great though, to grow up as part of a family?' Sally said wistfully.

Lockey returned the picture to the small table beside the sofa. 'I don't know, Teddy and I are pretty close I guess. But I was brought up more by a trail of nannies than by my parents.'

'At least you *have* parents...' Sally stated.

Lockey realised he had been tactless, 'I'm sorry Sally. Yes, I have a lot to be thankful for.'

Changing the subject, Sally picked up a clock from beside the bed. 'It's eleven. It's funny, I feel wide awake now I've sobered up.'

'Well I guess we must be about eight hours behind England, so it feels like it's still afternoon to us? You realise we travelled thousands of miles, in a matter of moments? Did you find any food by the way? I'm starving.'

'Instant noodles?'

Lockey pulled a face.

'Well, let's go back out. Get something to eat. Have a look around. I don't think either of us is going to be able to sleep anytime soon anyway.'

They both looked at the bed and there was an awkward moment of silence.

'I guess. I'm pretty shattered though.' As if to prove his point, Lockey yawned and stretched his arms above his head.

'Come on. Like you said, it's still like afternoon to us. Let's go and explore. I've always wanted to travel.'

Lockey nodded but didn't move. 'Sure. You're right.'

'Great. Just give me a few minutes. I'll freshen up.'

Sally squeezed into the miniscule bathroom and closed the door behind herself. There was a curtained off quarter-sized bath with a shower over the top, beside a toilet, and a small hand-basin opposite. Sally studied her reflection in the mirror on the wall. Her skin was in great condition and her hair cut into a sharp tidy bob. She was probably around forty to fifty pounds lighter than she had been just an hour or two ago. Sally was still gazing at her reflection when she was gripped by a sudden rush of dizziness. The blood drained from her face, turning her deathly pale. She broke out in a cold sweat and could hear her heart hammering in her ears, her head was pounding. She stumbled from the bathroom, her vision darkening around the edges, wondering, *what's going on?* A feeling like pins-and-needles was spreading up her arms and legs.

Sally spotted Lockey – his head lolled back against the sofa, his mouth had fallen open – and in an instant she realised what was happening. Lockey was falling asleep, he was shifting, and she was being dragged away with him. 'Lockey…' Sally struggled to get the words out, 'Don't go to sleep…' But it was too late. Sally's legs turned to liquid beneath her and she dropped to the floor.

18 ~ LOCKEY'S DREAM GIRL

Lockey was dreaming of her again. It was the same dream every time. He found himself standing on a residential street, beside a row of rundown looking terraced houses. Two young women were approaching. He felt he should move, but somehow he was completely rooted to the spot. One of the girls had her head bowed and Lockey couldn't see her face. But the other had her face turned up towards the sky, the sun bright on her cheeks and she was laughing. She had the most wonderful carefree laugh, it was so compelling. He felt inexplicably happy to see her. Did he know this girl? There was something about her. He certainly found her very attractive. She was unusual looking, with her huge brown eyes, messy platinum blonde bob and pierced nose. But it was more than just a physical attraction. He was captivated. As the girl passed by, she smiled and winked playfully. Their eyes met and something thrilling and unfathomable passed between them. Time stood still. The rest of the world melted away, leaving just the two of them.

But then her friend tugged on her arm lightly, and just as suddenly the spell was broken and she was moving away. He wanted to follow, but he was still stuck to the spot.

Lockey woke slumped across his desk at the laboratory. He opened an eye and winced against the stark morning light. He raised his head, his neck was painfully stiff and there was a sheet of A4 plastered to his cheek. *How long was I asleep like this?* he wondered, as he peeled the paper from his face. He discovered he was sporting a good few days' worth of stubble growth. He looked at the printout in his hand, but couldn't make sense of it as the ink had smeared and run. *I must have nodded-off working again,* he thought, feeling abysmal. His head was throbbing and it tasted as if something unpleasant and furry had crawled into his mouth and died.

Lockey yawned, stretched out his back and rotated his neck until it felt a little looser. It wasn't unheard of for him to work into the night and not make it home. But the odd thing was, he had no recollection whatsoever of what he was doing here. It looked like he'd been working on something important; his desk was piled high with files and covered in papers, and he seemed to have scrawled a frenzy of barely legible, incoherent notes. *Why can't I remember?* He tried to focus his thoughts.

Lockey was up on his feet the moment it all came back to him. *Are we back?* he wondered. *I know where I am, but when am I? And is this our reality or another variant?* It was all so peculiar still. It seemed to Lockey like just a moment ago he had nodded off on the sofa in the flat in Tokyo, and now, here he was back at the lab. Back at SALL, where it had all begun.

'Sally?' he called out, hoping that somehow they had both made it back. Lockey wandered out along the corridor. 'Hello?' He pushed open a couple of doors. 'Anyone here?' But the laboratory was silent. He was alone.

Lockey let himself into the cloakroom just beyond ALICE, and stopped in his tracks. The large double doors leading into the main testing area had been taped across with yellow caution tape and a large sign, handwritten in black marker, stuck to the doors read; 'DANGER. DO NOT ENTER.' Lockey reeled. *What happened here?* He thought back to Monday morning; the moment when Sally had somehow inexplicably fired up ALICE, and wondered for the first time what they had left behind when they'd shifted through into the first parallel reality.

He raced back through the building to the reception area, turned on the computer and while he waited for it to boot up, made himself a cup of tea. He found a pasty in the little fridge, he was pretty sure it was the same one he'd bought from the petrol station on the way to work on Monday morning. He opened the packet and took a bite, it tasted pretty disgusting, but he was hungry enough not to be too picky.

Five minutes later Lockey sat back down at the desk with his mug. He did a quick internet search with Sally's name, and almost sprayed a mouthful of tea across the desk as he read the headlines; *Office temp fighting for life after particle accelerator accident. Temporary worker, Sally Sullivan remains in coma three days after incident at physics laboratory. Safety concerns raised after woman left in critical condition...* he couldn't read anymore.

The door opened and Roy bumbled in. 'Morning Lockey,' he said dolefully. 'Did you pull an all-nighter?' Roy glanced at the screen over Lockey's shoulder, 'Any news?'

'Plenty of news, but nothing good...' Lockey said distractedly.

'Perhaps you should go back to the hospital and see if there's been any improvement? There's not a lot we can do about things here at the moment, until we hear back from the board.'

Lockey was barely aware of the drive, and arrived at the hospital within half an hour. A nurse greeted him as he entered the Intensive-care-unit, 'There's been no change I'm afraid Professor Lockhart.'

Lockey followed the nurse along the corridor and then, there she was. Her hair was a different colour from when he'd last met her, now a pale purple shade of blue. But he recognised her immediately. 'Nita!'

Nita looked up from Sally's bedside questioningly, 'Hello? Sorry, have we met?' she asked Lockey in confusion. 'Are you a friend of Sally's?' Nita was looking expectantly at Lockey, and he realised they had obviously never met in this reality – he'd said her name without thinking.

'I'm sorry, yes. I mean, no. Sally and I just met on Monday morning. I'm from the lab, where the accident...'

'Oh god, yeah. I wondered how I recognised you. I saw your picture in the papers. You're that Professor, aren't you? – the guy who Sal was working for?'

'Professor Lockhart,' Lockey offered his hand out to Nita, and she took it in her own delicate hand. Lockey was surprised by the force of her hand shake.

'Nita. But, you already knew that?' she said enquiringly.

'The nurse mentioned your name on the way in I guess,' Lockey fibbed, and then kicked himself, *how would the nurse know her name?*

But it seemed to be enough for Nita, 'Well nice to meet you.' She smiled sadly and turned back to her friend. Lockey looked at Sally too, lying there a mere shell of herself, with tubes and wires attached. And it dawned on him, that, if in this reality Sally was in a coma, then in their own reality, were they both laid out like this? And a sickening thought occurred to him; *how long do we have, before the doctors and our families simply give up on us, and let us slip away?* Lockey realised that he was responsible for all of this, he felt stricken. *How could I have let any of this happen? I should have been more careful.*

As if sensing his thoughts Nita turned to Lockey, 'It's not your fault you know. I know the newspapers were pinning all the blame on you. But it was an accident.' Her eyes were sparkling as she looked up at him. She wiped her tears away determinedly and sniffed. 'I keep thinking she's just gonna wake up any minute. Like nothing happened, and be all like – Neetz? what are you doing here?'

Lockey could see that Nita was putting on a brave face. It was obviously breaking her, seeing her best friend like this. He wanted to take her in his arms and tell her it was all going to be alright. But he couldn't. He thought back to the night in Brighton, when he and Nita had very nearly kissed – right before Sally threw up all over his brother – and he was suddenly hating himself for thinking about Nita, when he should be focussed solely on Sally. *What kind of a man am I?* he wondered. *When it seemed that just yesterday, I was married to Sally.* But could that have been? Although he'd meant every word, when he'd said – he'd be a lucky man to have a girl like Sally – Sally was right, it didn't really add up somehow. Maybe there was another explanation? Lockey thought of the family photo, *maybe my family adopted her when her parents died? Could that explain it?* He was pretty sure neither he nor Sally had been wearing wedding rings. But whatever that was in Tokyo, he needed to be here now and work out what was going on.

'Do you think she's gonna make it?' Nita asked, snapping Lockey back to the present. 'I wonder if she can even hear us?' she gazed unhappily at Sally. 'I've been gabbling away to her, and I brought in some old tapes I dug out – that we used to listen to when we were younger. I don't know… Is she in there at all somewhere?'

Lockey wasn't sure of much, but he had a hunch that somewhere, this version of Sally was shifting across parallel universes, just as they were. He wondered where this Sally was. Without him shifting with her, she'd be less limited, there'd be far more alternate realities to explore. 'She's in there Nita. I'm certain of it.'

Nita nodded and smiled at Lockey thankfully, and then stifled a yawn.

'Have you been here all night?' Lockey asked, noticing the dark smudges beneath her eyes.

'No. I rushed up here as soon as I heard. I had to find out from a newspaper that my best mate's in a coma. I've only been here an hour or so.'

'Her aunt didn't contact you?' Lockey had expected to find Sally's aunt here at her bedside.

'She mentioned her aunt to you?' Nita looked surprised.

'Only as a passing comment. But I was just wondering why there're no family members here?'

'Well Sal hasn't got much in the way of family. Only her Aunty Mary actually. But, no, now you come to mention it – I did think it was pretty off, her not letting me know. I mean, she's not the warmest or most communicative of women, but you would have thought at a time like this, she'd at least try and do the right thing. I asked the nurse on the way in if Mary was here, and she said she's not been here at all. That's a bit weird, isn't it?'

Lockey felt an anger bubbling up just below the surface. He'd never met the woman, and from what he'd heard she'd not treated Sally well, to say the least. But not even visiting her niece in hospital? What kind of heartless woman was she? 'Does Mary live far from here? Maybe we should go and pay her a visit? There's not really that much we can do here at the moment.'

'I don't know.' Nita looked at Sally hesitantly, 'What if she wakes up while we're gone?'

'Coma's, in real life, they're very different to how they're portrayed in the movies I'm afraid – it's incredibly unlikely she'll suddenly wake up, bright and alert, like she's just had a good night's sleep. When she wakes, it's going to be a gradual process, which could take days, weeks even,' Lockey said, and then added a little more gently, 'We'll leave our numbers and get someone to call us immediately if there's any change, okay? You've got a mobile phone?'

Nita nodded, but still looked unconvinced. Her stomach rumbled loudly. 'Sorry,' she laughed.

'We can grab something to eat while we're at it?' Lockey suggested appealingly.

Nita grinned now, looking a little more like the confident sassy Nita, Lockey had met in Brighton. 'Okay, okay,' she laughed. 'Sold.'

As they walked across the hospital Nita linked her arm through Lockey's, as if they were old friends, but somehow it didn't feel odd. 'So, what's your first name? I can't just call you *Professor*.'

'It's *Horace*,' Lockey said, bracing himself for her laughter. But Nita didn't laugh.

'Horace. That's pretty cool.'

'Really?' Lockey was a little taken aback.

'Yeah. It's unusual, kind of quirky. Sounds like you don't like it?' Nita looked up at Lockey questioningly as they walked, her short violet hair blowing lightly in the breeze.

'I suppose... it's not the name I particularly have the problem with, but the fact it's almost a family joke. It was passed down from some eccentric relative and somehow became a tradition to get passed on to the eldest son. Most people call me Lockey, it's a school thing, a play on my surname, Lockhart – Lockey, it just kind of stuck. My little brother calls me Ace though.' Lockey smiled fondly thinking of Theodore.

'Ace. I like that...' Nita smiled.

'You'd like my brother. Actually, I'm sure of it.'

'If he's anything like you, I'd definitely like him,' Nita fluttered.

Lockey missed the compliment, 'You would, he's great. He's the arty one of the family, got it from our mother.'

'So, what about you? You're a Physicist right? How'd you get into *that*?'

'I suppose it started when I was a small boy. I wanted to know how *everything* worked. Used to drive my parents crazy apparently; my constant stream of questions – why this and why that? Probably all kids go through a stage of this, when they're little, but mostly they eventually accept the answers; *Sometimes we just don't know why*, or, *it just is*. But I wouldn't accept that, it was never enough for me. I always felt like I was missing something. I had a kind of unquenchable thirst for knowledge. My parents would shoo me off to the library to search for answers. I spent hours poring over books. I collected facts like most kids collected stickers. I was dinosaur obsessed when I was a kid.' Lockey laughed, 'And that was long before Jurassic Park, when dinosaurs became cool. I bunked out of school when I was seven, took myself all the way to the Natural History Museum for the day.'

'Seriously!? How far did you travel to get *there*?!' Nita asked impressed.

'Ha, yes. It was a couple of hours on the train, plus a walk. I couldn't understand what all the fuss was about when I got back, my mother was in tears…'

'Jeez!'

'Then I got into astronomy, and mathematics. And then came science. I had the most brilliant teacher from the age of about nine. He had a real passion for the subject and it was contagious. With physics I started to get the answers I wanted, but with each answer came twenty new questions, I was hooked. That was, and still is what I strive for; to understand how the universe is put together. It's the ultimate question, isn't it?' Lockey stopped walking, they had reached his car. 'This is it,' he said, as he unlocked the doors.

Nita whistled. 'An Audi. Nice.' She slipped into the passenger seat, 'My car's at the garage. I think she might be terminally ill, poor old Bertha.'

'Bertha?' Lockey asked with concern.

'She's a Mini,' Nita laughed, 'But the old vintage sort, not one of those massive new Mini's they're making these days,' she said, as she adjusted her short skirt.

Lockey tried his upmost not to notice her bare thighs. 'We'd best be getting off I suppose.'

Nita raised a brow and laughed, 'I'm game if you are,' she said brazenly, a sparkle in her warm brown eyes.

Lockey realising what Nita meant, spluttered, 'I didn't mean...' He found himself blushing. *Good grief,* he thought, *how old am I?*

'Sorry Ace, don't mind me, I'm only joshing,' Nita twinkled.

Nita directed Lockey to Sally's Aunt's house.

'Is this where Sally grew up?' Lockey asked.

'Nah. Mary moved here about five years ago. Won some money on the lottery.'

Lockey clenched his jaw and nodded. They pulled up outside Mary's house. It was a semi-detached new build, on a tidy sparsely housed street with a park opposite. A tiny red car was parked on the driveway in front of the garage. 'Well, her car's here,' Nita shrugged.

Lockey followed Nita to the door. She rang the bell and they waited expectantly. There was no answer. 'Maybe she's gone away somewhere?' he suggested.

Nita rang again, repeatedly this time and shouted, 'Mary? Mary. It's Nita...' She bent and peered through the slot of the letter box, 'Mary?... Oh bloody hell Ace...' Nita straightened and looked up at Lockey wide eyed, 'I can see her feet. She's on the floor in there!'

Lockey took a look, and Nita was right, he could clearly see a pair of stockinged feet on the floor at the bottom of the stairs in the hallway. When he turned, Nita was clutching a brick she'd found from somewhere. 'What are you doing with that?!'

'I'm gonna smash the bloody window,' Nita held up the brick and was just preparing to take a swing at the frosted glass panel when Lockey took her wrist.

'Hold on,' Lockey said hastily. 'I don't know if that's going to work. It'll be toughened glass. Let's see if there's another way in first?'

Nita looked disappointed but begrudgingly agreed.

'If we can't get in, you can smash a window around the back, okay?' he offered consolingly. Nita flashed Lockey with a brief grin. He tried the front door handle just in case, but it was locked. He looked back at Nita and she held up the brick again hopefully. 'No. Come on,' he gestured towards the side gate and Nita followed.

The small back garden was half paved as patio, with a fastidiously manicured circle of lawn surrounded by potted plants. Lockey tried the glazed double doors, but they too were locked. Just along from the doors at the very corner of the house, he spotted a little window, it was pretty high up, but it was open, just a crack. There was no way he was going to fit through it though. 'If I bunk you up, do you think you'd be able to crawl in through there?' he asked Nita, gesturing towards the window.

'Sure. No problem,' Nita beamed. 'I still say it would be quicker and way more fun to just smash our way in though.'

Lockey interlocked his fingers. Nita had put down her brick and pulled off her Dr Marten boots. She trod a stripy socked foot into his hands. 'I've got you,' he said, and hoicked her up. She was surprisingly light. Lockey looked up and inadvertently caught a glimpse of Nita's knickers. He looked away quickly.

'Oy, naughty,' Nita laughed, 'You looking up my skirt?' She'd paused, clutching the window frame and laughed down at Lockey, and there was something there in her shining eyes. He hadn't been able to place it, but he realised now, it was where he'd recognised her from when he'd first met her in Brighton. It was her. Nita was the girl from his dreams. He didn't know how it was possible. *Perhaps I inserted her into the dream since we met in Brighton?* he wondered. *There had certainly been a spark there between us that night. It must be that; how else could it be possible?*

Nita wriggled through the small window and he saw her slide down on the other side beyond the frosted glass, and then she was out of sight. A moment passed. Lockey was expecting to see Nita appear at the back doors and open them. But she didn't come. 'Nita?' he whispered loudly at the window.

A blood curdling shriek came from inside the house, chilling Lockey to his core. A dog somewhere in the distance started to bark.

'Nita?!' Lockey shouted now, and he was running. He must have picked up Nita's brick, and he found himself smashing it through one of the glass kitchen doors. *Is there someone else in there? Why didn't we call the police immediately?* he thought, kicking himself for putting Nita in danger. *What the hell is happening in there?* He pulled his coat sleeve down over his hand and knocked the loose shattered glass aside, reached in and unlocked one of the doors. Lockey burst into the kitchen just as Nita appeared at the doorway looking ashen.

'What's happened?' he demanded in a panic.

'There's a bloody *massive* spider in the bathroom,' Nita said, wide eyed. And then she noticed the smashed backdoor and looked at Lockey quizzically, 'How come *you* get to smash your way in?' she pouted. 'That's so not fair.'

'I thought you were being murdered in here or something...'

Nita laughed, 'Oh Ace, I'm so sorry. You should see it though.' She shuddered.

Lockey looked back at the door he'd just smashed his way through and remembered why they were in here.

Nita was there at the same moment as him. 'Mary,' she said, and turned. Lockey followed Nita through to the front of the house.

'Oh god Lockey.' Nita was crouching at Sally's aunt's side. 'I think she's dead,' she whispered, visibly shaken.

The woman on the floor had a grey complexion and there was a dark streak of blood across her forehead, which had run down and soaked a patch on the carpet beneath her head. It didn't look good. 'Mary?' Lockey knelt beside her and tilted back her head to check for breathing. He checked for a pulse in her neck, and found nothing at first, but then he found it, very faintly, but it was there. He turned to Nita, 'She's alive Nita. Phone for an ambulance.'

Lockey wondered how long Mary had been lying there for. He took off his coat and covered her with it. 'Mary? Can you hear me?' he tried, but got no response. He found a couple more coats hanging beside the front door. Nita was pacing the hall and talking on the phone to emergency services now. Lockey piled the coats up on top of Mary in an attempt to warm her. Her head wound must have stopped bleeding of its own accord some time ago, he decided and didn't look to be as bad as he'd first thought. Her left ankle was black and blue and swollen, and twisted at a nasty angle. 'Mary?' he tried again, and this time her eyes fluttered open. She gazed up at him vacantly. 'Mary, I'm Lockey. You've had a fall. Nita and I are here to help you. There's an ambulance on the way. Mary, can you hear me?' Mary's eyes focused a little and she was looking at Lockey now. Staring. A look of fear flickered in her eyes and she groaned and tried to move. She was trying to say something, but her voice wasn't there.

'It's okay Mary, it's going to be okay. You just need to try and stay where you are for a little while, just until the paramedics arrive,' Lockey soothed. Mary tried to move again and he placed a hand very gently on her shoulder.

'It's you!' Mary finally managed in a rasp.

She must be delirious. Lockey thought. *Of course we've never met.*

'Hey Mary,' Nita said, peering over Lockey's shoulder. 'How are you feeling?'

And Lockey realised Mary must have been referring to Nita. They could hear the ambulance sirens approaching. *They must have been nearby,* Lockey thought thankfully.

The paramedics swooped in and took over with an impressive efficiency. A police car had arrived too, and Nita and Lockey told a couple of officers all they knew. Mary was packed off into the ambulance. A few neighbours had come out to see what all the commotion was about. Nita and Lockey walked back to the car in a stunned trance.

In the car Nita broke the silence, 'I still don't like her but, poor woman. That was horrendous. Explains why she hadn't been to visit Sally. God, I wonder how long she'd been there. Do you think she'll be alright?'

'I don't know Nita. We did all we could though, and she's in good hands now,' Lockey said. Nita looked completely exhausted. 'So, what now? Do you have family around here somewhere?'

Nita shrugged lightly, 'No, no family. I grew up in care.' She smiled, but Lockey saw a little chink in her tough girl exterior, something vulnerable rippling just beneath the surface, which he hadn't noticed before.

'We should get back to the hospital,' Nita said, changing the subject.

'Okay. But let's grab some food somewhere first? Or, I could take you back to mine if you need a lie down?'

Nita smirked and Lockey realised how badly that had come out. 'Now there's an offer,' she raised a brow.

'I just meant… if you're tired…' Lockey was suddenly feeling all hot under the collar. 'I wasn't suggesting anything untoward…'

Nita was grinning now, 'Oh?' Her eyes twinkled and she turned to look out of the window, 'Shame.'

19 ~ WHITE HOLE

They drove by a few unappealing looking restaurants and cafés, and eventually decided they might as well just brave the hospital canteen.

Lockey still couldn't get his head around why Sally from his reality wasn't here awake right now. It didn't seem to follow. In each reality they'd been in, it seemed to be that when either one of them went to sleep, they'd both shift. So surely it must follow that they both had to be awake? But maybe not. Or perhaps she was here, but in a way trapped just beneath the surface of consciousness? If he could just find a way to wake her. But he didn't know, his head was starting to hurt.

'You okay?' Nita asked with concern. Lockey looked up. He had been so deep in thought he'd been miles away. His sandwich sat half eaten on his plate before him. Nita had polished hers off already and was now wiping her mouth with a paper napkin.

'I'm sorry. I just keep thinking about Sally. I wish there was something I could do to make things right...' Lockey sighed.

Nita squeezed Lockey's hand, 'I know. Me too. I feel so helpless. I should have been around for her more... I always thought there'd be a time, that she'd break away from her aunt and start living her own life... but now...' Her wall crumbled and the tears started to fall. Lockey moved around the table, and he found himself holding her whilst she sobbed quietly against his chest. His heart ached for her.

Nita's tears had run out, she pulled back from Lockey and looked up at him with large watery eyes. 'I'm so sorry,' she laughed, and blew her nose on a napkin, 'I'm a right bloody mess. What must you think of me? I don't cry usually, you know.' She managed a faint smile.

'You've nothing at all to apologise about,' Lockey said earnestly.

'Sal's always been there for me. I had a pretty hard time growing up, moved around from home to home. She was the only constant in my life. I'd get pretty angry at the universe and Sal would lighten me up. She always stuck by me.'

'How long have you two been friends?'

'Since we were kids. Her mum and dad died and she ended up with Mary. She's a kind of a reverse Cinderella; went from a privileged start, and ended up as her aunt's servant. Her uncle was cool, but then he died too, a while back.'

'But from what I remember, Cinderella started out life pretty happy, until *her* parents died. Perhaps Sally just didn't find her happy ending yet?'

'Do you believe in happy-ever-afters? You're a scientist, surely you don't believe in fate and destiny? all that bull? I accepted years ago that life's no fairy-tale,' Nita said, ripping open three sugar-sticks and emptying them into her hot-chocolate. 'And It's fine. I'm happy. I'm making my own path.' She stirred her drink and looked up at Lockey.

'Well, no, I suppose I don't believe in fate and destiny as such. But I've realised recently that life's far more complex than I'd imagined. And happily-ever-afters? I'm not sure...' he trailed off searching for the right words.

'Don't get me wrong, I'm not anti-love or romance, or even happy-endings. I'm just against sitting around waiting for life to happen. I'm not looking for anyone to *complete* me. I'm going to enjoy life. All this with Sal's made me firmer than ever on that.' Nita ran a hand through her hair and folded her arms. 'My mum was always waiting for her *Mr. Right*, dragged me along through one disastrous relationship after another. Then she started heavily drinking, to fill the hole in her life I suppose. She was searching so desperately for happiness she couldn't see what she had. She was only twenty-seven when she died.'

Lockey winced, 'How old were you then?'

'Six,' Nita shrugged. 'I started working in art therapy a couple of years ago. I've been working with kids from similar backgrounds to myself; angry, lost kids, who need direction. They've been neglected, abused, overlooked, lost in the system. Some of them can't read, but they're clever kids, you know? So clever in fact they've learnt strategies to pretend, and they hide behind a wall of anger – pushing people away. But they're just kids. It's how I was, after my mum. I wanted to know *why* all the time too when I was younger. But there was no one there to give me any answers. I wanted to know why I felt so angry at the world, and how I was supposed to fit in. My need to understand was emotional. A need to make sense of my own emotions, I mean. I'm not good at expressing myself. I lock things away, bottle them up. That's how I got into art, it was my release. I can get out how I'm feeling and then I get to stand back and see, and it's all clear somehow. Like looking at someone else's problem rather than your own. It puts it all into perspective.' Nita took a tentative sip of her hot-chocolate.

Lockey wasn't sure he'd ever met anyone as brave as Nita, she was an inspiration. 'What sort of art do you make?' he asked sensing she wouldn't want any words that may sound like pity.

'I work mostly on large three dimensional pieces – I listen to music, poetry, even the news, and I interpret them into visual pieces. It's hard to explain, but it's kind of like I hear words as colours and shapes.' Nita's face had lit up talking about her work. She rummaged in her bag and pulled out a digital camera. She turned it on and quickly scrolled through some pictures on the screen. 'Here,' she said, looking suddenly almost shy. 'You may like this one…' she laughed as she passed the camera over to Lockey. 'I call it *White Hole*. You know like the opposite of a black hole?'

'White holes, ah the abominable snowmen of the theoretical physics world.' Lockey said with a laugh as he took the camera. Nita raised an eyebrow questioningly.

'Sorry... Wow! This is amazing Nita. You did this?'

'Yeah,' Nita beamed. 'That's the white hole, in the centre there. And all that spewing out of it, that's all the lost things; odd socks, lighters, pens. You see? I was watching this thing and they were talking about white holes, and how they could be at the end of every black hole. And it made me think, for some reason, of a miniature black hole sucking in all the things that keep going missing in life, and then a white hole randomly appearing somewhere else and returning them.'

Lockey was frozen, staring open mouthed. Was that the answer? Had ALICE simultaneously created a black hole out of one reality and a white hole into another? He didn't know why he hadn't thought of it before, but maybe it followed, that if the way in to all of this was through ALICE, it must also be the way out?

'I'm sorry. It's stupid, right?' Nita said, mistaking Lockey's dumbfounded expression.

'We need to fire up ALICE,' Lockey muttered.

'Who's Alice?' Nita asked in confusion.

'ALICE... Sorry, Nita, sorry. It's a work thing, I was thinking out loud. This,' he said gesturing to the picture, 'is not stupid at all. In fact, you're a genius!' he kissed Nita on the cheek and passed her camera back to her. 'Look, there's something important I've got to go and sort out.'

Nita looked momentarily dejected, but just a quickly it passed and she smiled. 'Sure. I should get back up to see Sal. Will I see you again?'

'I won't be long. I'll meet you there.'

Outside, Lockey dialled up the lab on his mobile phone. 'Roy. I need to ask a huge favour...'

'Lockey? Has something happened?'

'No, well yes. Look, I need you to fire up ALICE.'

'I'm not sure that's a good idea Lockey. It could be potentially dangerous, plus officially we're—'

'Roy. It's important.'

Roy sighed. 'Well, if you say so...'

'I do.'

When Lockey got back to Sally's room he heard the music before he'd even opened the door. Ace of Spades was blaring out of a ghetto-blaster at Sally's bedside. 'Nita?!' Lockey had to almost shout to be heard over the music. Nita turned and saw Lockey and switched off the cassette player, 'I'm not sure if this...!' Lockey's voice was still raised, 'Sorry,' he continued in a normal voice. 'I'm not sure that's very soothing coma patient music?' he suggested with a laugh.

'Oh, I like that one. Good point though.' Nita changed the tape and turned down the volume.

'Did you get your work stuff sorted out?' Nita asked, as some ambient music started to play.

Lockey nodded, 'I hope so. I know this track... Underwater Love?' He came to Nita's side.

'Yeah, Smoke City. It was one of me and Sal's favourites,' Nita said, and they both looked down at Sally. 'She looks so peaceful, like she's just sleeping,' she brushed a stray lock of hair aside from Sally's forehead.

Lockey studied Sally closely. There *was* something different about her now. Something had shifted. She looked somehow less vacant. Nita was right, she did look like she was sleeping. Dreaming even, Lockey realised as he saw her eyes flicker beneath her lids.

Nita was leaning in next to Lockey. 'Did you see that? I think she can hear us. Sally? Sally? It's Nita, can you hear me?'

Sally's eyelids had opened the tiniest crack and her eyes were rolling. Was she dreaming? or struggling to wake? Her head twitched, and then again.

'Sally? Oh god, is she having a fit?' Nita said in alarm.

'I don't think so. It looks to me like she's waking though, or at least trying.' Lockey turned to Nita and saw her pressing the button to call a nurse.

'Sally?' Nita said through her tears and clutched her friend's hands. Sally twitched again and then her whole body jerked this time. Her lips parted but no sound emerged. Lockey frowned – from the knowledge he'd gained about coma patients, when he'd been a doctor – this didn't seem to follow. It looked to him as if she were having some sort of internal conflict.

An alarming thought suddenly occurred to him; *Are both versions of Sally struggling to wake simultaneously somehow?* Lockey felt suddenly nauseous, *Good grief, what have I done? By starting up ALICE, did I just open up the portal to let this version of Sally back? And where would that leave my version of Sally? – where would that leave us both?* Sally's eyes opened, she took a huge breath and was tugging at her tubes. Nita was crying and hugging her friend. A doctor and nurse rushed into the room. And no one noticed that Lockey had crumpled to the floor.

20 ~ UNDER SEA SALLY

Sally had been having the most peculiar dream.

She was swimming the deep blue depths of a warm crystal clear sea. She could hear music playing from somewhere. One of her all-time favourite tracks. A single, teenaged Nita and herself had listened to over and over; Underwater Love. With an effortless flick of her mermaid's tail, Sally swam further down through a shoal of tiny silver fish, which scattered as she glided into their midst. A beautiful ray like creature soared towards her, flapping its large wings gracefully. Bizarrely, as the ray grew nearer, she sang to Sally, 'Follow me now…' and held out her tail for Sally to take hold of.

They slipped along together, Sally trailing behind – her arm extended – as the ray pumped her powerful wings, turned a loop, and rushed at great speed through the water. As they slowed Sally noticed a merman. He beckoned to her, and realising the merman was Harry, she released her grip of the ray's tail and swam to him, overjoyed.

Harry held out his hand to Sally and smiled. Their fingers touched and he pulled her into his arms. She could feel his soft skin against her own. Her fingers curled into his dark floating tangle of hair as they kissed. The water pleasantly boiled around them. She would have liked to have stayed here forever, floating far down in this underwater-world with Harry, in this passionate embrace. But then someone was calling her name, from somewhere far off, from some other world. Was it Nita? And Sally realised that her breath was running out.

With some effort she managed to pull her lips away from Harry's soft kiss. She looked up towards the surface. Far up she could see a white patch of glimmering light, which shimmered and sparkled through the ceiling of iridescent blue; the sun, its rays beckoning her, like fingers of light reaching down into the water. She could just make out the wavering shapes of two people, peering down through the water, and little clouds up in the pale sky above them. Nita and Lockey? She heard Nita calling her again. Sally was torn. She looked back to Harry and tried to speak, but all that escaped her was a small flurry of bubbles. She looked up as the bubbles wound their way toward the surface, the last of her air. Sally longed to stay, but she needed to breathe. Harry released her and gently pushed her away. He kissed his fingers and touched them softly to her lips and smiled, and then he turned and swam away.

Sally hung in the water for a moment, wanting to follow Harry, but knowing that she couldn't. She looked back up to where Nita and Lockey were still waiting for her above the surface, took one final look after Harry, and then flicked her tail and swam up towards the light. She rushed up and up, with the very last of her breath, and just as she was starting to wonder if she could make it, she broke through the waves and dove high into the air. The sun, hot on her cheeks.

Sally took a huge gasping great breath and woke on a damp bed in a tangle of sheets, covered in sweat. The sun was streaming in through a gap at the window, across Sally's face. She rolled onto her side into the shade. It was so warm. A mosquito net hung around the bed. Sally reached out and brushed it aside with the tips of her fingers. There were no curtains at the window and rather than glazing, the wooden window frame was screened with mesh and shaded by a wooden slatted shutter, which hinged from the top outwards. The shutter was propped open on wood blocks, supposedly in the hope of letting a stray waft of air into the stifling room. It was a simple room, with white painted wood panelled walls, and an un-carpeted floor. Sally yawned and stretched. She felt wonderfully rested. She climbed from the bed.

There was a large backpack on an old cane chair, in the corner of the room. Sally emptied it out onto the bed to study the contents. The luggage seemed to consist of mostly small items of clothing: shorts, t-shirts, vests, underwear and swimwear. But there were a couple of pairs of trousers and a jumper in the mix too. Plus, a camera, music player, mobile phone and a few novels. In a side pocket, along with a travel guide book on Fiji, she discovered a passport, which – she was relieved find – read Sally Sullivan. There were tickets tucked into the front cover of the passport. If the dates were right, this Sally had been in Fiji for three weeks, and still had another two to go. After that, she wasn't heading back to England, but on to New Zealand. Sally wondered what had brought her so far from home. Was she travelling alone? The idea seemed unimaginably brave.

There was a door off to one side of the room, which turned out to lead to a small basic en-suite bathroom. The girl that looked back at Sally from the mirror, was lightly tanned. Her body was slim but strong looking. Her hair short, messy and sun-bleached. Sally took a quick shower. There seemed to be no warm water, but the shock of cold was a welcome relief. She dressed in a pair of khaki shorts and an orange t-shirt, tucked her wallet into her pocket, and with nothing left to do, she left the room.

Sally wandered through the rambling old hotel. It was a far cry from the luxury of a modern city hotel, but it had an old colonial charm and achieved shabby chic effortlessly without pretentions. Everything whitewashed wood and furnished with a haphazard mixture from antique to cane. Large leafy potted palms and exotic flowers, dotted the polished wooden floors. Fans whirred on the high ceilings, struggling to muster a breath of air. The only sign that she was in this century; a large outdated television, which sat to one corner of the large communal sitting area. Sally was startled by a short rotund woman, who seemed to have shuffled out of nowhere to greet her, and kindly offered to bring Sally tea and toast.

Sally ate her breakfast out in the shade of a veranda. There was a slight breeze on this side of the hotel and it felt delicious on her skin, the fragrant air, sweet and salty. The hotel was surrounded by tall green palms and leafy bushes, some of which were flowered with outrageously large blossoms. Sally took a deep breath. It was so good to be able to have some time to take stock. It had been beyond a crazy few days. By Sally's estimations, it was now Thursday. Sally wondered where Lockey was, and realised guiltily that she was glad he wasn't here with her. She needed space to think things through – It's not often you meet a man on Monday, and wake up on Wednesday married to him. Sally still couldn't understand it. On one hand, it did kind of make sense, but it just didn't *feel* right.

Sally thought of Harry. She had never met anyone like him. She had had a few relationships over the years, but they usually followed the same pattern. She always went for the same sort of men: men who weren't looking to settle down, men who just wanted a bit of fun, men who had no intention of staying with her. They weren't even nice. Sally still couldn't bring herself to even think about Barry, or what would have happened if she had stayed with him – she shuddered, despite the warmth. And there was her last boyfriend Stew, who never introduced her to his friends or family and didn't even stop to pick her up in his car that time, when it was raining and she was trudging home from work with five carrier bags full of shopping, as he *"didn't want to wreck his car upholstery".* Sally was always the one to make all of the effort. But one person can't carry a relationship, however much they *will* it to work. Maybe she didn't trust a man who seemed to properly like her? Whatever the reason, she was just a magnet to them; the bad boys, who in fact were just nasty bastards. Arseholes, as Nita had rightly pointed out. But Harry was everything that the others had never been. Sweet, kind, funny, attentive. An open book with no pretences. Lockey too, he was all of these things, Sally realised. But it was different between them, and the idea of being with Lockey, like that, just felt wrong. She couldn't explain it, but supposed when it came down to it, Lockey just wasn't Harry.

The morning passed by delightfully slowly. It felt as if time stood still, in this corner of the world. Sally had taken a stroll around the gardens and discovered an outdoor swimming pool in a secluded part, shaded by banana plants and towering palms. She'd fetched her bikini, a sunhat and a book to read, from her room, and spent a luxurious few hours, alternating between reading and taking dips in the cool water of the pool.

She didn't see another soul all morning. It felt pure decadence to have the whole swimming pool to herself. Sally spent some time, floating around the pool on her back, gazing up at the deep blue sky and the woolly green mountains which rose up behind the hotel. Whatever all of this was, that was happening; she decided that she was going to try her best to enjoy it. Who knew what tomorrow held?

By the time lunchtime arrived, Sally had worked up quite an appetite. She made her way back to the hotel. She was sitting in the dining area, just finishing off a sandwich, and pondering, how quickly she seemed to adjust to these new lives and places, when someone tapped her on the shoulder. She turned, surprised, and looked up at a towering gangly man, maybe in his late twenties, with crazy blonde fuzzy hair.

'Sally. Are you not coming today?' He sounded Scandinavian. Swedish perhaps.

'Um, yes? I'm coming…' Sally said as way of stalling. Rule number-one, of interdimensional travel; don't let on that you have no clue who people are, or what's going on.

'Great,' he stood, and waited expectantly. 'They're all waiting, at the boat.'

'Er… Will you give me a minute? I need to change – I'm still in my swimmers…'

He gave Sally a funny look, 'That's okay, you're

fine as you are. You won't need anything else. Just your towel maybe.'

Sally scooped up the damp towel from beside her feet and followed him out of the hotel.

They walked along a dusty road. And within moments they were beside the brilliant blue sea. Sally had to walk at a brisk pace to keep up with his long, flip-flopped stride. The sun was scorching, 'Mad dogs and English men...' Sally mumbled.

The tall man slowed and turned to her quizzically, 'I'm sorry?'

'Go out in the midday sun? Sorry. It's a saying. I just mean, it's hot.'

'Ah more of your funny sayings!' he laughed.

The road followed around the coast and into a ramshackle little colonial town. The weatherboard shop frontages were painted in an array of pastel shades, with large old fashioned looking signs above their corrugated iron verandas. Sally felt as though she had stepped back in time, a hundred-odd years into some cowboy town in the Wild West.

He veered off when they reached a dive-shack. 'Here we are.'

Sally's heart sank. *We're going scuba diving?* She kicked herself for not making up an excuse, not to come. 'I'm feeling a little under the weather suddenly,' Sally tried, as they entered the dive-shack.

'Another saying? Come on, we have to hurry. They will have all of your gear on the boat already, so not to worry. Just need to put on our wet suits quickly.' He chucked Sally a damp black wetsuit, which was surprisingly heavy.

Sally had never worn a wetsuit before and it

proved quite tricky to wriggle into. She stepped out of the changing room self-consciously.

'Ah well done.' He reached over and zipped up Sally's back, without her having to ask. 'Off we go then.'

Sally almost didn't recognise him, all decked out in his wetsuit, his fluff of flaxen hair hidden beneath a red back-to-front baseball cap. She followed him out of the shack and around the corner, and then she found herself climbing into an open motorboat. There were half a dozen wet-suited people on-board, plus the driver.

'Ah, Axel. Sally… Glad you made it,' a lady with a commanding voice shouted. Sally assumed she was the diving instructor.

The boat sped out across the bright blue sea. Sally was sitting precariously on one of the boat's inflated sides and had to grip on with white knuckles to a woven strap to keep her balance. Her sunhat flew off her head into the water, as the boat zipped away from the shore towards the horizon. Sally looked back towards land wistfully, her hair waving around her face, and wondered – with a surge of fear – if she was going to survive this. The waves had become a little larger. The sea had turned a darker shade of blue. How far out were they going?

But then the sea returned to a lighter shade of turquoise, the boat slowed. The sea seemed calmer here, and was now an impossible shade of cyan blue, so bright it looked unreal, and suddenly the idea of getting into the water, didn't seem quite so dreadful after all.

Sally had no clue whatsoever about diving, other than what she had seen in movies. She decided her best bet was to copy what everyone else did.

'Okay, Sally and Axel. You want to go first?' the instructor shouted.

Sally froze.

Axel leant in close, 'Everything okay with you?'

Sally nodded mutely.

'Look, we've done this a lot of times already. It's easy, you remember. I'll talk you through it okay?'

Sally was so grateful she could have hugged him. Axel helped Sally get her tanks onto her back, and passed her a couple of pipes with breathing regulators on the end. He fiddled with some valves and adjusted her straps. 'Buddy check. All right buddy?' he patted her on the shoulder, handed her a weight-belt and gestured for her to clip it on around her waist. Sally mirrored Axel, as he put flippers on his feet, and pulled his facemask and snorkel onto the top of his head. He grinned at Sally as he yanked his facemask down and then put the snorkel in his mouth. Sally did the same. And then he disappeared backward into the water. Sally looked over the side.

'What's up Sally? Come on, go go go.' The Instructor was making her way towards Sally. Axel had surfaced. He blew out a spout of water from his snorkel and beckoned for Sally to get in, making a rolling gesture with his hand.

Sally put the snorkel in her mouth, took a raspy breath and then rolled backward off the side of the boat. She tumbled into the sea, and nearly inhaled a mouthful of salty water when she tried to take a breath through the snorkel. But she remembered what Axel had done, and instead of breathing in, she blew all her remaining breath out as hard as she could in an almighty puff through the snorkel and cleared the tube.

Sally was a natural once she was in the water. Before long the whole group were in the sea, bobbing about on the surface treading water. They replaced their snorkels with breathing regulators, and down they went.

It was a different world beneath the surface. Sally had never even swum with goggles at the pool before. She loved it instantly. It was as if all the cares in the world were irrelevant down beneath the waves. She felt a sensation of weightlessness, as if she could fly, and discovered, that when she breathed out she sank down a little, and then breathing in she rose. She kicked her flippered legs and flew through the blue sea, focussing on her breathing as she went. In and out, slowly and calmly. She sounded a little like Darth Vader – the thought made her giggle and a cloud of bubbles escaped her and wound their way up towards the surface.

Axel was by her side and looked at her through his mask, his eyes wide with concern. Sally tried a reassuring smile, but it came out as more of a grimace with the regulator in her mouth. She gave him a confident thumbs up. He seemed unsure and giving her a questioning look, he raised his own thumb. Sally nodded and reiterated with another positive thumbs up.

Axel grabbed hold of Sally and took her up to the surface.

Sally pulled the regulator from her mouth and kicked with her legs to stay afloat. 'Why did you pull me up?'

'You were in trouble?'

'No, I was loving it. I just laughed. I was thinking of Darth Vader…'

'Darth Vader… like from Star Wars?' he gave her a funny look. 'You said you wanted to go up.'

'No. I said I was okay, everything was good.' Sally raised a thumb again to demonstrate. *Surely thumbs up is a universal sign?*

'That means you want to go up.' He made a circle with his pointing finger and thumb, 'This means, okay… you remember? Where's your head today Sally? You drank a lot of that Kava last night?'

'I'm sorry, yes I guess I forgot. Can we go down again?'

They dove back down and joined the others and thankfully, no one seemed to have noticed they had been missing. They were diving over a coral reef now. This underwater world was teeming with life. It was like swimming in a gold fish bowl, a rainbow of vibrant colour; fish in almost fluorescent shades: electric blues, oranges, yellows, reds, pinks and purples. Fish of all sizes swimming together. The smaller ones flitting and flashing, swimming against the currents. Some of the fish were surprisingly friendly and occasionally hovered in front of Sally's mask, as if checking her out. A school of larger silver fish swam by and in a flash turned as one. Sally's attention was caught by a stripy yellow fish, nestling in an anemone. The fish poked out its head briefly and then shyly retreated to its hiding place among the anemone's wavering rubbery fingers.

Axel took Sally's hand and pointed, his hair waving about like a waft of yellow above his head. He made a fin with his hand in front of his forehead and pointed again. Sally followed his gaze and saw a shark with white tipped fins – just a few metres away – swimming gracefully by. Meandering languorously, it swam in a zigzagging motion and slowly disappeared into the blue. Sally was surprised, she would have imagined she'd be petrified, but the shark was so unfazed by them, she had no fear at all.

They swum on and Axel pointed out – what Sally at first took to be sea grass – hundreds of strange long thin fish dancing in an upright position, as if attached to the seabed. As Sally and Axel approached – like a vanishing act – the fish sank down out of sight into their holes.

Sally was blown away, she was hooked. As soon as they were back on-board the boat, she longed to be back down beneath the waves.

The boat bashed back across the sea towards land. The waves seemed quite a lot larger now. A breeze had picked up. The sky had turned an ominous brooding grey, dark clouds marching in from the distant horizon.

21 ~ A JOURNEY OF SELF-DISCOVERY

By the time they had reached dry land, the first drops of rain had begun to fall. And then it was as if the skies had opened. The rain fell in a torrential roar. The horizon had disappeared into a haze, beyond the rough pockmarked surface of the sea. Lightning lit up the dark grey sky, and a moment later, a deep low crescendo of thunder rumbled menacingly around. Laughing and shrieking as they ran, they all dove into the shelter of the dive shack. It was almost louder inside the shack. The hammering rain drumming, like an army of impatient fingers, upon the tin roof. Sally had peeled off the wetsuit and she hung it on a hook with the others, dangling in a row.

'Do you want me to walk you back to the hotel?' Axel had to raise his voice to be heard above the noise of the rain.

'No. I'll be okay.' She was confident she'd find her way back to the hotel, the route had seemed pretty straight forward.

Sally stepped out into the rain. It was still pouring down. She breathed in the smell of the rain – earthy and steamy – it smelt wonderful, and somehow familiar, although she had never been anywhere before so hot the ground steamed when it rained. Sally thought of Monday morning, the last time it had rained, before any of this had happened. This was far from the cold dank English drizzle. Sally had never experienced rain like this before. The air was still warm and humid, but the rain was surprisingly cool – it felt refreshing and cleansing, renewing even. Sally wasn't the only one out in the rain. Villagers huddled in doorways hiding behind translucent curtains of water, that poured from the veranda roofs. Others passed by, seemingly oblivious to the downpour. A group of children of varying ages, played gleefully together in the street, gambolling ecstatically, jumping and splashing in puddles. They smiled and waved at Sally as she passed them by.

By the time Sally had walked the short distance along the road to the hotel, her shorts and t-shirt were soaked through. She stood, dripping, on the wooden veranda, the rain thundering on the roof. She felt exhilarated, alive, and still slightly floaty from being out on the sea. She looked out across the shiny freshly rain washed tropical paradise, and realised for the first time, that she was happy that all of this had happened. She didn't know what would become of her, but she had learned and experienced so much in the last few days. It was as if she hadn't really been living at all before, and she never wanted to go back to being that Sally. She resolved that if she ever did make it back to her own reality, things would be very different. She would make sure of it. She would embrace life; make the most of each day: travel, smile and laugh more, follow her dreams, be self-confident, be assertive, see more of her friends and allow herself to love and to be loved.

Sally felt a hand lightly on her shoulder and turned. The lady who had served her breakfast, smiled affably and handed her a large white fluffy towel. Sally took the towel gratefully – overwhelmed by the simple considerate act of kindness – and smiled back. By the time she found the words of thanks, the woman had already turned and left.

Sally returned to her room. The bed had been made and a fresh stack of towels left upon the covers. She took another shower, prepared this time for the cold. Sally found herself humming *Time After Time*, and smiled to herself. *One day*, she vowed to herself, *I'll return to Tokyo and properly explore.*

Sally towel dried her short hair and sat on the edge of the bed. A strange noise startled her. Like an odd digital mew. She realised the noise had come from the mobile phone on the bed behind her, and picking it up she saw the battery was nearly empty. There was a text message symbol on the screen, and Sally started when she saw it was from Lockey. His name and number were stored in the phone. *So this Sally knows Lockey?* she wondered in confusion. *Are we together in this reality too?* Without hesitating Sally pressed call.

The phone rang and rang. Sally was just about to give up, when he answered. He sounded groggy, his voice thick with sleep.

'Lockey? It's me, Sally.'

'Sally?' He sounded befuddled, 'Is it really you?'

Sally started to worry about him, 'Lockey, are you

alright? Has something happened?'

He breathed heavily, yawning maybe. 'No, I'm okay. Just waking up. I can't see a thing... Is it the middle of the night?'

Sally heard a voice in the background then, a woman asking who it was. The phone muffled a bit and Sally heard Lockey tell her to go back to sleep. There was silence for a moment followed by rustling noises, then he was back. He spoke in a hushed voice now, 'Sorry, I'm just going somewhere I can talk. I don't know where I am. This is so weird still Sal. I just blanked out, and then, here I am. Wherever *here* is...' He lowered his voice even further to a whisper, 'And I have absolutely no clue who that was... Ow!' There was another silence.

'Lockey?'

'Stubbed my toe. It's pitch black here. I can't see a thing. I just felt my way down the stairs, but I've got no bloody clue where the light switches are...'

'Feel your hand along a wall. Lockey? Are you still there?' Sally heard a click.

'Ah that's better... I'm in a kitchen. God it's so good to hear you. You're alright? Where are you Sally? It's half-past three in the morning. And how did you find my number?' He yawned again.

'Yes, I'm fine. I'm in Fiji. It's afternoon here. Have you been asleep all this time? I just found your number on my mobile phone. I guess we know each other here too...' And then she remembered. It came to Sally in a flash, she did know Lockey. He was her oldest and best friend.

Her mother had died in the car crash when Sally was eight years old. Sally remembered the day of the funeral, everyone in black, her father's hand on her shoulder as they lowered her mother's coffin into the ground. Sally had carried on at Easthampton School and became a fulltime boarder; her father had to work. But she spent the school holidays with him. Each holiday he seemed a little more healed, and a little more relaxed. They were closer after her mother's death, perhaps because they realised they were all that each other had. He took her abroad in the holidays, to snowy mountains for skiing, or snorkelling off far flung exotic beaches.

Sally first became friends with Lockey the year after her mother had died. It was on the day when they had discovered they shared birthdays. It was the ninth of March, the Monday following their ninth birthdays. They had been called up in front of assembly – a moment Sally had always loathed – to receive a special birthday round of applause. Lockey had given Sally a look, as if to say, 'don't worry about it.' And it was always like that between them. They were just on the same wavelength. He was like a brother to her. Twins from different parents, they joked. They spent every moment they could together.

There had been a time, when they were thirteen and drinking stolen cider at a friend's party, a crazy moment, when they had kissed. But it had felt all wrong and without ever saying anything out loud to one another, they both agreed to pretend it had never happened. Conversely, the kiss didn't ruin their relationship, instead, it strengthened it. They both knew from then on, with an absolute certainty, that best friends was what they were destined to be. There were friends who were girls, that Sally would giggle with in the dormitory at night. But it was always Lockey and her.

There was one holiday when her father had to go away on business. And one way or another it was arranged that Sally would spend the holiday with the Lockhart's at Wentworth Hall. Sally and Lockey were beside themselves, it was one of the best weeks of their lives. Even better, after that it was agreed that Sally would return to Wentworth Hall each weekend with Lockey. The Lockhart's became an almost surrogate family to Sally. Sally supposed Lockey's mother had always longed for a girl; she had been told she would never have children, but with help from IVF she had been blessed with Lockey and then five years later, by some miracle, little Teddy had come along. Sally loved Theodore. He was only four when Sally had first met him, the sweetest, cheekiest little boy with red hair and freckles. He retained his childlike enthusiasm and humour as he grew over the years, until eventually he overshot Sally in height and then towered over her.

'Lockey? Are you still there?' Sally realised the phone had gone dead. She looked at the blank screen with disappointment. The battery had died. Looking around the room, she spotted a charger dangling from a socket with an adapter attached, and plugged the mobile in. But the battery must have been so drained it wouldn't even turn on now. She tutted in frustration and decided she'd simply have to wait and try again later. Sally was suddenly ravenous. She pulled on a fresh t-shirt and pair of shorts and made her way back downstairs to find something to eat.

After she had eaten a light supper, she decided to take a stroll. The rain had stopped. She wandered out into the gardens. Little fragments of memories came to her in flickers and flashes. This Sally was a far more confident version of herself. It felt as if she had shrugged off a heavy cloak of self-abhorrence, the relief was immense. She could see things so much more clearly now. It was strange to see Lockey in this new light. Sally knew him almost better than she knew herself.

Sally from this reality had been working for her father's firm for some years, but it had become boring. She needed something more, but she didn't know what. She was looking for something, but it wasn't a man. This Sally had had a few boyfriends over the years, but she had never really needed or wanted a relationship. She already had two men who were the world to her; her father and Lockey. With her father's encouragement, she had set off on a worldwide trip. She had already visited India, Malaysia, China, and Australia. After Fiji she was off to New Zealand where she was going to stay with an old school friend – Claudia. And then on to Vancouver, Los Angeles, Miami, and then South America; Rio de Janeiro, Sao Paulo, across to South Africa – Johannesburg and then up to Nairobi before flying back to the UK. Even though Sally had travelled extensively with her father, this was different. This was her doing something, under her own steam. A journey of self-discovery, as well as a trip of a lifetime. Sally felt as if she were on a similar rite of passage herself. She had certainly learned a lot about herself in just a few days.

There was an elderly man sitting alone in the garden before an easel. Sally looked over his shoulder. He was painting directly onto a canvas in fine strokes – creating a mirror of the view before him; green leaves, palms and flowers, with the sea, blue in the distance. He was very good, his work looked almost like a photograph, but had a dreamlike quality, the colours more vivid than real life. As if sensing that she was there, he spoke without turning, 'What do you think?'

'It's beautiful,' Sally replied honestly.

He turned now and smiled and extended a hand, 'Rodrigo.' His thick moustache quivered as he spoke,

'Do you paint?'

Sally shook his hand. 'I think maybe I do, but I haven't for a long time – if that makes any sense.'

'It sounds like you should,' Rodrigo said simply. 'Here…' He bent sideways, reached into a canvas bag beside his feet, and produced a watercolour pad and a pencil – He passed them to Sally. 'Take a seat,' he gestured to the low wall beside him.

Sally hesitated, but then thought – *what else have I got to do?* She accepted the pad and pencil gratefully and sat down beside him. She looked out across the gardens. It really was breathtakingly beautiful. Her hand began to move instinctively with the pencil, she looked up every now and then.

'Your Spanish is very good. Where did you learn?'

It took Sally a moment to work out what he had meant, she hadn't even realised that they were speaking in Spanish, until now. 'Oh… Thankyou. I… just learned recently. Something I learned in another lifetime…'

He gave her a funny look, 'There's a lot going on in your life. I could see it when I first saw you. You're searching for something, your purpose perhaps?'

'I suppose I am. Aren't we all?'

He looked over her shoulder at her sketch, 'Maybe it's this,' he gestured to her work. 'You're very good. You obviously have a natural talent.'

And maybe he was right. Maybe this *was* what Sally had been searching for. Somewhere deep down inside, it felt as though this Sally was agreeing. Maybe as well as learning and gaining insight herself, on this strange journey, Sally could also impart something of value to the versions of herself she visited? She hoped so – it seemed only fair that it should be a two-way exchange. Sally progressed onto painting, filling in the blank spaces on the page with dabs and strokes of colour. Hesitantly at first, but her confidence grew as she relaxed and lost herself in her work. They sat there companionably painting, for a couple of hours, until the sun sank down toward the horizon and the light began to fade.

Sally thanked Rodrigo, 'This afternoon has been wonderful, thank you so much.'

Rodrigo smiled, 'It has been a pleasure young lady. I'll be here again tomorrow; you'll be most welcome to join me.'

Sally wondered, *where will I be tomorrow. Will my alternate-self remember any of today?* She hoped so. But it was quite possible that she wouldn't remember a thing. 'I'd love that. Only, I have this thing... Sometimes I completely forget. I can lose a whole day. I'm afraid, I may not even remember you tomorrow.'

Rodrigo looked thoughtful, 'Well, *I* shall remember *you*. Maybe it means we shall get the pleasure of today all over, as if for the first time.'

'I may not even remember Spanish.' Sally cringed, *I must sound like a complete nutter.*

But Rodrigo smiled broadly, his thick moustache turning up at the ends, 'Then I shall speak to you in English. And you will sit with me again and we will paint, and talk, and enjoy this beautiful place.'

Sally thanked Rodrigo once more and said goodbye. She felt a little sad that she would most likely never see him again, and hoped that her other-self would get to meet him tomorrow.

Back inside the hotel, Sally played a game of

snooker with Vishal; a fellow hotel resident whom she had befriended a few days before. She drank a couple of Fijian beers and ate another meal. This time opting for a more adventurous local dish, which was delicious; sweet potatoes and vegetables in a creamy sweet coconut milk sauce. She was surprised that she was still feeling floaty from the dive – and after eating, realised she was completely exhausted, both physically and mentally.

Sally returned to her room. The mobile seemed to be fully charged now. She flopped onto the bed and turned the phone on. She had three missed calls from Lockey. It was just after ten o'clock and it seemed Lockey was twelve hours behind, so it would be mid-morning for him. She looked up Lockey's number. But scrolling through the address book, she came to 'Dad' first.

Sally pressed call, it rang briefly. And then he answered, 'Sal! Great to hear from you. Where are you now?'

It was so good to hear his voice, Sally burst into tears.

'Sal? What's up sweetie? Has something happened?' He sounded alarmed and this was the last thing she wanted.

Sally took a steadying breath and flapped air at her face, 'I'm okay Dad. It's just been a long day. I'm exhausted, I guess. I'm happy though, really – everything's good, it's just great to hear your voice… I've missed you…' Sally nearly lost it again but regained herself.

'Look, you know you can come back whenever you're ready? No one would think any the less of you. And there's always a position here at the firm, if you want it?'

'No Dad, honestly, I'm fine. It's great. You know, today I went out scuba diving... It was beautiful.'

'Oh Sal, I knew you'd love it. We'll both go one day... what do you say?'

Sally blinked back the tears and swallowed against the lump in her throat.

'Don't want to be seen with your old man?' he jibed.

'No, it's not that at all. I'd love nothing more. Tell me about what you've been up to?' Sally just wanted to hear his voice. She tried to picture him. She had seen him briefly on her first shift, older but still unmistakably her father. They talked for around quarter of an hour before he said he had to go.

'I'm so sorry darling, someone's at the door. This phone-call's going to cost a fortune anyway. In fact, is this still the work phone I gave you?' he chortled. 'Not to worry. Lovely to talk to you, Sal.'

'You too Dad.'

'I'll talk to you again soon.'

'Yes.' But Sally knew she never would. 'Bye Dad. I love you.'

Sally cried for ten whole minutes. It was so unfair that she had lost him.

Eventually the tears dried up. It was simply too hot to cry. It seemed the tears were evaporating before they got a chance to roll further than mid cheek. But she now had memories of a whole lifetime with her father; the most precious gift this odd journey into different dimensions had given her. And it was comforting to know that at least one version of herself would still have her father tomorrow.

When Sally finally recovered, she called Lockey.

'Sally! How are you? You cut off earlier…'

'Yes, sorry – the battery died. Did you remember anything yet?'

'No. Did you?' It sounded like he was somewhere noisy. The line had sounded surprisingly clear when she had spoken to him earlier on.

'I did. Lockey, we've been friends since school. My father didn't die. I carried on at Easthampton. Lockey, you're my best friend… Lockey?' Sally had been speaking in a rush, and she realised now that the line had gone quiet. She worried the phone had cut off again, 'Lockey?'

'Yes… Sorry, I'm still here. Sal, I remember. I remember it all now! I remember everything.' He blew out a breath, 'It's a lot to take in, isn't it? Monday morning, we were strangers, and now we're old friends. There's more Sal. I was somewhere else, in another reality just before this shift, and you… you were there, in a coma.'

Sally frowned, 'How could that be possible?'

'I don't know, but I think that might be where our bodies are, back in our own reality.'

'So you're saying we're in a coma? And just *dreaming* all of this somehow?'

'Not dreaming. I think we're travelling in pure energy form, but, we're going to have to get back, somehow.'

Sally couldn't make sense of it. How can she have been in a coma? How can she *be* in a coma? It was all too much to fathom.

She told Lockey all about her day; about diving, and painting, and about all the stuff she had come to realise. She even told him about Harry and Flora.

'But it's like with Cal, Sally,' Lockey reasoned, 'Harry and Flora... they're not yours really...' And then he felt the weight of his words and added more gently, 'Maybe you'll find him Sal, in our own reality, when all of this is over...'

'Perhaps. If we ever do find a way back, there's a lot I'll change. And I've got you now. You know, the Sally from this reality has given up on men. She's had about as many failed relationships as me. I guess some things stay the same. That's what was so good about Harry. He was just so different from the idiots I usually attract. Just Monday morning I was so lost and lonely. I've gained so much.'

They chatted away for almost an hour. Sally guiltily remembered the phone bill her dad would be shouldering. 'I should go. I'm so tired anyway...' Sally yawned.

'Are you going to sleep now?'

'Yes, I think I will.' Her eyes were stinging with tiredness. Then Sally remembered, that when she went to sleep, they would both shift. 'Oh. I can't, can I?'

'I'm on a train. It's going to look weird – but there's no way you'll be able to stay awake for several more hours, you sound like you're ready to drop...'

Sally tried to stifle a yawn.

'See. Never mind. It will just look like I nodded off on the journey I guess. People sleep on trains all the time. I just hope my alternate-self wakes before he misses his stop. I don't mind. At least I'm sitting down and forewarned. It's fine... Just lie down and go to sleep...'

'I'm already lying down,' Sally sighed dreamily. 'Night Lockey.'

'Night Sal. Hey, happy birthday for tomorrow. I'll see you soon.'

Sally hung up and pulled a corner of sheet over herself, not for warmth, but more for comfort. She was still pleasantly floaty from the diving – as if a part of her had remained out at sea – and surrendering to her tiredness, she drifted contentedly off to sleep. Over ten-thousand miles away, on the other side of the world on a train heading for London, Lockey drifted off to sleep too.

22 ~ HAPPY BIRTHDAY ~ FRIDAY

The temperature had plummeted from a sticky thirty-degrees Celsius, to what felt like a frosty zero. Sally pulled the covers up to her chin and shivered. It was still dark. Something had woken her, the cold possibly. She felt chilly and alert, but her head was spinning. Someone was snoring in the bed beside her. *Where am I now?* Sally reached out and fumbled around until her fingers located a bedside lamp. She switched it on and winced against the light and waited for her eyes to adjust.

The lump in the bed beside her shifted and groaned. A large arm, with a gorilla like hand attached to it, flopped across her, 'Uhgrrr… What's going on?' a deep voice growled.

Sally froze and then turned, not wanting to see. Her heart had sunk to her toes. Was it *him? Barry?* – possibly the worst of the worst of all her bad choices in boyfriends; the one that she, thankfully, had got away from. Sally wasn't sure, his hand was shielding his eyes against the light now, and she couldn't quite focus properly. Her head was pounding.

He groaned again and rolled towards her, 'Turn the bloody light off woman.'

Sally had often marvelled how anyone could wake up so angry, ready to fight from the moment his cold dark eyes had opened. She had thought him handsome at the beginning, had mistaken his quiet brooding frown for something deeper, poetic even perhaps, a troubled soul whom maybe she could mend. But Barry didn't run deep and once she had seen his true ugly self, there was no going back. What you saw is what you got, and it wasn't nice. Despite all of this, he had had a strange hold on her, he knew just the right things to say to put her down just enough, that she would doubt herself and think, "*maybe he's right: maybe I am lucky to have him. After all, who else would want me?*"

Quickly – her heart hammering in her chest, fingers trembling – Sally reached back towards the lamp to switch it off. The lamp fell from the bedside table onto the floor with a thump and went out, plunging the room back into darkness.

'What are you doing? You nutter.' His arm circled her waist and pulled her towards him. Sally felt his hot stinking breath on her neck and almost gagged. And then he kissed her, a rough, dry, selfish kind of kiss a million miles away from Harry's tenderness. Sally's knee went up instinctively in a sharp movement and connected with his groin. He groaned loudly, and then there was silence. Sally cringed at her mistake; he'd be enraged now.

'I'm sorry, I didn't mean to… it was an accident.' She cowered, but by some miracle this seemed to pacify him.

'Whatever...' he mumbled sleepily, 'Happy birthday...' He rolled away from her and farted, and then within moments he was snoring again.

Sally lay for a while listening to him snore, until she was one-hundred percent sure he was deeply asleep. And then she crept from the room.

The house was freezing. Sally remembered how he had never let her turn up the thermostat above thirteen degrees. How had she ever put up with him? And what in the world had possessed her to stay with him all of these years? It must have been ten, maybe eleven years since they had broken up. Sally tried a couple of doors, before she found the bathroom. Quietly she closed the door before she pulled the light cord.

Sally saw her reflection immediately and gasped. She had a black eye that a heavy weight boxer would be proud of, literally black and blue and swollen with a blood shot red eye at its centre. Her lip looked cut and swollen too. She grimaced at her reflection and her blood boiled. Had *he* done this to her? Barry had never abused her physically, but somehow *this* didn't really surprise her. She had seen it in her eyes many times, and knew that it would have come to this if she hadn't plucked up the courage to leave him. Her ribs ached. She unbuttoned her pyjama top and revealed an angry bruise, which spread across the entire right side of her tender ribs. She touched it gently and winced.

Sally wasn't sure how this was supposed to work, possibly rule number-two of interdimensional travel would most likely be; do not purposefully do anything that may alter the life of your alternate self. But luckily there *were* no written rules for any of this, and something most definitely must be done. The front door at the bottom of the stairs was semi-glazed with frosted glass, which let in an amber glow from a street light beyond. Without returning to the bedroom, even to look for clothes, Sally tiptoed silently down the stairs. She pulled a coat from a peg beside the door, shuffled into a pair of shoes and crept from the house, closing the door as gently as she could and cringing at the clack as it locked behind her, and she ran.

Sally was breathing hard, she had only been running for a few moments, but she had never been particularly fit. Her lungs were stinging and she felt sick. She slowed her pace and took to a fast walk instead. She was walking through a housing estate. It looked similar to Millside, only rougher – half of the buildings almost derelict looking, grubby, dilapidated and daubed with graffiti that was no-ones art. An upturned shopping trolley lay discarded beside the road; no doubt some drunken idiots had careered home in it from the pub during the night. A fox that had been ravaging a bin, froze when it heard Sally approach. It stared at her, wild eyed for a moment, before darting off into the dark.

Sally had no clue how long she had been walking, but the sky was lightening to a cold, battleship blue and surprisingly, somewhere not only were there birds, but they thought it appropriate to chirp in the arrival of the new day. There was a petrol station up ahead, its floodlit forecourt beaconing out across the dark. Sally was aware that she needed to vanish – Barry would come looking for her as soon as he discovered she had gone. And she wanted to be nowhere near, when that happened.

Sally entered the petrol station shop. A middle aged lady who had been slumped on a stool reading a magazine behind the counter, looked up indifferently as the bell at the door pinged. Sally felt self-conscious under the bright glare of the fluorescent lighting, suddenly very aware that she was wearing just pyjamas beneath the overcoat, which she realised now, must belong to Barry. But the lady seemed unfazed. Maybe it was a normal occurrence around here for people to wander about in the early hours of the day in their pyjamas?

'Can I help you?' she spoke in a bored monotone voice, barely looking at Sally, and sighed.

'Do you have a telephone I could use please?'

The woman closed her magazine and eyeballed Sally now. 'Car broken down?'

'No. I… I just, need to talk to someone.'

She gave Sally a long look now. 'There,' she pointed to a payphone attached to the wall at the back of the shop. 'You'll need money though.'

Sally felt a panic rising and put her hands in the pockets of the coat. Her fingers of her left-hand found a leather wallet. She pulled it out guardedly and opened it a crack. There was a wad of notes inside, mostly tens and twenties but at a quick count she made it to be about ninety pounds. She reached back into the right-hand pocket and withdrew a mobile phone. Sally was still staring at the phone when she felt the woman's eyes on her. Not only was she still watching her, but she looked deep in thought now – brow furrowed, chin resting on her palm, knuckles to the side of her mouth, elbow on the counter. She moved her hand around so that her knuckles were beneath her chin, and continued to stare at Sally for an uncomfortably long moment – her eyes boring into her. And then as if decided something, she raised her head.

'You're doing the right thing you know.' The woman folded her arms guardedly and leant on the counter, 'They never change. They say they will. But they never do.' Sally saw in the woman's eyes a kindred spirit, but then just as quickly she had closed herself off again. The woman sighed, her face hardened. 'Don't ever go back to him.' She looked at Sally for a moment with meaning, and then looked back down to her magazine and pretended to read.

Sally walked up the road a hundred metres or so and stopped in the shadows. She stared at the phone, its small screen lit up blue. *Who should I call?* And then she knew. From the last reality, she knew off by heart the telephone number for Lockey's parent's house – Wentworth Hall. Would the number be the same? Sally tapped in the digits. She could hear it ringing; that was a good start. It rang about a dozen times and then the line cracked, silence.

'Hello?' a woman's voice answered sleepily. It was Lockey's mother. 'Hello? Is anyone there?'

'I'm sorry. I'm looking for Lockey... Horace I mean... Is he there?'

'It's jolly early. It's six o'clock in the morning. Who is this?'

'Francesca, It's Sally.'

There was a brief silence. 'Sally?'

Sally realised that in this reality they had more than likely never met. 'I'm sorry, no... I'm a friend of your son's...' she found herself apologising again, and cringed inwardly at herself. 'I just really need to speak with him.'

'Okay, wait a moment. I'll see if … just hold the line. Sally did you say?'

'Yes, Sally.'

The line went quiet. Sally stood for a moment which felt like a lifetime, listening to the silence hissing through the phone. It had become really chilly. She pulled the coat in around herself. She was just starting to think that maybe Francesca had hung up on her, when Lockey answered. 'Sally? Where are you?'

'Lockey… I need your help.' Sally gave him a brief outline of what was going on. She still had no clue where she was.

'Is there anything around? Any street signs, or landmarks?'

Sally looked back towards the garage, she could just about make out the name and read it out to him. She heard Lockey conferring with his mother – did she know where that was? There was a low muttered conversation, she missed the most of it, but heard a mumbled – 'for goodness sake darling, it's not even light…' And then Lockey was back on the phone.

'Okay, I'm coming to get you. I'll be with you within the hour. Is there somewhere safe you can wait?'

'I'll be near the petrol station…' She wanted to add, please hurry, but didn't like the idea of him driving too fast. 'I'll be okay. I'll see you soon. Lockey… thank you.' Sally deleted Lockey's parents' number from the call list and then turned the mobile phone off and chucked it into a nearby bin.

The sun was just rising when Lockey pulled up.

The roads were still quiet and she heard the car before she saw it. She had been petrified that Barry would round the corner at any moment in a rage, and almost wept with relief when Lockey pulled up beside her in his mother's shiny silver Aston Martin – her very own knight in shining armour.

Sally removed Barry's coat and left it, along with his wallet, on the pavement beside the road. She wanted nothing of his. And she climbed into the car.

Lockey looked stricken when he saw Sally's face. 'Did he do that to you?'

Sally nodded. 'Yes, I think so.' She belted up and gave him a slightly manic smile, which was supposed to be reassuring. 'Can we just get out of here?'

The further they drove, the better Sally started to feel. Neither of them spoke for a good few minutes, before Sally broke the silence, 'Happy birthday, by the way.'

Lockey looked across and gave her a wretched look. 'Jesus Sally.'

'I know,' Sally replied grimly.

'Was Barry someone that you knew? in your own life?'

'Yes. I really was that stupid, for a time.'

'No I didn't mean that, we all make mistakes – look at me and Patricia…'

'We should introduce the two of them,' Sally suggested, 'Barry and Patricia, a match made in hell.'

Neither of them spoke for a moment.

'What *were* you thinking Sal? Sally and Barry… it even sounds ridiculous…'

Sally snorted, a mixture of a laugh and a sob. He was trying to make light of a very dark situation, in his own clumsy way trying to cheer her. Sally realised how close the name Harry was to the name Barry; one simple letter change and worlds apart. Barry; a name which she associated with fear and oppression. And Harry; love and compassion – two opposing sides of a coin.

As if reading her mind and trying to dig himself from a hole, Lockey added, 'But Harry and Sally is good.' Lockey glanced across at Sally, 'I can't stand the movie though; When Harry Met Sally…' he grinned, 'dreadful film.'

'No, you never could stand a romantic comedy. But you know, I've come to realise that love and laughter, they're really all that matters, when you really get down to it…'

23 ~ WENTWORTH HALL

They pulled into the long sweeping driveway of Wentworth Hall. It was properly light now and Sally marvelled at the neatly sculpted rows of bushes and miles of pristine, immaculate lawn disappearing into the distance. They rounded a corner and the breath-taking sight of the manor came into view. Sally recognised it immediately. She felt a thrill of excitement and remembered, in her other life, arriving here for the first time. She had been in complete awe.

Wentworth Hall was an imposing Elizabethan building, with row upon row of mullioned windows set into its soft grey stone walls. There were several tall chimney stacks, beyond the multiple peaked gables of its expansive red tiled roof. It was no less impressive. Sally had countless fond memories here.

Lockey rounded the large fountain and pulled up right before the manor's enormous oak front door. 'Come on, let's get you inside.'

The front door had opened. A couple of springer spaniels bounded out enthusiastically to greet them.

Lockey's mother – Francesca – stood on the threshold, her arms folded. Sally looked down uncomfortably, remembering she was wearing only the badly fitting stripped pyjamas and a pair of dirty old trainers. 'I can't meet your mother *like this...*' she said, suddenly mortified.

Lockey put a hand on her shoulder, 'It'll be okay, I promise. Besides, I already know that she'll love you.' He got out of the car, and reluctantly Sally joined him.

Francesca's hands went up to her face when she saw Sally, her cool reserve immediately thawed. Her face had fallen, 'Oh... oh dear. I think you'd better come on in.'

Sally could tell Francesca wanted to ask what on earth had happened to her – but was far too polite to ask. Lockey gave Sally a small reassuring smile, as if to say – *see, what did I tell you,* and motioned for Sally to follow his mother into the house. The dogs wagged around Sally's legs, nearly knocking her off her feet as she walked.

'Henry. Caspian. Leave the poor girl alone,' Francesca barked, and took the two dogs firmly by their collars. Francesca had led Sally through the immense wood panelled entrance hall into the drawing-room and gestured for her to take a seat on one of the large cream sofas before the ornate marble fireplace. 'I'll get someone to bring you a cup of tea and some toast, and I'll fetch you something to wear.' She paused, and then added gently but seriously, 'Do you need me to call you a doctor?'

'Oh, no! I'm fine, honestly – it's not as bad as it looks.'

'Well, if you're sure. You're very welcome to stay here for as long as you need to. We have plenty of room. I'll get a bed made up for you, so you can go and have a little lie down. I'm sure you must be tired.'

'You're very kind, thank you. I don't think I'd be able to sleep though...'

'I'll see if I can find you some sleeping pills.'

Sally and Lockey exchanged a look.

Lockey waited until his mother had left the room, before turning to Sally, 'Should we contact the police?'

Sally was taken aback. Should she? 'No, well, I can't really. I don't even actually know how this happened... It *is* still possible that Barry had nothing to do with my bruises... maybe it was a simple accident...' But she very much doubted this. What kind of accident could cause that kind of damage?

Lockey seemed unconvinced too.

Sally sighed. 'I'm really not looking forward to finding out... Maybe I should take your mother up on the offer of a sleeping pill...' But even as she said it, she knew she couldn't do that, this was something she needed to face. She needed to try and help this other Sally. 'I still don't know what on earth could have possessed me to stay with him...' Sally froze mid-sentence and blanched; she had just had the most sickening thought. 'Oh god, Lockey... I just left... I didn't think... What if there was a child... or children in the house somewhere?' *Could that explain why I was still with him?* Sally was horrified at the thought. *Did I walk out and leave an innocent child behind in the house with an enraged Barry?* She was appalled, 'I need to go back—'

Lockey cut her off. 'No. You're not going back there. Not ever Sally, not in any lifetime.'

Sally had never seen Lockey so angry before.

176

'I'll go,' he said darkly.

'No. Please don't. I don't want to make matters any worse...'

'What was the address?'

'I... I don't remember,' she lied, but then realised with relief that it was the truth. She didn't even know the street name. 'Honestly, I don't.'

Lockey sighed crossly. 'Well there must be someone we can contact, your aunt?'

Sally pulled a face; Mary was still the last person she was ready to see.

'Or a friend... Nita?'

'It's worth a shot. I can try and call her – the number was the same when I called here.'

Sally dialled Nita's number. *The number you have dialled has not been recognised...* She shook her head at Lockey.

Francesca came back into the room. 'Here,' she said simply, and passed Sally a pair of folded tweed trousers and a soft pink cashmere top. And then she opened her palm and held out a couple of pills. Sally was reminded of the pills that Harry had given her, and wondered for the first time what they had been. 'They'll help you get a little sleep,' Francesca prompted.

Sally looked nervously to Lockey and then back to Francesca, 'No. I'm okay... Thank you.'

Upstairs in one of the many guest rooms, Sally pulled on the tweed trousers and top – they actually fitted her very well, and even with the battered face, she looked much better out of the over-washed, baggy, men's pyjamas she'd been wearing. There came a knock on the door. 'Come in?' Sally called out.

It was Francesca. She stood a little awkwardly at the doorway and took in Sally's appearance. She seemed deep in thought. 'Much better.' She smiled a little sadly, 'You really reminded me of someone, and I couldn't even place who until now, but you look a lot like my little sister, Elsie.'

'I didn't know you had a sister...' Sally said, before she remembered this was supposed to be the first time they'd met.

Francesca eyed Sally quizzically, 'No, well I don't suppose you would. Not many people do actually. She disappeared when she was sixteen, fell in with a bad crowd and then simply dropped off the radar. I like to think that she's out there somewhere, living out an alternate reality. Here...' she passed Sally a small bundle, 'There's a new toothbrush and a few toiletries I thought may be helpful...' She cleared her throat. 'It's really none of my business... and forgive me for being forthright. But, this really won't *do* you know.' She gestured to Sally's face, 'No one deserves to be treated that way. I do hope you're going to put an end to it. I was serious when I said that you're welcome to stay here for as long as you would like to, in fact... I'd rather like to insist that you do. We can help you get back on your feet, but the changes have to start with you. You may not feel it right now, but what you've done today – walking away, it's your first step to breaking the cycle. Your first step towards living a life without fear. A life you deserve. You are far stronger than you know...' Francesca wrung her hands, 'I apologise if I've overstepped the mark.'

Sally's eyes had involuntarily welled with tears, she swallowed and gave a watery smile, 'Thank you Francesca.'

Francesca shut the door quietly behind herself as she left. Sally took a deep breath and exhaled slowly. Francesca was right. Nobody deserved to be abused, physically *or* mentally. She hoped with all of her heart that the other "her" would indeed break the cycle. There was still the terrible niggling feeling that she needed to go back to the house she had woken in and check that she hadn't left a child or children behind. She was going to have to be strong for her other-self.

Sally brushed her teeth and applied a little makeup, which Francesca had thoughtfully left for her. Apart from the bruises this version of herself looked much as Sally had looked on Monday morning.

24 ~ TAKING A STAND

'Are you sure about this?' Lockey had pulled over in the same spot where he had picked Sally up that morning. He looked across at her seriously.

'Yes. We need to check...' Sally had convinced Lockey to bring her back. Together they would try to retrace her footsteps, and hopefully they would find their way back to the house. It was nearing midday now. Maybe some memories would come to her, but she couldn't just sit around and wait for that to happen. Time could be of the essence.

As they walked past the petrol station, Sally looked across the forecourt into the shop. She could just make out the same woman, still slumped behind the counter. Sally wondered what *her* story was. How many women suffered silently behind closed doors? She wished there was something she could do to help. But she was. Right now, she was taking a stand.

Sally had made Lockey promise that he wouldn't get into a fight with Barry. Barry would be livid. But fighting violence with violence wasn't the answer.

They would check that there were no children involved, gather her things, and leave.

They walked together in mostly silence, the air around them weighted with anticipation. Sally recognised various daubs of mindless graffiti. Hastily sprayed, running paint lines, misspelt words, pointless sentiments. It gave graffiti a bad name. *If you didn't have anything clever or artistic to spray, why bother at all?* Sally thought sadly. And there was the upturned shopping trolley. They were getting closer.

They rounded the corner and Sally was surprised that she actually recognised the houses now. She felt a knot of anxiety. She wanted to turn back, to be whisked away once more to the safety of Wentworth Hall. As if sensing her thoughts Lockey touched her arm and stopped walking, 'We can go back. We don't have to do this. Or, you can go back to the car and wait, and I'll go.'

'No.' Sally took a steadying breath and felt a rush of determination. *I can do this.* She pointed to a house a few doors up, 'It's here.'

'Are you sure?'

Sally nodded, 'Yes. I nearly stood in that puddle of vomit just after I left the house.' She pointed at the pavement up ahead in disgust.

They stood before the front door and exchanged a look. Lockey rang the bell and they waited. They were just starting to think – perhaps wistfully – that Barry wasn't home, when they heard a shuffling noise from inside. Through the frosted glass they could just make out the indistinct shape of someone descending the stairs.

'Alright, alright. I'm bloody coming,' his muffled

voice came from within. Sally braced herself and stepped back slightly behind Lockey, and he stood a little taller.

Barry answered the door, but he wasn't Barry. He bore a vague resemblance to Barry, but Sally didn't recognise the man who stood before them in his boxer shorts. His small beer belly stretching out the front of his grubby looking t-shirt. He scratched his groin, stretched, and then rubbed the back of his head. 'Wha'd'you want?' he asked gruffly. He looked as if he had only just woken up.

Sally was just thinking she had picked the wrong house, when he spotted her. '*Sal?*' he looked confused, 'What's going on?'

Lockey stepped forward. 'We've come to get her things… and the kids,' he added, deciding to bluff it.

Not-Barry looked even more baffled, 'What kids?' He looked past Lockey to Sally, 'Sal? What the *fuck's* going on? And who's *he?*'

Lockey protectively stepped further in front of Sally, 'Not kids, I said kit. We've come for all of Sally's kit – her belongings. We don't want any trouble…'

Not-Barry scratched his head, 'This is mental…' He noted Lockey's menacing glare, 'Whatever, I'll get her stuff.' He turned and disappeared back into the house.

'He's not Barry,' Sally whispered animatedly.

'Well who *is* he?' Lockey asked, confounded.

'I've no clue,' Sally shook her head. Suddenly not sure what one earth was going on.

'He might not be Barry, but he's someone *like* Barry. We need to stand up for the other you. At least we know there're no kids involved…' Lockey broke off, Not-Barry was returning already.

The door opened again. Not-Barry was wearing a pair of tracksuit trousers now. 'Here,' he shoved a small bundle of clothes at Lockey, along with a pair of black strappy-heels and a small handbag. 'I didn't even know you'd gone already...' He looked a little dejected, 'Why'd you leave without saying goodbye Sal?'

Lockey leant forward blocking him. 'She left without saying goodbye, *because* you're a monster. What kind of a man does *this* to a woman?' Lockey gestured to Sally's black eye.

Not-Barry blinked hard. 'Sal?' he tried to address Sally again, but Lockey wasn't having any of it.

'I've half a mind to black both of *your* eyes...' Lockey growled.

Not-Barry shrank back. 'I never did that... Sal? Tell him,' he pleaded, visibly shaken. 'She fell out of a bloody shopping trolley. I told her it was a bad idea...'

Sally gasped and her insides shrank. An image flashed in her mind of hurtling along the dark streets in a clattering trolley, laughing uncontrollably, her hair blowing out behind her. 'Oh god Lockey, he's right,' Sally breathed, wide eyed, and pulled at Lockey's sleeve.

Lockey hadn't heard, he was still on the war path. 'Where's the rest of her stuff?' he held up the small bundle of crumpled clothing; what looked like a sparkly top a pair of black trousers.

'That's all that she left mate, honest.'

'I'm no *mate* of yours,' Lockey spat, and pushed Not-Barry in the chest.

Sally was still tugging at Lockey's arm. 'Lockey,'

she whispered.

Finally, Lockey turned to her, a little disgruntled.

'Lockey. I've made a terrible mistake…' Sally was mortified.

Lockey stared at her uncomprehendingly for a moment, before it slowly dawned on him.

Not-Barry, sensing that the tables were turning puffed himself up, 'Too right you made a mistake. You're a bunch of bloody nutters, the pair of you. Jeez Sal. It's over – not that it ever really started…' he looked crestfallen again. His eyes dropped to the ground and then flicked to Sally's feet, 'You're wearing my trainers?'

Sally's cheeks burned. She realised, that not only had she stolen this man's shoes, but she'd lost him his coat, wallet, and thrown his mobile phone in a dustbin. 'Lockey… let's go,' she pleaded.

'Yeah well, you can give me my shoes back first, can't you.'

Sally took off the trainers – they *were* a little on the large side when she came to think of it, but only a smidgen. She passed them back to him and inadvertently looked down at his tiny bare feet, which seemed strangely out of proportion to his stocky build and huge hands. *He looks rather like a less handsome Wreck-It Ralph,* Sally decided.

Not-Barry was working himself up to a full rant now, 'What kind of girl strings a guy along like that? I thought you was something special. And I don't s'pose I'll see my pyjamas again. Them were my favourites.'

'Okay, well we'd better be off now,' Lockey said with false cheer.

'You run off in my best pyjamas and turn up with

your… *whoever this is?* And drag me out of bed first thing in the morning and start throwing 'round mental accusations.'

Sally almost pointed out that it was more like lunchtime, than first thing in the morning. Lockey shot her a look and linked his arm through hers.

They were walking at a fast pace away from the house now. Sally thought again guiltily of the wallet, coat and phone. She was just starting to feel the tiniest bit sorry for Not-Barry. Until he shouted his next comment.

'I told you that last time I'd not hit you again, an' I'm a man of my word.'

Lockey stopped in his tracks and looked back, appalled. Sally feeling him tense, slid her hand down and gently enveloped his clenched fist. *Please just leave it. Please just leave it,* she silently pleaded. *He's really not worth it.*

Lockey took a deep breath and Sally felt him relax a little. His fist uncurled, he took Sally's hand, squeezed it slightly, and turned full on to face Not-Barry with a steely look in his eyes. Not-Barry who had stepped out onto his front path, started backing away – almost stumbling over himself – towards the safety of his house. Lockey's voice was low and calm, 'If I hear that you attempt to even so much as talk to Sally…' Not-Barry was almost back through his front door now. 'I'll be back to pay you a visit – now that I know where you live.'

'I won't. I promise,' Not-Barry yelped.

Lockey fixed Not-Barry with a final menacing look, and then turned and – still holding Sally's hand – walked away.

Sally felt a flood of relief as they rounded the

corner. She suspected that that would be the last that her other-self ever saw of Not-Barry.

Lockey had stopped walking, 'Here,' he passed Sally her shoes. 'You'd better put these on. I'm not sure it's a good idea to be walking bare foot along here. There's broken glass and all sorts of unsavoury looking things…'

Sally turned her nose up at the shoes.

'Unless you'd rather a lift to the car that is?' Lockey motioned to the upturned trolley.

Sally laughed and groaned, 'Very funny.' She held on to Lockey's arm to steady herself as she pulled on the black strappy high heeled shoes, which felt trashy and a little ridiculous teamed with Francesca's, country lady tweed trousers. 'What do you think?' Sally grimaced.

Lockey laughed, 'It's a good look, rather suits you.'

Sally smiled. 'Thank you for walking away Lockey.'

'Well you were right, he really wasn't worth it,' Lockey said distractedly.

Did I say that out loud? Sally wondered.

'Come on,' Lockey grinned now, 'I'm taking *you* for a slap-up birthday pub-lunch.'

25 ~ PIMM'S O'CLOCK

The drive back towards Wentworth had been pleasant, and with the weight of the morning's drama now lifted, the two had chatted easily. Lockey pulled in at a quaint country pub, somewhere nearby to Wentworth Hall.

They sat out in the pub's leafy garden at a wooden bench table. It had turned into a beautiful afternoon. The sun had broken through, and out of the cool breeze it was pleasantly warm. Sally looked up to the blue sky and closed her eyes, feeling the warmth of the sun on her cheeks. Lockey emerged from the pub with a couple of glasses of Pimm's and a menu tucked under his arm.

'Pimm's o'clock.' Lockey raised his glass to Sally as he sat down opposite her, 'Happy birthday!'

She clinked her glass to Lockey's and smiled, 'Cheers. And a happy birthday to you too.' Sally took a welcome sip, she hadn't realised how thirsty she was and the Pimm's was deliciously quenching and fruity. 'Well, that was quite a morning.'

'Hmmm, he was a piece of work…' Lockey frowned.

'Wreck-It Ralph?' Sally fished a piece of strawberry out of her glass and popped it into her mouth.

'Wreck-It Ralph?' Lockey raised an eyebrow.

'You know, small feet and comparatively massive fists.'

Lockey laughed and then grew serious. 'Well I hope there won't be any more trouble from him. Do you remember much yet?'

'I only got the glimpse of the shopping trolley incident…' Sally winced, and her hand went up to her eye protectively. 'How about you?'

'No nothing yet. Although my mother said something about a birthday party this evening. Would you like to come?'

'Perhaps, but…' Sally felt like there was something important she was supposed to be doing. Something she needed to remember. She frowned in concentration. And then it clicked – maybe she was getting better at this now. It felt a little like fine-tuning an old television this time, and all of a sudden the picture became clear.

Sally's life here was almost identical to her own reality. Her past seemed to match up to her own as an exact parallel, until a year ago, but she couldn't quite pinpoint what the turning point had been. She had the same friends – or more like lack of, these days – She even lived in the same flat. Except she wasn't temping anymore, but working as a waitress in the curry house beneath her flat. And, she now had a cat; an affectionate, docile, marmalade coloured cat, who would be starving by now.

'Tikka Masala!' Sally announced suddenly.

Lockey frowned at his menu, 'I don't see it... Is it on the specials?'

'No. My cat; Tikka... I need to feed my cat!'

'You have a cat? You have a cat, called, *Tikka Masala?*'

'Just Tikka for short... He was a stray kitten I found living out of the bins behind the Indian Restaurant below my flat. What time is it? He hasn't been fed since yesterday morning.'

Lockey insisted that Sally stay for lunch and then he'd drive her to her flat afterwards. So they ordered a couple of sandwiches. Sally wolfed hers down and fidgeted impatiently whilst Lockey finished his.

'Okay, okay,' Lockey acquiesced. He threw his napkin down on his plate and smiled at Sally, 'Come on then. Let's go rescue Tikka.'

26 ~ THE MAHARAJA

There was nowhere nearby Sally's flat to park – not that this was ever a problem for Sally, as she had never learned to drive and instead travelled everywhere by either bus or on her bicycle, which she stored behind the restaurant. Lockey parked up a few streets away and as they walked, Sally saw her neighbourhood with fresh eyes. It was all rather a sorry sight. Quite a few of the local businesses had gone bankrupt with the recession – or simply couldn't compete with the large supermarkets – and closed up. What had once been a bustling lively town; with its own bakery, greengrocer, and newsagent, was now more of a drive through ghost-town. Shop windows boarded up, and the few that remained were either offering closing down sales or huge desperate discounts, trying to lure in a few stray passing customers.

Sally opened the little squeaky side gate beside the Maharaja Restaurant, and Lockey followed her along the narrow alleyway and then up the iron spiral staircase to her flat on the first floor.

'Well this is it. Home sweet home,' Sally said, as she pushed open her front door with a slight shove of her hip. It smelt dank and of onions and curry. There was a meowling and a sound of tiny feet padding at high speed along the thinly carpeted corridor, and Tikka appeared. The cat snaked around Sally's ankles, purring. Sally loved animals and had always wanted to get a cat, but her landlord had said strictly no pets. In this reality Tikka hadn't given Sally much choice, he had simply moved in one day and had never left. Sally hadn't done much to encourage him – other than to feed him and offer him a warm lap to sit on in the evenings, which of course for a cat, was plenty. And he had gone from being a poor scrawny little thing, to quite a sizable tomcat in just a year.

Sally found a tin of cat food in the cupboard, scooped it out into a bowl for Tikka and placed it on a piece of newspaper on the discoloured linoleum floor of the tiny kitchen. Lockey was looking around. Sally could tell by his face that he was a little taken aback. He grew up in a manor house after all, of which the entrance hall alone was probably twice the size of Sally's entire flat. Tikka was tucking into his food with gusto and managing somehow to purr whilst he ate, like some crazy cat ventriloquist act.

'So what do you think?' Sally put out her hands.

Lockey didn't answer immediately, searching for the right words. 'It's very… cosy.'

Sally laughed, 'I'm teasing. I know it's hideous. But it's very handy for *the* best takeaway curry in the south of England. And, the rent is cheap.'

'Well it's larger than the flat in Tokyo, but I guess that wouldn't be hard.'

Sally gave Lockey the full tour, which took all of two minutes, and they found themselves in the small shabby low ceilinged sitting room to the front of the flat.

'How long have you lived here?' Lockey pulled aside a grubby net curtain and looked out of the window onto the road below.

'Well, it'll be two years in August.' Sally sank into her well-worn brown velour sofa and picked up a cushion, 'It's odd, apart from a few little things, pretty much everything is just as I left it—' There came a shrill ring of the doorbell. 'I wonder who *that* could be?'

Sally's landlord, and now boss – Sunny – stood at the door.

'SALLY,' Sunny said loudly and beamed. 'I'm hoping you will come and work this evening – we're very short staffed...' Sunny broke off when he saw Lockey, who had come to stand behind Sally. 'Forgive me, I didn't know that you'd be having company...'

'This is Lockey, he's a friend. He was just popping by... I was planning on going out this evening really...' Sally faltered when she saw Sunny's smile wavering. 'But, I guess, if you're really stuck...'

'Oh yes, yes we are. So we'll be seeing you at five o'clock?'

Sally glanced through to the clock in the kitchen, it was almost four already. 'Yes sure, okay,' she said with a smile, and wondered why she could never just say no.

Lockey had stayed for a cup of tea – which had turned out to be undrinkable as the milk had gone sour – and somehow all of a sudden it was twenty-to-five and time for Sally to get ready for work.

'Gosh where did the time go?' Sally said, as they made their way along the dingy corridor.

'Are you sure you can't just ditch work and join me for the party? I'd really rather you were with me; you know I can't stand parties,' Lockey beseeched.

'You'll be fine.' Sally poured the cups of tea down the sink and gave the mugs a quick rinse, 'I'm sure it won't be that bad. At least you don't have to work.' Lockey looked glum. 'I'll try and join you after I'm finished working, okay?' This seemed to cheer him a little. They said their goodbyes and Sally promised she'd try her best to get a taxi to Wentworth Hall after work.

Sally wasn't quite sure what to wear to work, but she found a black skirt and white blouse draped across the back of a chair in her bedroom, which looked clean, but smelt vaguely of curry, and she guessed they'd do. And with two minutes to spare she pulled a brush through her hair, put on a pair of flat black shoes and rushed down to the restaurant. Sally paused at the bottom of the steps, suddenly unsure whether to go in by the front door or in through the back, straight into the kitchen. She pushed the back door open tentatively, and almost jumped out of her skin.

'SURPRISE!' All of the Maharaja staff were huddled together in the restaurant kitchen and had shouted in unison when Sally had entered the room. And she certainly was surprised. There were balloons hanging from the ceiling and a few of the group were wearing party hat cones, including Sunny, who had pushed through to the front of the cluster, blew a party-blowout and let off a party popper above Sally's head.

'Wow!' Sally laughed, as a shower of streamers landed on her hair. She felt a little overwhelmed, nobody had thrown her a surprise birthday party before.

'Happy birthday SALLY!' Sunny grinned, and patted her on the back affectionately. 'I got you good. I was just kidding about you having to work tonight,' he laughed. 'Tonight *we* will be serving *you*. I have made up a special batch of your favourite.'

They were a really lovely bunch of people, and Sally was relieved that all of their names came to her easily. A few of them, she remembered seeing coming and going, to and from the restaurant in her own reality. There was Sunny's wife; Lavanya, who was a beautiful woman, as full of smiles as her husband. Lily; the newest waitress. The charismatic waiters; John and Krish. Rakesh; the well-built head-chef. Sam; the sous-chef slash kitchen comedian. Raj; Sunny's son, who tried his hand as second sous-chef. Manish; the enthusiastic kitchen porter. And Sid; the shy seventeen-year-old washer-upper.

The restaurant didn't open until six o'clock and in the meantime the staff shared a cake, after Sally had blown out the candles. Sunny hustled Sally through to the dining room and sat her before a beautifully laid out table, and Sally was served the most perfect meal she had ever eaten.

Sunny smiled as he walked past Sally's table, happy to see how much she had polished off. He was always telling her she needed a little more meat on her bones. It was in his nature to want to feed people. Sally had just a few forkfuls of curry left on her plate and she was really struggling now.

'No hurry, Sally. Take your time,' Sunny said, as he unlocked the restaurant entrance. And he was just turning over the sign on the door, from closed to open, when Lockey appeared on the other side of the glass, making them both jump. Sunny opened the door and smiled welcomingly, 'An eager customer! We've just opened—'

'Is Sally here?' Lockey spotted her as he spoke, he seemed agitated.

'Ah Sally's friend, Mr. Lockey.' Sunny gestured for Lockey to come in.

'Sally. I was halfway home when I remembered...' Lockey was saying as he strode over to Sally's table and took a seat opposite her. He broke off when he noticed that Sunny was stood beaming over them.

'Sorry, sorry. I will give the two of you a little room to talk,' Sunny said, suddenly realising himself and he bustled off out into the kitchen, leaving the two of them alone in the restaurant.

Sally was looking at Lockey quizzically, wondering what could have possibly got him so riled.

'Sorry, as I was saying, I was half way home, when it came to me. I don't know why it hadn't occurred to me, what with your life here being so similar—'

'For goodness sake. What is it Lockey?' Sally said, suddenly frustrated.

Lockey was so overexcited he could barely contain himself, 'It's the lab Sally. It's all here. Everything is the same. I've even been and checked. And, I think I've worked out how to get us back.'

27 ~ BACK AT SALL

Lockey drove like a man possessed – at the brink of speeding the entire journey to the lab – jabbering excitedly as he drove, more to himself than to Sally.

Sally's head was in a whirl. Of course she wanted to get back. She didn't want to spend an entire life moving sideways into borrowed realities. She needed to get back and start living her own life, but she just wasn't sure if she was ready yet.

They pulled up outside the lab. It was almost entirely dark now and the security lights came on as they walked towards the building. Lockey let them in.

The room was identical to the one that Sally had entered on Monday morning, except for the fact that the desk was neatly organised and the entire reception area immaculate. Lockey was rushing off, Sally had to almost run to keep up with him.

They were in the huge room now, with the particle accelerator – ALICE. Sally was no less impressed than the last time she had been in this room. Had it really only been four days ago? So much had happened since Monday. She had literally lived nine lives and now had almost the entire memories of six. She was amazed that her head could cope with so much information, but then, hadn't she once read that humans only usually use about ten-percent of their brains?

Lockey was at the emergency control panel now. ALICE was whirring at a low hum. 'Sally I'll be honest with you, I'm not entirely sure if this will work – I can't guarantee…' Lockey trailed off, only realising as he spoke, the real danger he was risking putting Sally in. He frowned, 'I don't know, maybe this was a bad idea.' His hyper energy was suddenly gone.

'I'll do it Lockey. I trust you,' Sally insisted.

'But I don't know if I trust myself. What if I'm wrong? I can't risk losing you Sally…'

Sally was a step ahead, 'But who knows when we'll get this opportunity again if we don't try now? How many realities will we find that are as identical to our own as this one? Plus, if you're right about us both being in comas in our own reality, how long do we have left to get back before it's too late? I'll accept the risk Lockey. It will be on me. We have to try.'

Lockey knew Sally was right. Who knew where they'd wake up tomorrow. But the idea of anything happening to Sally was unbearable, if he was wrong she could either end up stranded alone in another reality, or wake with no memories at all, or worse, be killed.

Sally could see his mind whirring away. 'Okay, it's down to odds. From what we know, what are the odds of us being somewhere entirely new tomorrow? And what are the odds of this working and you finding a way for us to get out of this?'

Lockey sighed, 'From what we know? It looks almost certain that we'll shift to a new alternate reality tomorrow, and from my calculations… I don't know I'm about ninety percent sure that I've worked it out…'

'Well that's good enough for me.' Sally smiled bravely, 'So what's the plan?'

He sighed again, this time in resignation. This was really the only way. 'Okay.'

Lockey gave Sally a rough outline of his plan. In order to get back to their own reality, he would have to first trace back along Sally's timeline until he could get to a point before anything had changed. Her birth. He likened the timeline to the veins on a leaf, or the branches of a tree. They were at present, hopping across the branches of time, and in order to find the right branch, they had to go back down the tree to a point before any of the limbs started branching off. He was convinced that he'd then be able to isolate the correct timeline and move her forward until he was sure. And then she should be home.

'You've worked out how to travel back and forward in time now!' Sally exclaimed.

'Not really forward. We can only travel as far as our own present. But backwards, yes, I think… I'm pretty sure I've worked it out.'

Sally was impressed. 'Okay, how do we do it? And what about *you*? You sound like I'm going alone?'

Lockey was silent for a moment. 'You have to Sally. I need to be here on the controls…'

'But how will *you* get back?' Sally pushed.

Lockey looked shifty.

'Lockey?'

'When you're back in our own reality, you'll just need to fire up ALICE and I should come back… I think. But apart from the unthinkable fact, that this may possibly kill you, if it does work… if everything goes to plan, there's still a very real chance that you won't be able to remember anything…'

Sally's heart wrenched at the very thought. To go back to how everything had been – to her sad, empty life – and to remember none of this at all, and worst of all to loose Lockey and not even remember that he was lost. Her resolve started to waiver.

'Maybe this *is* a bad idea,' she said quietly. 'I'd rather be lost in time *with* you, than lost in my own time without you.'

'But you're right, I don't know how long we *can* keep this up for. And, I've a theory that the further sideways we travel, the further we'll get from ever getting back. If I'm right, this is possibly our only chance. We'll be both taking a huge risk, but… I think we have to.'

Reluctantly they agreed. Lockey and Sally hugged. Sally wished she could stay in his arms, just like this for ever. But they had to get on. Time was ticking by.

Lockey had instructed Sally to go to the exact spot where it had all happened, and recommended that she lay down. He gave her a mobile phone which he told her to just hold on to. And so, here she was, lying on the cold hard floor beside ALICE, staring about the high ceilinged room, marvelling at this amazing machine that Lockey had created.

Lockey had gone off to the control room. He had explained that he'd attempt to send her backwards a few stops, until he could establish the correct time thread, at which point, he should be ready to get her back to their own present. But as this had never been attempted before, he had no real way of knowing how it was all going to go.

'Just don't do anything that might change anything,' Lockey had said, 'It's really important. No confronting your aunt, promise?' Confronting Mary was still the last thing Sally felt up for, so it was an easy enough promise to make. But perhaps she'd get to see for herself what had happened.

Sally heard the warning signal, the machine was firing up to full working capacity. And she felt it now, the odd pulling feeling, and the soft ticking sound was starting up. A thought suddenly crossed her mind; *what if he only gets me back to just before this all started? And I get off the bus again, oblivious, and it's Monday morning and it all happens again in the exact same way. Will we become stuck in a time loop? What if all of this has already happened? Could that explain why Lockey had seemed so familiar when I first met him?* Sally felt panicky suddenly, she needed to talk to Lockey. She tried to raise her head, but found that she couldn't seem to even move. The ticking and tocking had become louder now and Sally felt as though she were being pulled in all directions. Her vision was blurring. She was vaguely aware of the phone buzzing in her hand. Everything distorted and went blank.

28 ~ THE PAST-TEMP

It felt different this time. Sally felt as if she were
weightless and rushing at an amazing speed, hurtling
through an indistinct tunnel of light. Every now and
then she thought she caught a glimpse of something
familiar; a face, a hand, a tree. More shadows of the
mind than three dimensional images. And then she
stopped.

Sally was still weightless; it was the strangest
sensation. She was a being with no physical entity.
And rather than looking out from eyes, it was as
though she could see simultaneously all around in
every direction. She found that she could move by
simply thinking herself to a different place, but she
wasn't walking.

She was in a sunny glade, tall trees waving their
boughs up to a deep cornflower blue sky. The heady
scent of pines and of earth and ozone filled her very
being. The trees hushed in the wind. She could hear
birds chirruping, the flap of a wing, crickets, a stream
burbling somewhere nearby. She wasn't alone. Sally

focused her thoughts and found that she could see in one direction now.

There was a boy there, perhaps seven years old. He hadn't seen her yet, he was playing by a small brook, sending sticks racing along its lazy current. The boy as if sensing her, raised his head and looked around. He didn't see her immediately, and then a look of fear clouded his eyes.

'It's okay. Don't be scared.' Sally's voice sounded strange; a soft ethereal echoed whisper, but somehow it reassured the boy.

Emboldened, he straightened and took a step closer. 'Is you a ghost Miss?' he asked, full of wonder.

Sally tried to shake her head, but wasn't sure the movement came off how she'd intended and smiled instead. 'No. I'm not a ghost. Are *you* a ghost?' she asked, for she noticed now that the boy was dressed in what appeared to be Victorian costume; a button down shirt, knickerbocker style shorts with long socks, and a wool cap on his head. There was something familiar in the boy's eyes, he reminded her of someone.

'What's your name?' Sally asked vaguely.

'Me names Lawrence Lockhart Miss. An', *I* aint the ghost,' the boy answered boldly.

Lawrence Lockhart, that was it, his eyes; they reminded Sally of Lockey's. *But why am I here?* she wondered. 'What year is it?'

'It's eighteen-seventy-three.'

Sally reeled. Lockey had sent her back too far. Over a hundred years too far! She hadn't even been born yet.

The boy was still eyeing her in wonder. 'So *is* you?' he asked.

'Am I what?'

'A ghost?' he was starting to look a little fearful again now.

Sally felt a need to reassure him, 'No. I'm not a ghost. I'm from the future. I was sent here by, maybe your great, great-grandson. He's a very clever man. He invented a time machine.'

'A *what* machine?' the boy asked sceptically.

'A time machine. It can send people through time. Like it could take you to yesterday.'

The boy looked thoughtful, and strangely he seemed to take it all on-board with little doubt or surprise.

Sally felt the familiar pulling sensation starting again. 'I think I'm going now,' her voice was thin and flimsy, and she felt even less substantial. And then the glade became out of focus and once more she was rushing along the translucent tunnel of light.

Sally was unaware of stopping, but she was standing in a hospital corridor now. A nurse pushing a trolley almost drove straight into her. Sally shifted out of the way at the last moment, but the nurse didn't seem to have seen her. A door to the side of the corridor opened and a lady emerged; probably about the same age as Sally, she wore the same uniform as the nurse who had almost run into her. The nurse was carrying a fresh baby, bundled up in a blanket like a little parcel, only its tiny face exposed. Sally realised that the nurse was a midwife, and that the midwife was in fact a much younger Aunty Mary.

'Mary?' Sally's voice was barely a whisper.

Mary faltered for a moment and looked down at the tiny baby thoughtfully. She glanced along the corridor both ways. She didn't seem to notice Sally either. And then Mary moved off hurriedly and disappeared into a room a few doors down and shut the door behind herself, leaving Sally alone. Sally looked to the end of the hall, there seemed to be a bright light up ahead, but she couldn't quite make it out, and then she was hurtling onward again.

'Hello?' A little girl's voice broke her reverie. Sally looked around and found herself in a bedroom, it was oddly familiar. She recognised the curtains and the wallpaper, with its bizarre print of cherry blossoms and contemplative Pierrot characters. And she realised that this was her old bedroom, many years ago. The little girl was sitting at a low table playing with a doll, the table laid out with miniature teapot and cups. The girl poured an imaginary cup of tea and offered it to Sally, and Sally suddenly recognised that the little girl was a four or five-year-old version of herself.

Would you like a cup of tea?' Little-Sally asked indifferently.

'You can see me?'

'Yes,' she pulled a face, 'but you look a bit *funny*. My mummy locked me in my room because I gave her a headache.' Little-Sally looked suddenly as if she might cry.

Sally knelt before the little version of herself, 'You'll be okay. One day you're going to have great adventures. And you needn't ever feel lonely, because I'll always be looking out for you.' Sally smiled warmly and felt a rush of love for this little her, she reminded her a lot of her own daughter; Flora – from another life. Sally felt the familiar pull, she was off again. Little-Sally looked up with big eyes and smiled back up at Sally.

The journey was shorter this time. Sally was suddenly in the back of a moving car. Her parents were there, she was surprised to see, in the front, her father driving.

'We already *have* a child of our own,' her father was saying crossly. And then his eyes flicked up to the rear-view mirror and he seemed to look straight at Sally. His eyes grew wide with fear, and then there was a smash and the whole world seemed to turn on end, over and over. The car was tumbling sideways, and then Sally was in the tunnel once more.

Everything was black. Sally moved back a little, she was standing behind herself now, and she knew exactly how old she was. She was eight-years-old. It was the day of her parent's funeral. Sally trailed behind the small group as they walked toward the graveyard to bury her parents. She could feel the grief emanating from her small self's form, both raw and at the same time numb. Sally placed a hand on her shoulder, 'You're strong. You'll get through this,' she said gently, and wished with all of her heart that there was more she could do to ease her eight-year-old-self's pain.

Sally zipped the next time, transported in the blink of an eye a few years on. She was in the local park, she recognised it immediately. It was a beautiful summer's day. Sally spotted herself not far off, she was eleven now, and out by herself taking Chewie for a walk – Chewie was Joe's dog, aptly named as he looked like Chewbacca's twin. Sally raised a hand in a wave to her younger-self, but she obviously couldn't see her anymore, *maybe only younger children have the ability to see?* she wondered. But then something happened. Chewie stopped walking. He strained on his lead and whined, staring directly at Sally. And then with a sinking feeling, Sally remembered this day, and she saw it all in slow motion from the outside, powerless to do anything. There were a small group of boys up ahead. One of which was Brandon Winkelman; the boy of Sally's *younger-self's* dreams. Younger-Sally tried a little smile and a flick of her hair and she hadn't noticed that Chewie was straining at his lead. She had hoped she'd see him out today, she'd worn her new skirt, the one she'd modified to resemble something short she'd seen Madonna wearing, in one of her magazines.

Sally knew what was going to happen. Chewie whined again and strained a little harder on his lead, and Sally realised that *he* could definitely *see* her. *Maybe I can do something.* Sally gestured for Chewie to calm down, but this made it instantly worse and suddenly he was off; running towards Sally and dragging along her poor younger-self behind at the end of his lead, her skirt now up around her waist. And Sally realised that it was *her* who'd spooked Chewie, all of those years ago. *So I was here before like this? What does that mean?* But she didn't have time to ponder further, as she was being pulled away again, back into the tunnel. She seemed to be going faster and faster, until she couldn't tell which way she was travelling anymore, or where she even ended or began. Everything became a blur of colour and light. She was careering out of control. All thoughts ceased completely. She was everything and everywhere, both tiny and huge. Everything seemed to rush into a dot as small as a pinprick. Sound morphed, as if an aeroplane door has been shut mid-flight. For the briefest moment all was absolutely quiet and still. And then she was off again, falling now; tumbling and turning, hurtling towards the earth.

29 ~ AUTUMN LEAVES

Sally woke with a start in a cold sweat. She knew she had been having the most peculiar dream, but already it was gone. Her head was pounding, her mouth dry. Groggily, she pulled herself from her bed and made her way unsteadily through to the bathroom.

Turning on the tap she drank deeply from shaking cupped hands and splashed water onto her face. She looked in the mirror, her face was ashen. *Am I sick?* She rubbed her temples. There would be no calling in sick today, although part of her wished she could.

Times were tough and the company were having to make serious cutbacks. Unfortunately, that meant 'pruning back' (as the general manager had called it) the staff – and it was down to Sally to break the news to the five long-term employees today. She dressed quickly into her formal navy skirt suit, and five minutes later left the flat, still eating her toast.

The day was going far worse than Sally had imagined; poor old Fred had actually cried when she'd broken the news to him. Her apologies, no consolation for the pitiful compulsory redundancy he'd been fobbed-off with. He had been working for the firm for ten years. These were hard times for everyone. Sally knew.

Sally left the building on her lunch break for some fresh air. The day was pleasantly warm for mid-September and the sun felt good on her face. She walked across the park. It was quiet now; all the children had gone back to school, and the majority of tourists had left. The leaves were just beginning to turn their autumn colours. A light breeze ruffled the trees and a stray leaf blew across Sally's path. She bent and picked it up and for a moment stood studying the intricate pattern of veins which branched out across its surface. Sally was reminded of something, but what was it? It felt like there was something important she needed to remember. It was just the stress of work, she decided. She released a pent-up breath and let the leaf flutter to the ground. If things didn't improve at work soon, she feared she'd be heading for a burnout – she had said as much to her manager.

Sally continued to stroll through the park, intuitively stepping out of the path of an inattentive cyclist. *Was there something else I was supposed to be doing today? Somewhere I was supposed to be?* Her stomach felt as if it were tied in knots. She frowned in concentration, and closing her eyes, for some reason she thought of Uncle Joe. *Had I arranged to see him?* She hadn't, she was sure of it. But she was suddenly positive that she had to, and gripped by an unnameable fear she found herself running.

She wasn't sure where she was running to, but she kicked off her heels as she ran. And she ran, harder than she had ever run before, not even thinking about a destination, her stockinged feet pounding the pavement. A few minutes later she rounded a corner, and hesitating for just an instant and panting for breath, she looked up at the hospital building, before crossing the road and running through the automatic doors.

Aunty Mary was pacing the corridor, her mobile phone in hand.

'How did you know?' she asked in confusion. 'I was just about to message you. Sally, it's t-terrible,' she stammered. 'He's had another heart attack. He's...'

Sally had already pulled away from her aunt and rushed down the corridor towards the intensive care unit.

It was sickening to see Uncle Joe – usually so full of life – laid out with all sorts of wires and tubes attached to him. Sally felt so helpless. She squeezed his hand, and her heart lifted when she felt his fingers squeeze back, just a little. His eyelids fluttered open and with some effort he smiled at Sally.

'Sally...' His voice was weak and hoarse, but he looked up at her intensely.

Sally leant in close.

'You're a good girl Sal.' He squeezed her hand a little more urgently, 'You need to go Sally... go out into the world... and grab every moment.'

Sally reeled, had she heard him say this before? Again the niggling feeling.

'Promise me,' he persisted.

Sally nodded mutely, too afraid to speak for fear of breaking the fragile dam which was holding back an ocean of tears.

'I'm so happy you came.' He smiled tiredly and then his eyes fell closed as if in a slow blink. But they never opened again, he simply slipped away.

Sally stood and gazed uncomprehendingly at her uncle for a moment. How could he be gone? She was vaguely aware of a hand on her shoulder, and in a daze, absently turned. Her aunt was there, a look of utter desolation on her face. In a trance Sally turned on her heel and numbly, as if sleepwalking, she wandered from the hospital.

Sally found herself in her aunt and uncle's house – her old home. *Did I walk all the way here?* Still disorientated, she climbed the stairs and went to Mary and Joe's bedroom. Reminders of Joe's sudden and terrible departure were all over the place; the slippers by the bed, the unfinished crossword and half-read novel on the nightstand. Sally picked up Joe's favourite jumper and hugged it to her chest, it smelt of Joe. Sally was comforted, fleetingly. Feeling suddenly cold, she pulled the jumper on. *Where did my jacket and shoes go?* she wondered.

Sally didn't know what she was looking for, but she searched her aunt and uncle's little bedroom from top to bottom – careful to leave no trace of her search.

It was under a loose floorboard that she discovered it – she quite literally stumbled upon it – and reaching into the dark space beneath the floor, she'd pulled out the dusty old metal biscuit tin; its innocuously jolly exterior belying the dumbfounding secrets it held within.

Sally learnt of her aunt's deceit; of the money which she should have inherited. It was all there in black and white in her parents' will, which she held in her shaking hands. An heiress. But where had all of the money gone? – Mary and Joe had always lived so frugally. And *how* had she, on some strange and deeper level already known this? *Am I out of my mind?* She couldn't explain it, but somehow she *remembered* her future-self already realising that Aunty Mary had defrauded her. And it was then that Sally remembered, everything. Memories, within memories, within memories, that came, not from *her* past, but from her future, and from her future-self's alternative pasts and presents. It was as if a bomb had gone off in her brain. It was too much to comprehend.

She didn't know how long she'd just sat there for, staring into space. She was in an utter state of shock. But then something pulled her back to the present – it was the sound of the front door closing. Sally blinked, slowly regaining herself, suddenly aware that she was no longer alone in the house. Her aunt had returned home.

Sally was hastily returning the will to the tin, when a letter caught her eye; a hand written envelope, addressed to herself. On impulse she shoved the letter into her handbag. She carefully returned the tin to its hiding place and crept from the room. Sally waited until she was sure her aunt was in the kitchen; she heard the kettle being filled, and a chair scraping across the kitchen floor. Her aunt would be sitting at the small table now. Quietly, Sally tiptoed down the stairs, every creaking step memorised in her teens. She held her breath as she let herself out, and softly, she closed the front door behind herself.

She needed to get away, as far and as quickly as possible. She knew she couldn't escape her own mind, but she couldn't stand the idea of seeing Mary. She needed to collect herself. She wasn't ready for a confrontation. Besides, something told her it would be a mistake, and all she could do now was follow her intuition. It was the most peculiar feeling, to be both her past and future self simultaneously. But she was in unchartered waters here; she had no recollection of the present, as this had been the lost time, her *Fugue State*. Memories came to her just as they were happening, like re-watching an old movie you thought you had never seen. Sally headed for the train station. She stopped at a cashpoint machine and withdrew as much cash as it would allow her, and then, not caring even where it was headed, she bought a ticket on the next train out of town.

30 ~ THE LETTER

Sally had hurried onto the train just in time and had been thankful to find an empty carriage. She rested her forehead against the window and tried to untangle the jumble of memories and thoughts which were churning around inside her mind. As the train rushed out of town, she felt relieved to be moving, no particular interest as to where she was headed other than forwards, forwards and away.

Sally heard her mobile phone vibrating and fumbled in her bag for it. The screen flashed up with Aunty Mary's name. She let it ring off. There were four missed calls; three from Mary and one from work. She turned the phone off completely and returning it to her handbag, she remembered the letter. The envelope had already been opened. She pulled out the letter and unfolded it. It was handwritten in a flowing looped cursive, the blue ink slightly smudged in places, but still legible;

Dear Sally,

When I read in a paper recently of your parents' awful

death, I felt like I had to write to you…

Sally's eyes flicked back up the page, there was no forwarding address, but it was dated just a few months after Sally had moved to Millside to live with her aunt and uncle. She read on;

I was just seventeen when I got pregnant – too young to be anyone's Mum, I could barely look after myself. I agreed to the adoption quite early on, my midwife told me she found the perfect home for the baby, with a loving couple who were desperate for a child.

It wasn't until late in the pregnancy that I began to have my doubts. I told the midwife that I'd changed my mind; that I wanted to keep the baby, but she told me in no uncertain terms that it was too late, all the paperwork had been signed. It was a long birth and at the end of it the baby was just whisked away from me, I didn't even get to see it.

I didn't know it at the time, that the couple were actually related to the midwife, her sister no less – Sylvie and David Sullivan – your parents, Sally…

Sally stopped dead and re-read the last sentence, her heart hammering. She continued reading in disbelief;

I don't know if they ever got to tell you that you were adopted, and I'm really sorry if they didn't, but I'm your birth mother. It's a cruel and ironic twist of fate that you are now in the care of Mrs. Grundy, the very midwife who stole you from me. Please know that I always regretted giving you up. I have nothing left but to trust that Mrs. Grundy will take good care of you. I will be looking out for you from afar Sally. I hope that one day this letter will find its way to you, and that you will find it in your heart to forgive me.

Yours

Rosemary Addison.

Was this for real? Had her life not just completely

fallen apart enough?

Sally realised that she had been holding her breath and exhaled deeply. Her mind whirred, her heart raced. How could this be true? She almost succumbed to the tears – but there would be time to cry later, she told herself. Sally sat and forced herself to breathe calmly, trying to allow only one thought at a time have its say.

Whether it was fate or luck, or simply a fluke, the train pulled into the station at Southampton Airport and on impulse, Sally got off the train. She threw her mobile phone into a bin as she strode off towards the Airport.

31 ~ SALLY ADDISON

The lady at the desk was initially unhelpful. When Sally had asked for a ticket on the next available flight, going as far away as possible, she had eyed her with an equal measure of suspicion and disinterest – taking in her dishevelled appearance; the oversized jumper, her lack of luggage or even shoes. But Sally had nowhere else to go. She had looked at the lady beseechingly, and then miraculously, she had softened. Maybe she had recognised something in Sally's eyes, a sincere desperation, this was not a dangerous person, but a woman in need of help. Or perhaps it was the fistful of notes. Either way, Sally had been relieved when the woman had changed from uncooperative to amenable in the blink of an eye and was suddenly tapping away at her keyboard. 'Do you have your passport?' she'd asked Sally dubiously, but not unkindly.

Sally shook her head. All she had was what she'd taken to work that morning, not much at all.

'Without a passport you'll only be able to take an

Internal Flight.' The lady continued to tap away, staring at her screen, 'I could get you on the 14:50 to Kirkwall.' She glanced at her watch, 'But there's not much time.'

Sally didn't know where Kirkwall was, *Ireland possibly?* she thought, as she ran through the small airport to the departure gate. The flight was already boarding – the gate just a few minutes from closing – Sally made it just in time and was rushed onto the plane.

The journey passed by quickly and soon enough she was landing again. She hadn't even realised that she would have to change planes a couple of times. But it was good to have the time to think, with so much new information to process. Even more memories had come to her on her first flight, filling in the blanks. She had now managed to organise her thoughts quite successfully. In fact, she was now feeling surprisingly good, more confident somehow, perhaps buoyed by the newly acquired wisdom of not just her own twenty-eight years, but by the experiences of multiple alternate-selves; in a way she was now over two-hundred-years-old.

She remembered how it had begun; the particle accelerator, and Lockey. She had almost turned back, gone to search for him. He would be here in this reality, of course. But Lockey would know nothing of any of this, as for him it had all yet to happen. And hadn't Lockey himself explicitly warned her not to do anything that may disrupt the timeline? No, her best bet was to vanish, to step out of her life completely, surely that way she wouldn't risk altering anything.

It was with this thought in mind that on her first

change-over, Sally had stepped into the airport boutiques and bought herself not just a new outfit, but a whole new identity. For too long she had squeezed herself into a mould that she'd never really fit; the smart clothes, the expensive haircuts and uncomfortable heels. But Sally felt like a new person now, with a new found optimism and lightness of heart. She found herself now drawn to clothes that she would never normally have dared to wear; bright colours, clothes that were built for comfort, rather than the dull and restrictive urban camouflage she'd normally opted for. In an act of self-rebellion, she bought a bright coral pink hoodie, a couple of soft cotton t-shirts, some comfy well-fitting jeans, and a pair of red canvas pumps. She would disappear in plain sight, she decided.

Sally changed into her new clothes in a toilet cubicle at Manchester Airport. She ditched her laddered tights and hesitantly removed Joe's jumper, but then changing her mind she pulled it back on over her new orange t-shirt and zipped her hoodie into the rucksack. With a pair of craft scissors, she'd bought in a stationary shop, she hacked her hair into a short choppy bob. She washed off her heavy makeup and applied just a touch of mascara and lip balm. Sally surveyed herself in the mirror. The girl that stared back at her looked at least ten years younger than her ashen faced self from just that morning. And her self-cut hair looked surprisingly decent. Yes, she decided – as she left the toilets, her transformation complete – somehow all of this was going to work out.

Sally was feeling so relaxed, she had almost missed her next flight. She slumped into her allocated seat, somewhat disappointed not to have the window seat. 'Ma'am. You need to stow your backpack away in an over-head locker,' a flustered stewardess said loudly, making her way down the narrow aisle towards Sally, 'And fasten your seatbelt as quickly as possible please.'

Sally blushed, realising that the stewardess had meant her. She stood hastily, pulled open a locker and attempted to shove her bag into the already tightly packed space. A folded overcoat dislodged and fell out onto the head of an unsuspecting old lady sitting below. Sally was still apologising profusely when she found herself being helped by a pair of strong capable arms. The man from the seat next to her had stood, and effortlessly he'd stowed Sally's bag and the offending coat away and slammed the locker shut in one swift movement. He turned to Sally and grinned; his eyes twinkling mischievously. Sally's heart flipped. It was *him*; Harry!

Sally almost blurted out his name, she was so happy to see him. She wanted to throw her arms around him. But *this* Harry hadn't met her before. But she knew *him*. She tried her best at a polite smile, but it came off as more of an inane grin.

Harry liked Sally immediately, this funny kooky girl in the oversized man sweater. He stuck out his hand, 'Harry Scott.' He flashed her a winning smile.

'Sally,' she paused and then on the spur of the moment added decisively, 'Sally Addison.'

'The girl so nice they named her twice.' His handshake was hot and firm and sent tingles right up her arm to her very core, 'Very nice to meet you Sally, Sally Addison.'

Sally sank into the seat beside him. The flight

attendant had made her way to Sally by now, wearing a fixed smile which didn't quite reach her eyes, 'We're preparing to take off ma'am, please fasten your seatbelt,' she said, pointing unnecessarily to the illuminated fasten seat belt sign.

Sally fumbled with the belt ends ineffectually. Harry reached over, 'Do you mind?'

Sally smiled, 'No. Please.'

Competently, he clicked the belt buckle together and firmly tightened the belt.

'So, are you going all the way?' Sally asked.

'I beg your pardon?' he grinned, and raised his brow.

'To Kirkwall, I mean. Or are you getting off at Aberdeen,' Sally felt herself flushing. She had known this man for almost five years – in her future alternate reality – and still he managed to make her blush. Although, she mused, this was also their first proper meeting. She almost laughed out loud at this odd revelation.

'Aye, Orkney. I'm there for the Flappers,' he said.

Sally raised her eyebrows now.

Harry laughed, his deep hearty belly-laugh. 'Sorry. Flapper Skate; *Dipturus intermedia*. I'm a marine biologist.'

The last bit of course Sally knew and she had heard of Skate, but Flapper Skate? 'As in the fish and chips, Skate?' she asked, to goad him.

He pretended to look outraged, 'You *eat* them? You know they're on the critically endangered list? Chondrichthyes.'

'Pardon?'

'Con-drick-thees,' he said more slowly. 'They belong to the same family as rays and sharks you know.'

So this was how they had met. Sally had wondered if she would ever find him again. And here he was. She knew now that she was headed in the right direction. Whatever was to happen, over the next eleven months, was yet to be written. Or was it already written and she just couldn't remember? She still had little grasp on the complexities of travelling through dimensions or time. Either way, she'd have to take each day as it came. But lingering in the back of her mind she *knew* the deadline; the date which she would return to her aunt Mary, a mere shell of herself. She pushed that thought as far back as possible, threw it in a trunk and sat on the lid. She would deal with that when the time came – for the time being, she intended to enjoy herself for once.

And enjoy herself she did. The remainder of the flight went by in a blur. They laughed and talked. Sally could talk to Harry all day long and not get bored. She nodded and smiled at the stories she had heard him tell her before, giddy with the love she felt being together again with this funny, kind, intelligent man. With the experience of nine lifetimes, she knew just what a special and rare thing this love was.

They dined together at the Aberdeen stop-over, in an airport bar, and rolled onto the next flight in a bubble of love and beer. Their love went up and beyond a mile high, on their last flight. The steward gave them a mock stern look as they returned to their seats snickering like children, and brought them a couple of complimentary drinks.

Harry gave up his window seat to Sally. He pointed out the islands as they approached the Orkneys, laid out like bright emeralds in the sparkling blue sea. The plane descended through wispy cloud and they touched down at Kirkwall at 19:35, just as the sun was setting.

32 ~ MERRY DANCERS AND MERMAID'S PURSES

Harry had rented a small cottage in Birsay, on the north coast of mainland Orkney. And with nowhere else to go and more importantly no one else in the universe – or even multiverse for that matter – that she would rather be with, Sally had happily accepted Harry's generous offer to join him.

They were met at the airport by a friendly local; a fellow marine biologist, Jack. His melodic accent so thick, Sally had difficulty understanding him. If he had been surprised to find that Harry had a guest with him, he hadn't shown it. He hustled them into his beaten up old car and drove them across the island to the cottage. It was dark by now. They drove past a handful of villages and occasional small clusters of houses, but mostly it was black and Sally could nothing of the countryside.

Jack had pulled up in front of the cottage – there were a few buildings dotted around in sight, but it felt like the most remote place in the world – and then he had driven away and left them in the dark. The only sound; the distant roar of the sea. And the sky; Sally gasped in wonder and was reminded of her night out on the waves, when she'd floated on a starry sea. There was no light pollution here and the relatively flat landscape offered a 360-degree dome of night sky, studded with a billion stars which twinkled overhead and around them.

The days and weeks went by. On days that Harry wasn't working, they walked together by the shore collecting Flapper Skate egg-cases; Mermaid's purses, Harry told Sally they were nicknamed. Occasionally they spent entire delectable days cocooned in the cosy cottage, only surfacing for supplies. And on the days that Harry drove off to work in the clapped-out old Renault-five – the *company car* he called it affectionately – Sally walked alone, marvelling at the rugged beauty of this strange and breath-taking place. And she began to paint – and to sing – on some days, she walked and she painted and sang. Sally had never felt so totally at peace with herself. And her love for Harry at times almost overwhelmed her. When Sally had first met Harry; in the alternate future, all of this had been a blank. She had known him and loved him wholeheartedly, he was her best friend as well as the love of her life. But this was different from the comfortable worn in kind of love, which grows with the years. This was the thrilling unquenchable passion of a new love.

Sally was shocked to realise that she had been in Orkney for two months, and even more shocked when it had finally dawned on her that she may be pregnant. A basic test kit, which she'd managed to get hold of at the nearby shop, had confirmed it. And it was then that she knew. She had to tell him – not just about the baby, but about everything. She risked him thinking her totally out of her mind, but he had to know. She had to prepare him.

They talked into the early hours. Mostly Harry had just listened. He didn't dismiss what she had told him offhand, he could tell that she sincerely believed every word that she spoke. But it was hard to swallow. Sally could offer no immediate proof to support or back up her words, she knew nothing of what was to come over the next eight months. They had until the end of July, in this little bubble of theirs. After that, there were some things that Sally remembered; little snatches of information which only time would confirm. What Sally said, scared Harry, he didn't want it to be true, any of it. And how could it be? All he knew was that she wasn't lying, and crazy or sane he was besotted with her. He would just have to take it on faith – humour her perhaps – for the time being, and see how it played out.

They didn't speak of it again for a few months, but there was now an underlying unease, a sense of foreboding, a storm on the distant horizon. Autumn turned to winter. Sally's tummy grew a little rounder. The nights grew longer. On clear nights, they would often wrap up warm and take their cocoa outside to gaze up in awe at the night skies. Occasionally they were treated to the most magnificent show on earth – the sky, illuminated with the brilliant eerie green bands of light, dancing across the night sky; the aurora borealis.

They drove into Kirkwall for supplies and

antenatal appointments. Sally had even started to sell a few of her paintings. Most days it seemed to rain and they were blasted by the relentless prevailing winds. And so the days went by.

They spent Christmas, just the two of them, holed up in the cottage, the wood-burner roaring. Harry had cooked them up a feast – and they exchanged gifts. Sally had painted a small but beautifully detailed, surreal picture; as if viewed from the sea, the little cottage, under a sky full of stars and the twisting streaks of green, pinks and purples of the northern lights, a few flapper skate picked out amongst the swirling dark blues of the North Sea.

And Harry had produced a ring. 'Not an engagement ring,' he had explained, as he'd slipped the silver Celtic band onto, not her left, but her right ring-finger. 'But a promise, that whatever happens after July, I'm never going to give up on us.'

It was mid-February when they finally spoke of it again; the elephant in the room. They had just been for the twenty-week ultrasound scan. The sonographer had told them everything was going well, and that the baby was – as far as she could tell – a girl. Sally had smiled sadly, the tears in her eyes mistaken for tears of joy. She already knew.

'We're having a little girl, Sally,' Harry had said happily in the car. He saw Sally's face, 'You, *knew?*'

Sally nodded. 'Flora Rose.'

He puffed out a breath. 'Flora... My Granny was called Flora... Look, we can't ignore this any longer. Everything you told me, you still stand by it?'

Sally wished with all of her heart that it wasn't true, had even almost convinced herself that she was wrong, or that perhaps she would live the alternate version; where the three of them got to stay together. But deep down, she knew. She remembered trying to put her life back together around the gaping hole of her lost time. She hated the idea of not remembering these precious months; of forgetting Harry, and of not even knowing of her little girl's existence.

'Yes,' her voice cracked, and the dam broke.

Harry held her whilst she cried, until the tears ran out. He took her face and gently wiped her wet cheeks with his sleeve, 'We need to make a plan.'

Harry's contract in Orkney was drawing to an end. They needed to decide where they wanted to have the baby, and where they wanted to be in August, when whatever was going to happen or not happen, came to pass. They drove to a little Internet Café in town. Harry discovered that there was a position coming up, based on the Isle of Wight, as a conservation advisor. It would be less pay, but he would be able to pretty much choose his hours and, as he pointed out, maybe they should be nearer to Sally's old home.

Sally had tried a quick search on her birth mother's name; Rosemary Addison. But nothing came up. Maybe she had married? Sally typed in: Horace Lockhart, and, Wentworth Hall. She paused momentarily – *it couldn't hurt to look*, she thought – and hit enter.

She found a few irrelevant articles on Wentworth Hall itself, and the family history, but they weren't what she was looking for. And then she saw it, half way down the page; Mr. Horace Bartholomew Ernest Lockhart to marry Miss. Patricia Lorena Smythe. Sally's eyes bulged. She stared at the article, trying to fathom what this meant.

Harry came over and kissed her neck and looked over her shoulder, 'What you found?'

'I, I don't understand. It says here that he's getting married. But that's not what happened...'

'Well, maybe that's a good thing? Maybe this means it's not going to happen how you thought...'

Sally looked at him doubtfully, still trying to understand what was happening. 'If Lockey marries... That means no lab... Which means no ALICE...' she said, thinking out loud.

'Alice?'

'ALICE was what he called the particle accelerator... I don't know Harry, something's gone wrong. And I've got a feeling it's not a good thing.'

Harry was still unconvinced that this wasn't in fact a positive thing. Maybe things weren't going to happen the way she'd predicted. Maybe they would be okay?

But Sally persuaded him that they needed to find out more. A trip down south would be needed for an interview for the position on the Isle of Wight – which was more of a technicality really as they had basically told Harry, on the telephone, that the job was his if he wanted it – so stopping by Lymington, for a little poking around, would fit in well with their plans anyway.

Sally herself couldn't risk seeing Lockey, after all, they weren't supposed to meet until that first day she had temped for the lab, still four years from now. Sally thought of that day. *Was it really only five months ago?* But of course it hadn't even happened yet. And if it never happened, then what would that mean? That she had no hope of ever remembering Harry again after July?

And so, they travelled south. Sally felt sad to say farewell to the Orkneys, it had been her safe haven and now, they were heading into the unknown.

33 ~ CUCKOO

It took them a little while to track Lockey down. But finally they found him. He looked older somehow; face drawn, shoulders hunched, as though he carried the weight of the world. A man resigned to his fate.

Sally slumped down in the seat of their rented car, to hide, and shoed Harry out.

'Go on,' she urged.

'But what am I going to say?'

'We've been through this. Look, hurry. Just, make it up as you go along.'

Sally had watched them, peeking out over the top of the steering wheel. Harry fell into step with Lockey, and then he was obviously introducing himself. The two men shook hands and had stopped walking, now deep in conversation. They talked for about five minutes. Sally wished she could lip-read. There was quite a bit of animated hand gesturing going on. Lockey seemed very enthusiastic and was writing something on a piece of paper. What *were* they talking about?

Harry squeezed back into the car and shut the door. Lockey had walked away now, a spring in his step. He had turned to wave at Harry, and Sally had slumped further down in her seat.

'What on earth were you talking about?' Sally finally asked, stroking her rounded tummy, relieved to be able to sit up straight again – little Flora seemed to be doing the Highland-fling in there.

Harry was holding a scrap of paper in his hands. He didn't speak immediately, he seemed troubled.

'Harry?'

'I opened the conversation, saying I recognised him from an article I'd read on his work – which *is* actually true. I had wondered where I knew his name from, when you first mentioned him. I didn't put two and two together until just then. He's got some pretty progressive theories – the bright young thing in particle physics. Anyhow, he said he's stepping back from his work for the time being; family commitments he said. Didn't look too happy about it. And yes, the wedding does appear to be going ahead. He mentioned he's getting married at the end of August. Loves talking about his work though, turned into a different man when he thought I was a fellow physicist.'

Sally looked at Harry questioningly.

'I may have told a little white lie about my profession,' Harry admitted guiltily.

Sally breathed into her knuckles. So, the wedding *was* still going ahead. Maybe he just hadn't found out what Patricia was really like yet? It would be best to keep a watchful eye from a distance, Sally decided, and see how things played out.

The next stop was the one that Sally had been dreading. But she needed some answers and felt that she could avoid it no longer. The inheritance, her adoption, so many secrets and lies. She didn't want to make trouble. Lockey had told her specifically to avoid confrontations – but perhaps this was how it was meant to be? It was time to visit Aunty Mary.

And so, Harry drove Sally into Millside. Sally wasn't sure if everything had become more run down, in the months that she'd been away. Or, was she just seeing it all with fresh eyes? He pulled up outside her aunt's house. 'Are you sure you want to do this?' he asked.

'No. But I feel like I have to.'

'I'll park just over there.' Harry pointed to an empty parking space across the road, several houses down. 'Good luck.' He kissed her furrowed brow.

Sally took a deep breath and rang the doorbell. She was just starting to hope that maybe Mary wasn't at home, when the door opened.

'Sally.' Mary's face was pinched, unreadable. 'Where have you been all these months?' Mary's eyes darted down to Sally's obvious bump. She pursed her lips.

'I'm not back. Not for now at least. There're a few things we need to talk about…'

Mary shifted uncomfortably, 'I think you'd best come in.'

Sally followed Mary into the small kitchen. 'Of course you missed poor Joe's funeral,' Mary was saying.

'Yes. Look, I'm going to get straight to the point. I know about the money.'

Mary's eyes darkened, but she said nothing.

'The money I was left. The trust fund? I've seen the *will*, Mary.'

If Mary was feeling guilty she didn't let it show, in fact, she seemed more irritated than ashamed. She sighed noisily, but still she said nothing. This wasn't the reaction Sally had anticipated.

'And I know about my mother… my *birth* mother.'

Mary looked at Sally sharply now. 'And how *is* it, that you know all of these things Sally?' she spat the words out bad-temperedly.

'I can't explain how. That's not even important right now. I just need some answers.'

'Always such an odd child you were.' Mary seemed to be talking to herself now more than to Sally.

Sally looked at her in disbelief, 'I beg your pardon?'

'Sometimes I rue the day I brought you into our family. Nothing but a curse to us all you've always been.'

Sally stepped back, stung.

Mary went on, 'You should be grateful. I saved you from a life with that haughty cold woman. And why should *she* have got two babies? – when my poor sister got none…' Mary trailed off, perhaps sensing from Sally's face that she'd said too much.

'*Two babies?*' Sally asked incredulously. 'Look, I'm confused. What are you talking about? And tell me what happened to the money.'

Mary laughed a single hard, bitter laugh. 'You never should have gotten any money. The way I see it, they weren't really even your real parents. But you know that now. So why do you think you should be still entitled to their money? She was *my* sister. Why should you, a cuckoo, get anything?'

Sally felt nauseous. 'But they were my parents, they were all that I had. They adopted me for goodness sake. So, no matter what *you* thought, legally and emotionally we were family. And besides, it was you that brought me into this family anyway?'

Mary looked uncomfortable again. She filled the kettle, flipped it on and gestured for Sally to sit. 'Poor Sylvie was desperate for a baby, but it was impossible. Adoption was the only way. I would have done anything for her not to have gone through all that. They did love you, you know.' Mary had softened, she looked ashamed now. 'For what it's worth, I am sorry. I never meant to keep it, you know. All the money, it's still there. At first I was resentful that you were to get everything. And then it became more… After Joe got ill, I just got scared that you'd go, and I'd have no one to look after me.'

'But how could you think that? I wouldn't have just taken the money and gone. You and Joe were my only family. I know you and I didn't always see eye to eye, but I always tried to do right by you.'

'I know.' Mary was looking wretched now, 'I guess I just got used to that. And how could I suddenly tell you? I was just waiting for the right moment…'

Mary went upstairs, and returned holding the familiar biscuit tin. Sally was still sitting at the table, feeling sad and confused. What a strange and messed up woman her aunt was.

'It's all in here,' Mary announced.

Sally barely cared about the money anymore, it just made her feel miserable. 'And my mother? My birth mother, I mean?'

Mary looked like a rabbit caught in headlights.

'Rosemary Addison?' Sally persisted.

Confusion swept Mary's expression, 'Rosemary?' She looked unsure.

'My birth mother,' Sally persisted, 'Rosemary Addison. Do you know what happened to her? I found a letter from her.'

Something like – relief? – flashed in Mary's eyes. 'You read that? Rosemary, yes… Rosemary Addison. Last I knew, she was living in Southampton. But that was a long, *long* time ago Sally. I've no clue where she'd be now.'

'Surely there's a way of tracing her though? Do you not have any information at all that may help?'

'No. I told you all I know,' Mary said impatiently. 'I think there's a list you can put your name on – but she'd have to want to be contacted. Was there not an address on the letter?'

Sally shook her head.

'Well there you go then. Doesn't sound like she really wanted to be found. I wouldn't bother delving around in all that, it'll only bring you heartache.' Mary stood and rinsed the cups, 'More tea?'

Sally shook her head, 'No, actually I need to use the bathroom.' She gestured to her pregnant tummy as she rose from the table.

When Sally returned downstairs, Mary was stood in the kitchen doorway, her arms folded. It was obvious she wanted Sally to leave now. 'So what are you going to do with it?'

Sally thought she meant the baby for a moment.

Mary saw her place a protective hand on her bump. 'All the money, I mean.'

What *was* Sally going to do with all the money? She stroked her tummy, 'Is it really that simple. It's all mine?'

'Yes. Of course. All though, there was also a little more, that I had saved away…but…'

'Oh, just keep it.'

Mary gave a simple nod. She had written down the solicitor's details for Sally; Mr. Whittaker. Apparently he had dealt with all of Sally's financial affairs.

'So I suppose you'll be going now,' Mary stated.

Sally suddenly remembered something. 'And, you said *two babies*, what did you mean by that?'

Mary shot Sally a look which she couldn't decipher. 'Did I?' she asked vaguely.

'You said; why should *she* get two babies and your sister get none?'

'Oh, I just meant she already had a child…'

'But, she was only seventeen?'

'Well there you go then.'

'So I have a brother or sister?'

'I don't know anything else. As I said already, it was a long time ago.' Mary folded her arms – it was clear Sally would get no more from her – and changing the subject asked, 'When will I be seeing you again?'

Mary had looked almost sad to be seeing her go, almost. 'You can only have two or three months to go?' she looked pointedly at Sally's stomach.

'That's the thing. I think I'm going to be back on the first of August. But I'm not going to be myself for some time. And, I'll be, alone…' Sally felt tears prick her eyes. 'I can't explain…'

'Then I shan't ask you to,' Mary said brusquely.

'And Mary, this is really important, we need to never talk of this again. I won't remember anything. You can keep all the money in your savings, on the one condition that we never talk of this again – not the money, or any of it. You didn't even see me today.'

From Mary's house Sally had gone straight to the Solicitor's; Mr. Ralph Whittaker, a genteel man in his early sixties, with an old school integrity. He held open his office door for Sally and gestured for her to take a seat. A little polite small talk was made and two teas ordered. 'So Sally. For what do I owe the pleasure of your visit today?' he asked.

Sally kept it brief and explained as little as possible. She firstly needed to know the value of her assets. She had almost choked on her little biscuit, when Mr. Whittaker announced her net worth; over two-*million* pounds. But Sally had already decided what to do with the money, even though the amount had far outreached her expectations.

It had been Mr. Whittaker's turn to be surprised, when Sally had informed him of her wishes, but he had regained himself almost immediately, and – a true professional – had been all business. It was not his place to question his clients' biddings – plus, a not insubstantial amount of Sally's worth had, no doubt, lined his pockets over the years. By the end of their meeting, Sally had signed everything over to Harry, and left precise instructions for when and how he would be contacted. If Sally wasn't going to be there to care for them, at the very least, she could see to it that they'd wish for nothing financially.

Sally had told Harry of her visit to her aunt, and a brief outline of what had been said, but when she tried to tell him of the money, he hadn't wanted to hear. 'I don't care about any money Sally. I just want you – our little family to be together.'

And that was what Sally wished for too, more than anything. She ached at the thought of what was to come. 'Okay, well let's just call it an *if*. If things happen as I predict, you're going to have to be dad, and mum, to our little girl. At least for a few years. Maybe I'll make it back, I just don't know. I'm so sorry Harry; that I got you caught up in all of this.'

'I'm not, Sally. I wouldn't change a thing.'

'If something does happen, I'm going to need you to contact Aunty Mary. I won't be able to remember, and you mustn't try and make me. It all needs to happen as it should. I can't even meet you for three years. If I don't follow the same path, then I'm not sure I'll ever have a chance of making it back… And my mother, promise me you'll keep looking for her? for me. I don't want to give up. At least maybe our daughter will get to meet her grandmother… even if I…'

'I'm not going to give up on you either Sally. Neither of us ultimately knows what our future holds. I'll find a way. We *will* all be together.'

The last few months passed by far too quickly. They had moved to the Isle of Wight in March. Welcomed by the bright nodding heads of the yellow daffodils which lined the roadsides, and the undersized trees waving their boughs of blossom cheerily.

They had initially rented a house in the rolling green hills of the north-west side of the Island. Sally fell in love with the Isle of Wight immediately. It was far from the remote beauty of the Orkneys, but it had its own charm. It seemed to be on a different pace to the rest of England, a slower more relaxed pace, as if it kept its own time. And time at this point was what Sally longed for more than anything. Harry had taken up the position, which only took up a few precious hours a week. Every moment together a treasured gift.

Their little girl came into the world on the ninth of June, Flora Rose. Flora had gazed up at her, and Sally had been overwhelmed by the rush of the love she'd felt as she held her in her arms for the first time. Sally was now in a baby haze of nappy changes, feeds, and surviving on very little sleep. She didn't mind the not sleeping, quite the opposite, she cherished every moment awake and often found herself gazing at little Flora, when she herself could have been sleeping.

Sally had barely noticed spring turning into summer. Time had crept away. Harry had turned over the page on the calendar that morning, on the first of August. 'Sally. It's August. We're okay… you see! You're still here.' He smiled and hugged the two of them, 'We're all still together.'

Harry had been so relieved. Now they could start living for the future. Surely now Sally would have to see that she'd been wrong. A strange trick of the mind, probably as he had suspected, a breakdown, triggered by her uncle's death. She had been through a lot. But he was here for her now, and little Flora. And she seemed so well, so happy. Yes, he decided. It was all going to be fine.

It started in her fingertips, a tingling. Sally ignored it at first – she had just been accepting, that perhaps, it *had* all been in her head. As Harry had pointed out, she had been through an awful lot. She'd much prefer for that to be true. She would see a doctor, maybe get some counselling. She was still here, with Harry and Flora. But then the tingling had spread up her hands to her wrists, and her feet had started too. She was walking, but it felt as if the floor had turned to sponge and her feet were treading right through it. The fizzing had started in her head now. Her face felt cold and numb. She sat down on the bed and felt as though she were rushing backwards. Harry came into the room carrying a freshly bathed Flora, still wrapped in a fluffy white towel.

Sally's vision was starting to go now, she had to concentrate hard to focus. It was as if she were draining away. The harder she tried to fight it, the worse she felt. The ticking had started now. The chorus of the ticking clocks. She shook her head slowly, as if trying to shake out the noise. She heard Harry saying her name. But It was no use, she was going. Unwillingly, wrenched from herself. *Harry.* She tried to call out but couldn't form the words. And then she was falling, falling into space, and rising up simultaneously, spreading out and contracting inwards. And she was gone.

34 ~ LITTLE BERTIE

Sally came-to, kicking and screaming – a writhing, angry heap on the floor.

'Sally?' It took Lockey a few attempts to get close enough to embrace her. 'Sally, it's alright.' He hugged her to him, until the fight had left her. What on earth had he done? Her muscles twitched as she slowly relaxed and then slumped into his arms. 'Everything's okay, Sally. You're back.'

Sally pulled away and vomited on the floor. She looked up at him blearily through her tears, 'Lockey?' But she could say no more, choked by an uncontrollable bout of ragged sobbing.

'Sally, I'm so sorry. There was a power outage. I got you back as soon as I could. I almost lost you... What happened in there? You didn't *do* anything, did you?'

'I was there for going on eleven months. It would have been impossible to *do nothing.*'

'Eleven-months! You were gone for just over ten minutes... Oh Sally. I should never have risked it.'

Lockey hugged her again.

Sally was calming now, but she felt freezing cold and couldn't stop shivering. Lockey had led her through to the reception area, where it was a little cosier. He wrapped her in a blanket he'd found from somewhere, sat her down, and made her a hot cup of tea. She had felt so disorientated when she first came-to, but now things seemed a lot clearer.

Lockey listened carefully as Sally filled him in on all that had happened. She started from the beginning. He was shocked that he had sent her as far back as eighteen-seventy-three. And he was even more astonished to hear that she'd met Lawrence Lockhart.

'Lawrence Lockhart!' Lockey exclaimed. 'I told you about him, didn't I?'

Sally shook her head.

'He was my...' Lockey thought for a moment. 'Great-great-great-grandfather... it was him who started the family name, Horace – which I got lumbered with. He had a lifelong obsession with time travel, and named his first born son Horace, because it means; time-keeper. Anyway, and this is the crazy bit. The story goes, that he met a time traveller when he was a boy. Nobody believed him of course, but he told his friend Bertie all about it, and well, he must have sparked something in little Bertie, because when *he* grew up, he wrote a very famous book; ever heard of, The Time Machine?'

'As in, "The Time Machine" by H G Wells?'

'Herbert George Wells; little Bertie no less!' Lockey laughed in wonder, 'Sally, I think I may have *you* to thank for my name!'

Sally filled him in on the rest of her journey. Lockey didn't seem too fazed about the further little proofs that this had all happened before; like the instance with Chewie – in fact, he seemed positively excited.

'It doesn't mean we're in a loop that we're stuck in Sally, it just means everything is playing out as it should,' Lockey enthused.

Something was gradually dawning on Sally. Why hadn't she thought of it before? She wasn't sure whether to laugh or cry. 'Lockey. The lab… it's called *SALL…*'

'Yes, SALL?' Lockey said, no clue where she was going.

'And that stands for?'

'Scott Addison Lockhart Laboratories…' Lockey froze as it all fell into place. 'Harry Scott! *Your Harry,* is Harry Scott? The *Scott* of *Scott Addison Lockhart Laboratories?*'

'Yes, I think so. And, when I met Harry… I introduced myself as Sally Addison; it was my birth-mother's name.'

'So *you're* Addison? – the laboratory's silent partner? Now my mind is fully blown!' Lockey was staring into space, and then he frowned. 'But how could Harry have come up with the huge amount of money he invested in SALL? That's what I can't figure out…'

'Well, I set him up with my inheritance, which was well over two-million,' Sally offered.

'Yes, but we're talking *millions,* like; a lot more than that…'

Sally wasn't really listening, that was just a detail. She felt a little like she was going to be sick again. But she knew now what she had to do. 'Harry's waiting for me… he, *believed* me. He must be waiting for me in our own reality… and Flora. Lockey. I have to go back.'

Lockey was very reluctant to put Sally through it all again. They had been lucky the first time. But they were so close now, and they couldn't just give up. Ideally, they'd get a good night's sleep and try again in the morning. But of course, that wasn't possible, as tomorrow they would be, who knew where. And so it was back to ALICE for a second attempt.

Lockey had deftly mopped up Sally's sick puddle. And he was now crouched beside her on the floor. 'I've got all the data from last time stored. So in theory, this time it should all be more straightforward. I'm pretty sure I pinpointed your birth-point successfully, so… first stop is there, and then, well we should be on a home run.' Lockey squeezed Sally's hand, 'You sure about this?'

'Yes. I've never been more sure of anything in my entire life. And Lockey, I'm going to bring you back, okay? I promise. I'll find a way.'

The two hugged and then Sally lay back on the floor. 'This isn't goodbye Lockey. I'll see you on the other side,' she called after him, as he walked from the room.

35 ~ THE BIRTH

Sally recognised the maternity ward immediately. She was back where it had all begun, at the very beginning of her story; this was the day of her birth. She caught sight of her aunt Mary, and this time decided that she would follow her. She needed to see. This is where all of the answers were hidden. Behind one of these doors, she would find her birth-mother.

It was a busy afternoon on the ward; Sally could hear by the noises coming from behind each of the doors she passed. Aunty Mary seemed flustered and rushed along the corridor muttering something indiscernibly to herself. Sally floated along unseen after her and glided in close behind, as Mary hurried through a door.

There was a young girl in the room on a bed, in an obviously painful, advanced stage of labour, sweating and swearing profusely. A midwife by the girl's side looked over and exchanged a look with Mary.

Mary pulled on a pair of thin gloves, strode toward the girl and took a look at the business end of things,

'Now, now, Rosemary. All of this fuss isn't going to do you any favours. You've to save your energy for pushing,' she said patronisingly.

Sally froze. *Rosemary?* she thought, *so this is my mother.* She gazed at Rosemary and her heart went out to her. *Seventeen had she said, in her letter? She looks so young, almost a child still herself.* The girl's pale blonde hair was plastered to her forehead with sweat. She puffed out her a breath and swore again, louder this time, and then wailed as a savage contraction ripped through her. *Why doesn't she have a birth partner with her? Surely her mother should be here? or a friend? or the father? … my biological father,* Sally realised, and wondered about him for the first time. Where was *he* now? She had most likely inherited her looks from him, she decided, as Rosemary couldn't have looked more dissimilar to her, with her large blue eyes, rounded face and flaxen hair.

'You're so nearly there now, one more big push.' Mary sounded a little more encouraging now. With the next contraction the girl gave a loud bovine like moan, pushed with all of her might, and the baby slithered out into the world. Mary caught the baby and wrapped it in a towel.

The girl was crying now and shaking. 'My baby. I want to see her…' she reached out piteously.

Give me to my mother. Sally silently pleaded to her aunt, as she looked on in distress. *At least for a moment.*

Mary exchanged another fleeting look with the other midwife, who then placated the girl, 'There, there. You did ever such a good job…' and gave her an injection of something.

Mary swiftly scooped up the baby and slipped out from the room. Sally followed behind irately. *Where are you taking me Mary? Rosemary wanted to see me, you didn't even give her a chance.* Mary had paused outside the door, she looked down at the tiny bundle in her arms and swore under her breath. Sally looked too. The baby was tiny, and silent, and absolutely still. Sally felt as if she were holding her breath – even though she had no physical lungs or body – and she willed the baby to cry just a little. But the baby somehow hadn't made it. Sally stared uncomprehendingly. *How can this be? How can I have died, when I lived?* Fear gripped her now as she wondered what was happening. *Has history changed somehow?*

Mary looked down sadly at the little bundle in her arms and sighed. And then, her face hardened, her jaw set in resignation. She looked nervously either way along the corridor and then she was walking again, quickly.

Sally trailed after Mary and found herself in another room. This room was a nursery. *Perhaps Mary is going to resuscitate this tiny me somehow?* Sally thought, and her heart lifted a little. There were several cribs in a neat row, the babies all sleeping. Mary glanced surreptitiously over her shoulder as she approached a crib. And Sally watched in disbelief at what happened next. Mary lay the silent bundle in the crib beside a sleeping baby, turned, and at a desk wrote on some tiny identity bands. She returned to the crib, deftly snipped the bands from the sleeping baby, and replaced them with a new set. And then just as quickly put a set on Rosemary's poor little baby. Sally strained to read the tags and gasped inaudibly. F I Lockhart.

Mary blew out a breath and then picked up the sleeping baby, and strode from the room. Sally followed Mary as a furious gust of incomprehension. Mary was hurrying off along the corridor and opened a door at its very end. It was a bright room, a shaft of sunlight seeped through from a large window, and Sally saw her adoptive parents; David and Sylvie, half silhouetted against the bright light. Mary passed the sleeping baby to a beaming Sylvie. The baby awoke and started to cry.

Sally didn't want to see anymore. And as the room melted away and she felt herself being pulled into the tunnel of light, her very last thought was; *I am female infant Lockhart?*

36 ~ COMA ~ SATURDAY

Sally stirred. She couldn't seem to open her eyes, but she knew she was in a hospital; she recognised the smell. Heavy with sleep, she groaned and moved her head to the side. There was something attached to her face. With great effort she managed to prise her eyes open to just a squint, and winced against the brightness of the dimly lit room. She tried to call out, but her voice emerged as just a coarse faint whisper and she gagged against something in her throat. She was so groggy and ached all over. Her hand went to her face and she found a tube emerging from her nose, and another larger one taped to her mouth. She felt a wave of fear and nausea. *How did I get here?* She coughed and gagged as she pulled the tube from her nose and then ripped away the tape and oxygen pipe from her face.

'Okay Sally. It's okay. Everything's alright. You're in hospital...' there was someone by her side now. A woman. Sally struggled to focus. Everything very clearly wasn't fine. 'Doctor!' the voice was now hastily calling, and didn't sound at all convinced that everything was fine either.

Sally's throat was so sore; she could barely swallow. She tried again to talk, but could muster no more than a rasp. The room was starting to come into focus now, and the woman by her side; a nurse with a furrowed brow. 'You need to calm down. Everything's going to be just fine,' the nurse continued to soothe.

Sally finally managed to speak. 'Where am I?' she wheezed. 'I mean… I'm obviously in hospital… but, why am I here?' It was a great effort to talk. Sally tried to pull herself up the bed, but had no strength. A doctor had appeared in the room now and the tiniest flash came to her, and she realised that, she *recognised* him. 'My legs,' Sally said flatly, 'I'm paralysed, aren't I?'

The doctor frowned and looked through her notes. 'No, no, I can assure you; you are not paralysed,' he said distractedly.

Sally had the most peculiar feeling, as if this had all happened before. It was on the very tip of her mind, if she could only remember. 'Look what's going on… I remember speaking to you…' She paused for breath. 'And you were talking about rehabilitation and brain injury? I'm confused.'

'A fair amount of disorientation is to be expected. In fact, it's incredible that you're even this lucid and compos mentis. Try and stay calm Miss. Sullivan.' The doctor turned and spoke to the nurse, 'Maybe a little something to help her relax?' And then to Sally, 'There was an accident at the laboratory you were working at…'

Sally was trying to piece everything together. 'I

remember going to work this morning, my coat got trapped in the bus door… And I met my new boss, who was really nice…' Sally closed her eyes trying to recall his name.

'Well I'm afraid, that wasn't *this* morning. It's now Saturday morning.' The doctor was flicking through Sally's notes again, 'You've been in here for five days. You've been in a coma Miss. Sullivan.'

Five days! Sally opened her eyes again and stared uncomprehendingly at the doctor, 'I've been in a coma?'

'Very unusual case. No signs of brain swelling or trauma…' he was speaking more to himself now than to Sally.

Sally felt a sharp prick and looked down to see that the nurse had given her a shot of something. She felt it almost instantaneously. A huge wave rolled over her and she drifted away.

When Sally awoke the next time, she had been moved to a small ward with five other beds, four of which were empty. But the bed beside her had its light blue curtains drawn, so she couldn't really tell if it was occupied. She felt a little clearer headed. The tubes from her face were gone, but she still had a cannula in the back of her hand with a drip attached.

Sally located the bed control buttons and adjusted her backrest, rearranged her pillows, and sat herself up a little. She still felt as though she had been run over by a truck, but the aching had definitely lessened. There was a single window at the end of the room and she could see that it was now night time. She gazed about the room. It looked much like any other hospital ward; uniform beds, white sheets, polished floor, stark and clinical. There seemed to be no personal items at all, no flowers beside her bed even. Sally wondered briefly where her aunt was, had she even been here to visit? She still had the feeling as if there was something very important she was supposed to be doing.

'Hello?' a small voice came from behind the curtain, 'Is there someone there? Please…'

'Um, *I'm* here…' Sally ventured. 'Are you alright? Do you want me to call a nurse for you?'

'You can understand me?' the woman sounded dubious.

'Of course…' Sally stretched out toward the curtain, but it was just beyond her reach.

'You're Japanese?' the woman said, with equal measures of relief and uncertainty.

'No… I'm English?' Sally replied to the curtain.

There was a brief silence. 'But your Japanese is very good. I can't understand anything they've been saying to me, and no one has been able to understand… I need to see my family… I thought they would have found me an interpreter by now, but I've waited and waited… Are you an interpreter?'

'Yes. I worked in Tokyo for four years translating…' Sally trailed off, the words were out of her mouth before she knew what she was saying. *Where did that come from?* She thought in confusion. And there was that niggling feeling again. What was it? She closed her eyes and concentrated until it almost hurt. But still nothing came to her. And then she tried a new tack, and taking a deep breath she just let it all go. She imagined a blank wall; a perfectly white, clean and tranquil room. She let her breath rise and fall, like waves on a beach. She was vaguely aware that the woman behind the curtain was speaking, but she was impervious, the words rolled off her and faded into the distance.

It started in her very centre. At first it was nothing more than a mild tingling sensation. Sally continued to breathe steadily, still focussing on the blank wall, until – ever so slowly – it began to grow; a radiating ball of energy, churning and burning, gathering mass and momentum. And then it came to her as a huge surge, a thundering tidal wave of all-encompassing adrenaline and memory. It was as if an explosion had gone off in her brain. She felt an almost blinding flash of light, and then just as suddenly all was calm once more. And she remembered everything.

'Lockey!' Sally exclaimed. *How had it taken me so long? Am I too late?*

37 ~ KOEMI

Sally knew what she had to do. She had to get out of the hospital as quickly as she possibly could, get to the lab and *somehow*, fire up ALICE. Simple? Perhaps not.

Throwing back her covers she discovered her very first obstacle. Taking a deep breath, she grimaced and tugged on the tube of her catheter. She winced and then muttered as the end of the tube flicked out and sprinkled wee on the white sheets, 'Oh—'

'Is everything okay over there?'

Sally had entirely forgotten about the woman behind the curtain. 'Um, yes…' she lied.

'So you will help me, won't you?'

Sally carefully plucked out her IV drip and cannula, and pulled herself up onto her weakened legs, buoyed by some supernatural energy. She opened the small bedside cupboard. No clothes, 'Oh, come on!'

'Hello?' The woman behind the curtain was not going to let her off easily. Sally felt a stab of compassion and awkwardly pulling the back of her robe closed with one hand, she slipped through the curtain.

The woman in the bed before her was young, perhaps mid-twenties. She had long dark hair and a pale, sweet, kind face. 'Hi, I'm Koemi,' she smiled up at Sally.

'Sally.' Sally extended her hand. Koemi took it and shook it limply. 'Look, I really have some things I have to do, Koemi. If I help you... will you help me?'

'Of course,' Koemi said earnestly. 'What do you need?'

With Koemi dictating, Sally transcribed a note introducing Koemi and most importantly giving details on how they could contact the girl's family. In return, Koemi leant Sally some clothes – which she just about squeezed into – a pair of skin tight neon pink trousers, a white micro t-shirt, and a teeny-tiny cropped green cardigan. There was no way the shoes were going to fit. Sally felt a little like one of the ugly sisters, and was still fruitlessly trying to cram her size sixes into an obvious three, when all of a sudden there was someone just beyond the door. They were just about to enter the ward, when thankfully they started up a conversation with someone passing by. Sally jumped back into bed and pulled the sheet up over herself and the discarded catheter, just in the nick of time.

The nurse entered the room and strode over to Sally, 'Ah, you're awake. How are you feeling Sally?'

Sally was resting back against her pillows and faked looking groggy. 'I'm rather hungry actually. Is there something you could get me to eat?'

The nurse looked quizzically at Sally's IV drip, her eyes darting along to where the tube now hung loosely, rejected at the floor. She pursed her lips. 'Sally did you pull this out?' she asked in exasperation, holding out the end of the tube.

Sally was just grasping desperately of something she could say, when Koemi started making an almighty racket on the other side of the curtain. Startled, the nurse swished the curtain aside. Sally caught Koemi's eye for the briefest moment, *GO!* Koemi willed her with a glint. And Sally went.

She didn't run, only a foolish person runs. Rather she sloped from the room, and walking at a fast steady pace she made her way along the corridor on bare feet, trying to imagine herself invisible, and cringing at the reality of how she may appear; in her undersized brightly coloured ensemble. She could still hear the commotion Koemi was making back in the ward and felt a huge flood of gratitude and relief.

She was nearing the lift doors at the end of the corridor, when something made her look back across to one of the closed doors. She paused, she should really just go, but, something was stopping her. She found herself at the door, she pushed it open, and there was Lockey. He probably looked very much as Sally herself had, not so long ago; wired up, spread out, tubes and machines connected to him. His face, blank. His mouth, agape with breathing tube taped in place. Sally wandered to his side. 'Lockey?' she whispered, and clutched a lifeless hand. And it was at this moment that the final pieces fell into place, and she realised for the first time, that Lockey was her brother.

'Lockey? Can you hear me?' Sally breathed. But he wasn't there. She felt a tear escape and wiped it away furiously. 'I'm going to bring you back Lockey. Just hang on, okay?' And then she was running, foolish person or not, she ran.

38 ~ RIGHT HERE

Thankfully, the lift had come remarkably quickly and the hospital corridors were deserted. It almost seemed too easy and within no time, Sally had slipped out from the hospital building. She needed to make a plan; she had no clue how she was going to get into SALL, let alone how she would start up ALICE. But first off, she needed to get some shoes and get changed; this crazy lady look wasn't going to do her any favours.

She was just about to jump into a waiting taxi when she literally bumped headlong into her dear friend Nita. 'Sal?! What the? I thought you were supposed to be in a coma?!' Nita threw her arms around Sally and wrapped her in a bear hug, 'Oh Sal, I was so worried. I came as soon as I heard. Your landlord contacted me, Sunny?'

Sally wondered about her aunt again; *So I've been in a coma for five days and Mary didn't even think to notify my friends?* But she didn't have time to think about that now. 'Neetz, I'm in kind of a rush. But you can come with me if you like?'

Nita raised a perfectly arched brow. 'What's going on? Should you not be in *there?*' she gestured back at the hospital and seeming to notice Sally's outfit for the first time, gave her a funny look.

'It's a long and very weird story. But I'll try and explain as best as I can on the way.'

The taxi driver eyed Sally warily as she climbed into his cab. She gave him her address but he still seemed hesitant. 'You got money?'

'I will have, when I get there. I'm in quite a hurry…' Sally tried an encouraging smile.

Nita had climbed into the back of the taxi beside Sally, and glowering at the driver, ordered, 'Come on, what are you waiting for? You heard the lady. I've got money. Just go.'

This seemed to do the trick and suitably chastened, he shifted into gear and sped away from the hospital.

Sally gave Nita a largely edited version of events, and noted the taxi driver's eyes growing larger and larger by the minute. She pretty much expected her friend to order the taxi driver to turn around and return them straight to the hospital, when she'd finished telling her story. But Nita nodded, deep in thought.

'So what's this brother of yours like then?' Nita grinned wickedly. 'Lockey,' she tried his name out suggestively,'

Sally rolled her eyes and laughed, 'Seriously!? I tell you all of that, and *that's* all you've got to say?'

'Well, you're either bonkers, or you've got a new – quite possibly hot – long lost brother, whom I can't wait to meet… Just think, I could be your sister in law…'

'And you think it's *I* who might be bonkers…'

The taxi pulled up outside the Maharaja, which by the looks of it was in full swing. Sally got a delicious waft of curry and felt suddenly starving.

'Will you wait here?' Sally asked the driver. 'I just need to pop in and get changed…'

The taxi driver looked at his watch, 'Sorry love, got another job.'

With Nita in tow, Sally hurried around the back of the restaurant as quickly as she could and struggled up the stairs – her muscles screaming with every step. *You'd think that lying about in bed for five days, I'd be nice and rested,* she thought, panting.

Nita took her arm and looked properly concerned for the first time, 'Sal? Are you *actually* all right?'

Sally put on a brave face, 'Sure.' And managed a convincing smile.

'What the hell happened to your toaster?!' Nita suddenly asked in wonder, thankfully distracted by the scorched, half melted remains of the toaster, which Sally had hastily thrown out of her flat on Monday morning.

Sally shrugged as she let them in with the spare key from under the plant pot, 'You know, me and toast…' The door was stiffer than usual and she had to barge it with her whole weight, hip and shoulder.

The flat smelt fustier than ever, but other than that everything was just exactly as she had left it, when she'd rushed out to catch the bus on Monday morning. But so much had changed since then. She was a different person now, changed irreversibly by her experiences. And although she was home, it no longer felt like home to her. She had outgrown this little flat and her empty life, perhaps even this country. She would miss her quirky landlord and his family, but she had a life to start living, a whole world to explore.

'Cor! It's a bit pongy in here,' Nita commented bluntly.

'Well, I *was* in a coma for five days,' Sally laughed in mock offence, 'Forgive me for neglecting the housework.'

Nita had only visited Sally here once before. They hadn't seen enough of each other over the years. Sally vowed to herself to change this. Sally realised that Nita had gone quiet, which with Nita was a cause for concern. 'What?' Sally asked.

'Sal, were you really in a coma? I thought somehow it must have been a mistake...' Nita actually looked as if she might cry.

'Hey, look, I'm okay. I promise.' Sally hugged her friend and added firmly, 'You are going to help me aren't you?'

Nita seemed to have bounced back. 'You try and stop me.'

Sally shimmied out of Koemi's clothes and pulled on a pair of black trousers and a dark fitted sweater, washed her face and scraped her hair back into a ponytail. She still felt horrendous, lightheaded and both hot and cold. But an image of Lockey lying in hospital, flashed in her mind and she was driven on. She found Nita in the sitting room.

Nita looked up approvingly. 'I like it. Very milk-tray-woman-esque,' she laughed.

Sally pulled a face.

'No seriously, it's a definite improvement. Where *did* you get that whacky get-up, you were wearing before anyway?'

Sally glanced at the kitchen clock; quarter past eight – and she was just looking for something Nita and her could quickly eat, when her landlord; Sunny, burst into the room brandishing a cricket bat.

Nita screamed and jumped behind Sally.

'SALLY! I thought you were in hospital...' Sunny exclaimed in bewilderment. 'I heard footsteps up here, and your front door was open... I thought... Oh Sally, it's so good to see you!' Sunny dropped his cricket back and hugged Sally a little too tightly. 'But what are you doing here?' He released her and studied her face, 'Surely they didn't let you go? You were in a coma?'

'I'm okay,' Sally tried to reassure him.

Sunny didn't look convinced, and exchanged a concerned look with Nita.

'Really. Look, Sunny – I haven't got time to explain it all to you, and I doubt you'd believe me anyway. But I've got something really important to do. There's somewhere I need to get to...' Sally started looking around for a number for a taxi.

'Well I will give you lovely ladies a lift. When do you want to go?' Sunny offered immediately.

'Really?' Sally looked up at his expectant face.

'Sure, for my favourite tenant,' he smiled broadly. 'Lavanya and Raj will be able to hold the castle here without me for a while.'

'Sunny, that would be great! Thank you. Can we go now? And... do you have a crowbar?'

He didn't batter an eye, 'Yes I think there's one in the car. I'll go start her up.'

Sunny had pulled his pink 2CV up outside the front of the restaurant – Sally had never been in his car, but knew that it was his pride and joy – he tooted his horn and beamed at Sally and Nita as they emerged from the side of the building.

'Oh my god, this is such a cool car!' Nita laughed, as Sally pushed her into the back and climbed in beside her.

'So…' Sunny asked eagerly as he riffled through a pile of cassettes, 'Where are we headed?'

Sally gave Sunny the address of the laboratory, and was just wondering if he was even listening to her, when he pushed a tape into his ancient cassette player and grinned. 'Okay! Let's go!'

Fatboy Slim's; Right Here, Right Now, began to play. Sunny cranked up the volume, put his foot down, and singing along loudly, accelerated off into the night. The car rattled along, it felt as if they were travelling at around a hundred miles an hour, but when Sally looked across at the speedometer they were well within the speed limit. And it was all so hilariously unexpected, that Sally and Nita couldn't help but roar with laughter.

'I didn't know you were into dance music Sunny!' Sally shouted over the music when they'd finally contained themselves.

'Oh yes. The dancing music also makes such very good driving music, I find,' Sunny bellowed. 'Raj installed these top of the range speakers for me.' He glanced at Sally and Nita, suddenly unsure, 'I can turn it off though, if you don't like it?'

'No,' Sally laughed. 'It's perfect Sunny!'

As they revved into the laboratory complex, Sunny turned the volume down. 'Is this it?'

Sally nodded, nervous suddenly, 'You can just drop us here...'

'Oh no, I'm not leaving you young ladies out here in the middle of nowhere. Besides, I'm here to help.'

'It could be dangerous, Sunny...'

'Well then, I'm definitely not leaving you.'

'And possibly very illegal...'

Nita grinned, obviously thrilled by the prospect of criminal activity.

'Are you sure this is something you have to do?' Sunny asked Sally, seriously. But he didn't ask her if she might actually be completely out of her mind, and she was thankful because there was always the possibility that in fact she was.

'Yes,' Sally answered more certainly than she felt.

Sunny parked up in a dark secluded stretch, surrounded by trees, a few hundred metres from the main laboratory building. He reached into the back and pulled out the crowbar. 'You still need this?' he asked.

Sally pulled a face, 'Maybe?'

Nita grabbed the crowbar delightedly.

Sally realised she hadn't really thought any of this through at all. There were bound to be alarms and all sorts of security measures in place. How was she supposed to break into the laboratory, with only the help of a crowbar and two inept accomplices? Still, with no better ideas she climbed from the car.

It was a cool and clear, dark moonless night, and apart from a distant hum it was absolutely silent. Sally beckoned for Sunny and Nita, and led the way, silently creeping, mindful to walk on the grass verge rather than on the stony drive and careful to keep to the shadows. Sunny followed close at heel, his corduroy trousers swooshing together noisily. Nita couldn't seem to stop giggling. Sally glanced back at them and raised a finger to her mouth.

Sunny nodded back. 'Yes, yes, we must be very quiet,' he said a little too loudly.

As they neared the building, Sally was surprised to find that there was light coming from within. She had imagined it would be deserted by this time in the evening. She looked back at Sunny and Nita, puzzled. 'Looks like someone's here already...' she whispered.

'Is that not good?' Sunny asked.

Sally shrugged, 'I think we'd better ditch the crowbar, and go with Plan B.'

Nita reluctantly surrendered the crowbar and Sally stashed it in a clump of shrubbery.

'What's Plan B?' Nita whispered excitedly.

'Knock on the door and explain that I need to come in and fire up the particle accelerator?' Sally muttered, 'What could possibly go wrong?'

The security light came on as they approached, dazzling them all. And they were almost at the door, when it flew open. Sally shielded her eyes against the glare of the lights, straining to make out the figure standing in the doorway, she was sure she recognised him.

'Sally?' It was Roy, Lockey's assistant.

39 ~ RANDOM REQUEST

Roy was unexpectedly pleased to see Sally, and welcomed the three of them in enthusiastically, 'Sally! I can barely believe my eyes that you're here. This is remarkable! When did you wake up? You're looking extraordinarily well! How are you feeling?' he said in a rush.

'Um yes, I'm fine,' Sally said a little taken aback.

'Well I must say, I'm pretty relieved to see you. They're wanting to shut us down; after the incident. We've had them coming at us from all angles. So, what brings you here? Surely you should be in hospital still? And, is there any news on Lockey?'

'Um, no news on Lockey, no.' Sally was unsure where to start, or how much she should even say, 'This is going to sound *really* odd, but we need to fire up ALICE...' She had expected some kind of protestations, but Roy was still looking at her eagerly.

'Okay,' Roy nodded. 'Now?'

Sally was dumbfounded. What was going on here? *He's not even going to argue? Has he secretly alerted security or something?* Sally wondered. *Mad lady, attempting to breech the lab...* 'Um, yes, now,' she finally managed with a hopeful smile. Sunny and Nita were looking just as disconcerted as Sally felt.

'Not a problem.' Roy turned and began walking from the room. And then, sensing that they weren't following, he faltered and looked back questioningly, 'Are you not coming with me?'

Sally exchanged a look with Nita and Sunny, and raised her shoulders. 'Yes, sure, of course.'

They trailed along the corridor behind Roy. Sally still had no clue what was happening, but had decided to just go along with it all for the time being. This was all very bizarre.

'Oh, I think this may be yours?' Roy passed Sally her mobile phone. 'I found it under ALICE, after they'd taken you to hospital... I've charged it. The battery was dead and I wasn't sure whose it was.'

Sally turned over the phone in her hand as they strode along, a relic from another life.

'Mr. Scott's coming here too actually. He should be on his way.'

Sally stopped in her tracks, 'Harry?'

'Harry Scott, yes. Held up by the ferry. Should be here within the hour though I expect.' Roy gestured forward, 'Shall we?'

Nita was desperately trying to get Sally's attention. 'Who's Harry?' she whispered.

'I'll tell you later,' Sally uttered. 'And no, he's not single.'

Nita was looking amused. 'You dark horse.'

Sally followed Roy blankly, *Harry is coming here?* Her mind was a whir.

Sunny leant in as they walked, 'Is everything okay Sally?' he asked softly.

Sally nodded mutely.

Roy swiped his card beside the large double doors, pushed them open and gestured Sally and Sunny through into the cloakroom area. He handed them all white coats. Nita pulled hers on and gave a twirl, 'What do you think? Geek ce chic?'

'I don't really know why Lockey always insists we wear them, but we'd better stick to protocol,' Roy laughed as though he'd made a joke. Sally made towards the double doors at the end of the room, but Roy stopped her, 'Not that way.'

Sally turned.

'We'd better head to the safety of the control room this time Sally. Don't want any more *incidents* on my shift.'

Sally could bear it no more. Roy's peculiar acquiescence and familiarity were making her feel beyond nervous. She had to ask. 'Roy, what's going on here? Why haven't you chucked me out? Or at least questioned why on earth I'd want to come in here and randomly fire up a particle accelerator?'

Everyone seemed to be holding their breaths.

Roy looked a little befuddled, 'It's not my place to question the orders of a superior. And I doubt your request is random, *is it?*'

'Well, no, it's not actually random. But, what do you mean by *superior?* You do remember that I'm just a temp, right?'

Roy smiled now a little, 'Ah, *that.* Is this a test?' he looked about, as though he may be being secretly filmed, but when he saw that no one was laughing he went on. 'Lockey explained everything to me. He told me to just go along with everything when we first met. Said that we were to pretend that you were just here as a temp. And if anything were to happen to him, that of course, I was to report directly to you, and do whatever you ordered.'

Sally was astounded. '*When* exactly did Lockey say all of this to you?'

Roy thought for a moment. 'Well, I suppose it was a few days before it all happened. The Friday before last? Yes, that's it. Said you'd be coming in on Monday. I was intrigued to finally get to meet the elusive Ms. Addison, I had been starting to wonder if you even existed,' he laughed.

Sally struggled to make sense of what Roy was telling her. And then she figured it out. Lockey was trying to get back. He'd found his right timeline, gone to a week ago and paved the way with Roy, so that Sally could start up ALICE. 'Okay. Let's get to the control room and fire her up. How long will it take?' Sally said with renewed determination.

Roy seemed pleased that they were back on track. 'Fifteen minutes if we hurry.'

'Right. Well let's hurry.'

40 ~ TERAELECTRONWHAT'S

They ran almost the entire way to the control room, with poor Roy panting and puffing as he shuffled along. Sunny was still very bemused by the whole adventure, and Nita seemed to be enjoying herself immensely.

Sally had expected the control room to have a huge window looking on to the giant ALICE, but in fact the room which they found themselves in had no windows at all. Sally blinked. Every inch of wall seemed to be covered almost entirely with monitors and screens, which were emitting so much blue glare it was almost like entering a solarium.

'Ah I like it in here,' Sunny said in awe. 'I feel like I'm in a James Bond movie… Double-oh-Sunny…' he quipped.

Nita guffawed and Sally rolled her eyes and smiled despite herself. 'Let's just let the man work, shall we?' Sally suggested. The three of them watched enthralled, as Roy set to work; pushing buttons, tapping on keyboards, adjusting levers. Sally was expecting a big bang, or something dramatic to happen, and it felt a little anticlimactic when Roy turned and announced it was done.

'Are you sure?'

'Yep. All up and running. How long shall I keep her running for?'

Sally realised that Lockey wasn't just going to appear here, as if by magic before their very eyes like in a Star Trek transporter. The only way she was going to know if any of this had worked, would be to get back to the hospital.

'How long *can* you keep her going for? An hour?'

Roy looked concerned, 'No, not an hour. I can keep her stable like this, for about twenty-minutes tops.'

Sally did the maths; the journey to the hospital alone would take at least half an hour, depending on traffic, not including time to get to and from the car. That meant that if they got to the hospital and Lockey hadn't made it back yet, the window for his return would be closed already. 'And how long a break, before you can get her running again after the twenty minutes?'

'If I push it to the twenty minutes, we're talking an hour minimum cool down. We're running at record breaking teraelectronvolts here.'

'Teraelectron-what's?' Sunny quizzed.

'Teraelectron-*volts*,' Roy corrected distractedly. 'Not to mention the fact that we're right at the brink of this whole project being closed down.'

'Okay, just do what you can.' *Maybe he's already made it back,* Sally hoped silently.

Sunny had to practically run to keep up with Sally and Nita's fast stride. 'Where are we going now?'

'Back to the hospital,' Sally called back over her shoulder.

'Are you feeling okay Sally? I have to admit; I still have no clue what's going on.'

'You're not the only one,' Nita piped in.

They were just rounding the corner into reception, when Sally saw the front door open. And there was Harry. Sally had stopped mid run; she could barely believe her eyes, and Harry it seemed, felt the same way.

'Sally! Is it really you?'

Sally nodded and then a smile spread across her face, 'Yes. I'm back.' The pair embraced. Sally could feel his heart pounding against her chest.

Harry pulled back a little and gazed at Sally in wonder, 'You're here. I've waited, so long. Three years Sally, Little Flora...'

'Is she... is she here?' Sally looked around half expecting a little blur of copper locks to come running at her.

'No, my mother's looking after her.' Harry couldn't take his eyes off Sally.

'Your mother?' Sally asked in surprise, and realised that there was still a lot she didn't know about Harry.

'I'll explain later,' Harry smiled. 'Where were you off to in such a rush anyway? You know they want to shut it all down?'

'Who's Flora?' Nita was sounding frustrated now, realising she'd missed something important.

Sally nodded (choosing to ignore Nita for now), 'Yes. And we've got to get Lockey back.'

41 ~ TAKE ME TO THE HOSPITAL

Harry – it turned out – had been dropped off by taxi. And so the four of them made their way to Sunny's 2CV. Nita introduced herself to Harry as they marched. Sally climbed into the back of the car and Harry piled in beside her.

'I'm not letting you out of my sight again woman,' he grinned.

Nita craned around from the front passenger seat and beamed at Sally and Harry in the back, '*So* how did you two meet?'

'Long story,' Sally and Harry said in unison, and then laughed. Harry pulled Sally in and kissed her.

'Okay, no canoodling back there please,' Sunny announced, as he changed the cassette. 'Everybody belted up?' And tyres flicking up a shower of gravel, he skidded out onto the stony drive in a spectacular handbrake-turn, music blaring once more – Sally recognised that it was the Prodigy playing, but hadn't heard the track before, then a deranged Dallik like voice started up with; *Take Me to the Hospital*, and they all fell about laughing. Nita's raucous cackle setting them off again each time they were all nearly laughed out.

'Sunny!' Sally eventually cried, 'Enough!'

'You don't like this music?'

'Maybe not just now,' she laughed. Sally felt a little like they should all be taking this a lot more seriously – Lockey's life could be hanging in the balance – but she was finding it almost impossible, sitting in the back, squashed up next to Harry, his hand resting casually on her knee. She was telling herself to get a grip and focus, but she could barely contain herself. Sally felt a tingling in her thigh where their legs were touching and grinned at Harry inanely.

'Is that your phone ringing?' Harry laughed, and started playfully probing Sally's pocket.

'Oh,' Sally blushed, as she realised he was right. She hooked her phone out, it was still set to vibrate. She didn't recognise the number on the screen and answered it apprehensively. It was an automated marketing call. Sally hung up crossly. And it was then that she saw the missed call icon and remembered that Mary had been calling her on Monday morning, right when it had all happened. There was a voicemail waiting. Sally had to press the phone to her ear and cover the other, to hear over Nita and Sunny's bantering in the front.

'*You have a new message. Sally? ... Sally? It's Mary...* Oh, it's gone through to voicemail,' Mary mumbled. There were some rustling noises and then she was back on the line. 'Sally. I've had a little bit of an accident. Managed to fall down the stairs. My head's bleeding quite a bit, but I guess heads do tend to bleed...' There was another silence and Sally could hear Mary breathing. 'Thing is; I can't seem to get up. Silly old woman. Anyway I won't bother you, you're at work by now I guess. I'll phone the doctor.' Mary's breathing was sounding more ragged and she seemed to be struggling to catch her breath. 'Anyway if you could give me a ring when you get a moment. But Sally, I… I wanted to apologise… I made some pretty bad decisions in my life. I know I could have done better. But… I just wanted you to know that, actually, although the way you came into our family was wrong, it wasn't *you* that was ever wrong for the family… You're a good girl Sally, and I feel, well, I'm sorry… Sorry for everything… Oh… It sounds like my battery's just about to run out. Just give me a c—' and the line went dead.

Harry was studying Sally with concern, 'Is everything okay?'

Sally shook her head, 'I'm not sure.' She gazed out of the window and realised where they were. They were just about to pass the turn off to Mary's house. Sally was momentarily torn. She was desperate to get to the hospital to find out if Lockey was back, but then…

'Sunny. Take the next left. I've just got to make a quick stop to check on something.'

Mary's house was in darkness. Sunny pulled up outside. 'Here?'

'What's going on Sal?' Nita asked.

Sally briefly explained the voice message. 'I've just got to see…' And she silently climbed from the car.

She pressed the bell and waited, but she didn't know why she was bothering, as even if Mary was already asleep, there would be a light on. She'd always left a light on downstairs, ever since Joe had died. Sally rang again and then tried knocking a few times.

'You looking for the old lady who lived there?'

Sally looked around and saw a teenage boy standing in the gloom, his hands in his pockets. *Lived?*

'They found her yesterday. She'd been in there four days 'fore anyone found her 'parently.'

Sally felt nauseous suddenly, 'Is she...'

'Dead. Yeah. Did you know her or somfing?' the boy said unthinkingly.

Sally felt a ripple of grief. Mary had done some truly horrendous things. But she had also been there for Sally a lot of times too. And what a sad way for anyone to go. Alone and forgotten. Not even missed for four days.

'Yes, something like that,' she said numbly, as the boy slouched away into the darkness.

Sally wasn't sure if they had heard the brief conversation with the boy, or whether they could just sense what had happened, but when she returned to the car they were all waiting in absolute silence. A dog barked somewhere far off in the distance. Sally stood for a moment and looked up at the moon – which had just risen and looked huge and beautiful, mournful and somehow wise – and she said a silent goodbye to her aunt, surprised at how easily forgiveness had come. She just felt sadness for Mary now, rather than anger. *What a waste.* Mary had become a sum of her mistakes, and it had turned her into a very miserable and bitter person. Sally vowed that she would try and do her best to make the most of her gifts; her newfound wisdom and all of the wonderful people she had to love. But right now, she had to get to the hospital and see what she could do about getting Lockey back to the here and now, to where he belonged.

Sally climbed into the car and still none of them said a word. Nita gave her an empathetic look, and Harry wordlessly wrapped her in a hug.

Sally took a deep breath. 'Right.' She mentally shook herself and managed a small smile, 'Take me to the hospital.'

42 ~ LOCKEY LOST IN TIME

Lockey had found himself at his mother's side. And as she puffed and panted, he realised that this was his birth. He could see why they called this labour. It was strange for Lockey to see his mother like this. Not just younger, but even in obvious agony – and even though she was fierce and determined, and using some pretty inventive language – she was also somehow more relaxed. The version he had always known of his mother had been, not cold exactly, but uptight, always in control of her very British stiff-upper-lip.

A baby slipped into the world, shiny and new. There was a whole team of midwives in the room and one of them now held the baby towards Lockey's mother and smiled. 'Congratulations. It's a beautiful little girl.'

She's made a mistake of course. Lockey thought. *I have no sisters.*

His mother managed a smile as the midwife carefully passed the baby onto her chest. 'Hello beautiful.' She was crying as well as laughing now, and tenderly she kissed the top of her brand-new baby's head, 'My little girl. Sophia…'

Something inside Lockey shifted. He was frozen to the spot. *This must be a mistake?* he thought.

His mother was blowing out a long breath now, it was starting up again.

The midwife swooped back in, 'We'll give her back shortly, I promise.' And gently she removed little Sophia and whisked her away.

'Okay, let's get this next baby out now, Francesca.'

Lockey watch transfixed and realised that his poor mother had to go through all of that again. *Why was I never told that I was one of a twin?* he thought in confusion.

The door opened and Lockey drifted out into the corridor, unable to bear seeing anymore, knowing for a fact that he has no sister, he couldn't face seeing what must be inevitably going to happen. His father was pacing the corridor in a state of agitation. *Just go in there and give her a bit of support,* Lockey tried to will him.

Time stretched on. Lockey was ready to leave, he'd seen enough – but try as he might, he couldn't seem to move on. His father was finally by his mother's side, and Lockey saw a side of him that he'd never glimpsed before, a proud tenderness; he kissed his wife and looked down adoringly at his perfect twins.

Still Lockey was at the hospital. He was starting to feel well and truly bored of this all now. He wafted up and down the corridor, willing himself to leave. A couple of midwives emerged from his mother's room with the pair of babies, the new-born versions of himself and the sister whom he never knew. Lockey followed along to the nursery and watched on as the babies were carefully placed into adjacent cribs. He stayed in the nursery, it seemed as good a place as any to wait. And, he thought, *this is the only time I will have with my sister.* Lockey looked down upon the sleeping babies, they looked remarkably alike one another. They could almost have been identical – although the baby version of himself was a little longer and chubbier than his baby sister.

Lockey didn't know how long he'd been there for – it could have been minutes, or hours, days even – and then the nursery door opened. A midwife entered the room. Lockey watched her impassively. She had a baby in her arms and he was supposing that she'd come in to place the baby in a crib. But then he saw how very still and blank the baby was, and he realised that it was dead. He wanted to look away, but somehow he couldn't. He noticed now that the midwife was looking shifty somehow. Glancing around, she approached his sister's crib. Lockey watched in horror – unable to do a thing – as the midwife swapped the tiny name tags between his sister and the lifeless baby, and then blowing out a breath she plucked his sister up and marched from the room. Lockey tried to follow, he could see a bright light at the end of the corridor, but then he felt himself being pulled away.

Everything moved faster, after the seemingly infinite last stop. Lockey saw flashes, glimpses of himself as a boy growing up: riding a horse, running with a kite, meeting his little brother for the first time. It was an odd sensation, to see his life like that; like watching a video montage of his memories, but viewed neutrally from the outside. And between each stop he hurtled on a rollercoaster of space and time.

Lockey woke, and stretched as he opened his eyes. He recognised where he was immediately. He was at his family home. But the matter of *when* he was, was a little harder to ascertain. Over the years, not much had been allowed to change within the walls of his family's grade-one-listed manor. He climbed from bed and realised that he was certainly younger. *I haven't felt this good for quite a few years,* he thought. *My knees aren't even creaking.*

Lockey regarded the younger – tauter and smoother – version of himself in the mirror. *I must be about eighteen,* he mused, *judging by this embarrassing bleached quiff.* He grinned experimentally at his reflection and was dazzled by his straight and very white teeth. *Why didn't I take more care of these?*

Whole days stretched on. Lockey couldn't understand it, but he seemed to be stuck. A week passed by, and determined not to change a thing he found himself play acting the role of his younger self. *Will I ever make it back to my own present?* he wondered. Lockey thought of Sally. *How did I ever expect her to get into the laboratory and start up ALICE?* He kicked himself for being so foolish. *I will be stuck here forever, I suppose now. Locked in time.* Living life over had its perks, it was nice in some respects, but it was also a little boring. He wondered where Sally would be now, in this time. *It couldn't hurt to just look in on her, could it?*

Lockey felt a little like a stalker. Although he knew the general area where Sally lived, he had no clue of the address. He found himself staking out the neighbourhood, unsure what he was hoping – that he'd just randomly bump into Sally somewhere? He suddenly got the strangest feeling that he'd been on this street before, but he was certain he hadn't. And he was just about to head home, when he spotted two teenage girls approaching. And there she was; Sally, and her friend Nita.

Lockey heard Nita laughing and smiled, remembering their time together in the alternate futures. He meant to step out of the way, but somehow he was rooted to the spot, mesmerised. Lockey realised that he *had* been here before. This, was his recurring dream. And it all played out exactly as he'd dreamt. Young-Sally had her head down and didn't even seem to notice him, but as they passed by, Nita gave Lockey an approving look and winked, and then their eyes locked for a brief moment and Lockey felt himself flushing. *For goodness sake,* he thought, *please let me be a grown man again – this teenager me has way more intense hormones surging about.*

Lockey waited until they were almost around the corner before he followed, and then he hovered behind a tree, pretending to adjust his shoes – which wasn't really such a smooth move, as his shoes had Velcro fastenings. He watched furtively as Young-Sally and Nita stopped before a house. They chatted for a little while longer and Lockey was just starting to think that he'd best stand up and walk on, before he alerted suspicion, when he heard Nita saying a loud goodbye to Sally before carrying on her way. Sally waved, and stood for a moment looking on after her friend. Her shoulders drooped as she turned and walked to the front door and let herself in. *Number forty-two. An easy number to remember.* Lockey thought, *the answer to the ultimate question of life, the universe and everything* – he was probably around this age when he'd first read The Hitchhiker's Guide to the Galaxy.

Lockey returned again for the next few days, just checking in. But on the third, Sally wasn't there. *She must be running late.* There was a woman emerging from Sally's house and Lockey recognised she was Sally's Aunty Mary. Looking a lot younger and healthier than when he'd first met her – she was now far from the grey faced old lady version of herself, whom he and Nita had found unconscious on her hallway floor – but he supposed that must have been fifteen years from now. Mary was muttering something to herself. She paused at the gate, looked either way along the street, and it was then that Lockey realised who Mary was. He hadn't seen it before. But somehow seeing her now, younger and fully conscious he realised, that *she* was the midwife. *Sally's Aunty Mary is the midwife who stole my sister.* Lockey felt as if he were about to be sick. What were the chances? He wondered again what had become of little Sophia, and it finally dawned on him. The shared birthday. The connection and familiarity. And he was suddenly absolutely certain, that Sally was his twin sister.

Maybe he'd already known on a deeper level, as somehow he didn't really feel all that surprised. It all made sense. Lockey stood and watched Mary as she approached. She gave him a withering look as she passed by. *I hate this woman,* Lockey thought, and he realised now that he had never actually hated anybody before. Something animal had awoken inside him and he didn't like the feeling. As if what she had done to their family wasn't bad enough, Lockey knew from Sally, that Mary had systematically ruined her life. He remembered the money – Sally's inheritance – a meagre consolation it would have been, for sure. But it would have been something. Lockey thought of teenage Sally and her apathetic demeanour – Mary was responsible for so much wrong – and before he knew what he was doing, he was running after her. He skidded up right in front of her blocking her path. She looked up irritably.

'You're in my way,' she grumbled.

But Lockey wasn't budging. He tried to tell himself to walk away, but he was in some kind of zone. 'I know what you did,' he heard himself hissing.

Something flickered in her eyes; fear? remorse?

'What are you talking about, boy?'

Yes, he thought, *she's scared.* He could almost smell it. And perversely, it pleased him. 'I'm talking about a midwife swapping babies at a maternity ward, eighteen years ago, Mary.' He'd definitely got her now. The colour had drained from her face; she'd turned grey – looking more like the future alternate Mary he'd saved. She rocked forward slightly on her feet, and thinking that she was going to fall, Lockey reached out instinctively to steady her. He reprimanded himself immediately for caring. He had hold of her arm now anyway, so he turned the movement into something else. 'Let's go back to your house, and we can talk about this a bit more,' he ordered, just making it up as he was going along.

Mary didn't argue and allowed Lockey to lead her back to the house.

They were sitting in her gloomy little kitchen, which smelled like chip fat with an undertone of, dank dog perhaps?

'So how did you find out?' Mary asked flatly, not even attempting to deny it.

'That doesn't matter. I know about the money too.'

Mary looked uncomfortable, but didn't say a thing. Lockey wasn't sure what he'd expected her to say. He'd wanted to watch her squirm he supposed, but this vacant submission was disconcerting. *What do I do now?* he thought, *I can't just get up and walk away. And it's not like I'm really capable of anything sinister.* But the idea of Mary keeping Sally's money and laughing behind her back, while she spent it all on cruises, was too much to bear.

Lockey took out his wallet from his pocket and withdrew his bankcard. 'Do you have a pen?' He wrote down his account details on a scrap of paper. 'You're to transfer every last penny that you've leached from Sally, into this account. I'll be checking the balance and if the money's not there, I'll be going to the authorities.'

Mary fixed him with an indignant eye, 'And what proof do you have of any of this, anyway?'

'Proof? That will be easy enough. A simple DNA test will show Sally's true identity, won't it? Combine that with the embezzlement… It's your choice though. You transfer the money and you never hear from me again, or… it's an almost definite stretch in prison.'

Mary nodded in submission and took the piece of paper from his extended hand.

Back at home Lockey went over and over it all in his mind. *Did I make a mistake? I should have just walked away. But how could I? At least now I can make sure Sally's money ends up in the right place.*

He checked his account balance the next day, and although it was what he was waiting for, he was shocked to see that it was all there; Three-hundred and sixty-thousand pounds. A lot of money for an eighteen-year-old boy. But he'd worked out exactly what he was going to do with it. And it was all easy enough. He invested the entire amount in shares with a technology company, which, coming from the future he knew for certain was going to give a huge return. By his estimation, in ten years, it would be worth millions, and with Harry's contribution, they should be looking at enough to set up SALL. Lockey then contacted a solicitor with instructions to sign it all over to Harry Scott, in August ten years from now. And he wondered again, had this all happened before?

Lockey still knew little of how any of this worked, but when he went to sleep that night he drifted away.

The next morning, he woke up and thought, *I'm back?* He was certainly home in his apartment. But his digital alarm clock beside the bed, told him it was the thirty-first of February, *It's the Friday before Sally's first day at SALL,* he thought, *three days before it all began.*

Everything seemed to be exactly as it should. Lockey hoped he hadn't caused too much trouble with his little blackmailing Mary episode. He still didn't know what had gotten into him. The earth was still spinning, but it was stupid to have taken such a huge risk. He decided he'd stick to his day as exactly as he could. But oddly – even though it was only a week ago – try as he might, he couldn't for the life of him remember what had happened today, the day was a complete blank. Lockey was starting to get a bad feeling. If he didn't get out of here before Monday, there was a very real possibility that Sally and he could get stuck in a time loop. Should he do nothing and risk that happening? *Maybe I could prevent Sally from going anywhere near the lab,* he thought, *I could call the temping agency right now and say we don't need her anymore.* And then something else occurred to him; *Or perhaps, today I should see to it that Roy will help Sally to start up ALICE in the present, opening the portal for my return.*

43 ~ SOPHIA

Sunny dropped Sally, Nita, and Harry off in front of the main hospital entrance – he still had little clue what exactly it was that had been going on – but he wished them good luck. The three of them rushed into the hospital and back up to the wards. As they bundled out of the lift and along the corridor, they were stopped in their tracks by an obstinate looking nurse. 'Can I help you?' she asked wearily.

'We've come to see Lock— I mean, Horace Lockhart.' It dawned on Sally that it must be really late by now and would be way after visiting hours.

'Are you family?' the nurse looked unconvinced.

Sally nodded, 'I'm his sister.'

The nurse narrowed her eyes, 'Hang on, aren't you Sally Sullivan? You weren't supposed to leave...' She was looking about, for backup possibly? 'You two have brought her back I should hope?' She gave Harry and Nita a reprimanding look. 'You were in a coma Sally. It's some kind of miracle that you're even up on your feet so soon. It's really not advisa—'

'Look. I appreciate your concern, but I didn't come up here for a lecture,' Sally cut in, surprisingly assertively. 'It's really important that I see Horace Lockhart.'

'I'm sorry, but it's family members only in the ICU at this time of night.'

'But, I told you that I *am* family. I'm his sister…' Sally was getting quite riled now, for perhaps the first time in her life. Nita looked impressed.

'It's okay Nurse.'

Sally spun around and came face to face with Francesca.

'If they want to see my son, that's fine. I shall take them in.' Francesca gave the nurse a look which somehow couldn't be argued with. She turned back to Sally enquiringly, 'And *you* are?'

'I'm…' *I'm the daughter you thought had died?* But of course she couldn't say that. 'I'm, Sally,' she said simply instead, and put out her hand.

Francesca still looked perplexed. She politely shook Sally's hand, but then didn't let it go, 'I don't know how you know him. But my son… he's not doing well at all I'm afraid.' Sally could see now that it was taking every ounce of effort Francesca had, to hold it all together. 'We're preparing to turn off his life-support. It's what he would have wanted…'

'Can I see him? Please?' Sally said quietly, and gently squeezed her mother's hand.

Francesca led the way and didn't seem to mind that all three of them were trailing along after her.

Sally had already seen Lockey like this, but it was no less startling. She picked up his hand and kissed his knuckles, and willed him to open his eyes.

Francesca placed a hand on Sally's back, moved to tears by her obvious affection for her son, 'How *do* you know him?' she asked gently.

'He's my twin brother,' Sally said absently, before realising herself. But the words had already left her mouth and there was no unsaying them now.

Francesca took Sally's face in one of her soft hands, gently raised her chin and studied her daughter intently for a moment. 'But...' her voice broke. 'How is this possible? Can it be true?'

Sally blinked back the tears, 'The midwife... she swapped babies, and I was taken away and adopted.'

'Sophia,' Francesca whispered, openly weeping now. 'My baby.' And she folded Sally into her arms – Lockey's limp hand still clasped in Sally's, trapped between the two of them now – Sally felt the tiniest movement, a flutter of Lockey's fingers. And then he squeezed her hand. Sally pulled back from her mother's embrace and looked down to Lockey, his eyes flickered open.

'Lockey!' Sally cried.

Lockey blinked and dazedly looked around the room. His eyes settled on his mother and he smiled. Francesca discovered a whole new reserve of weeping. It was the first time she had ever fully let go of her emotions.

Lockey was looking at Sally curiously now.

Does he remember? Sally swallowed nervously. 'Lockey? Lockey... Do you remember who I am?'

Lockey struggled to speak, he cleared his throat. Sally helped him un-tape his breathing tube, and then leant in closely so that she could hear him better.

'The temp...'

Sally's heart sank.

But then he continued, 'The temporary lives we've lived, Sally.'

And Sally saw the glint in his eye. He remembered. He was back.

44 ~ NEET AND ACE

There wasn't a dry eye in the room. Even the impervious nurse – who had been watching from the respectable distance of the doorway – was quietly sniffling.

Nita blew her nose noisily, and strode over to unashamedly check Lockey out. 'Hi. I'm Sally's best friend, Nita. You can call me, Neetz,' she announced brazenly and offered Lockey her hand. And Lockey took it. Sally was surprised she hadn't seen it before, but there was most definitely something there between the two of them. It was almost a *get a room* moment.

The pair were still gazing intensely at each other. 'Horace Lockhart. You can call me Lockey, or Ace,' Lockey twinkled.

Sally smirked and looked away, so he *had* heard.

'Neet and Ace,' Nita grinned.

Harry was at Sally's side now. Sally found herself leaning back against him, and realised – now that all of the excitement was over – just how wiped out she was really feeling. And she didn't even argue when the doctor appeared and ordered her straight back to her bed. There would be plenty of time for talking. For, now they had all of the time in the world. Their futures were unwritten and stretched out before them all, adventures for tomorrow. But today, Sally was going to sleep.

45 ~ METAMORPHOSIS

When Sally awoke the next morning in hospital, she had never felt better. Harry was by her side, and yes, she still ached a fair bit, but she'd woken up feeling completely invigorated, rejuvenated even.

As the saying went; today was the first day of the rest of her life. Sally felt as if she had finally awoken, not just from the coma; her journey across time, but awoken from the half-life she'd been living before any of this crazy adventure had begun. She had been living in a cocoon for so many years. And finally she had emerged. Metamorphosed. Not into a fragile butterfly, but into a moth; strong and resilient, and drawn to the light. She'd dance towards the flames and just have to hope that she wouldn't get burnt, for she was finally, fully alive and any risks that came with that would be worth it.

Sally thought of the reality with Harry she'd experienced, happy but numb. And she suddenly felt an immense wave of sadness. She looked up at Harry, the most beautiful soul she had ever met, and it tore her in two to have to admit, but she had to be honest, not only with him, but with herself.

'I don't know if I can be the person that Flora and you need me to be, Harry. To live in suburbia with two-point-four children and mortgage repayments. But equally, I don't know if I can live without you.' There, she had said it.

But Harry seemed unfazed. He smiled, 'How about one child, and a bit of exploring the world with your crazy Scott husband? I've been offered a job in the Galápagos Islands… Of course, I wasn't going to take it without you, but…' Harry took Sally's face gently in his hands and kissed her, so softly she thought she may implode.

Sally blinked back her tears and laughed, 'Yes. Yes, that sounds like a much more suitable place to start.'

EPILOGUE ~ THE FUTURE-TEMP

Sally Scott gazes through her reflection as the little glass-bottomed-boat slips across the calm, crystal clear shallows of the turquoise sea. She hugs her daughter in a little closer and breathes her in, as they lean in together over the boat's small hull window; marvelling at the pristine underwater world beneath them.

A whole year has passed by since it all happened, and it's been quite a year. They've been here for two-months now, and have another three to go. Then it's back to the UK for a while, for Lockey and Nita's big wedding. And then? Well they haven't decided yet, maybe on to Spain, or perhaps back to Orkney. Sally is more than content spending her days with Flora, and she's writing and illustrating a series of children's books about an endangered flapper skate and her mermaid friend.

Sally thinks of all she has to be thankful for and smiles, deeply happy with the way her life is going. Every decision she has ever made in her life has led her to this point in time, and here she is.

Printed in Great Britain
by Amazon

25703650R00179